MORE STORIES FROM THE ROUND BARN

More Stories from
THE ROUND BARN

Jacqueline Dougan Jackson

TRIQUARTERLY BOOKS
NORTHWESTERN UNIVERSITY PRESS | EVANSTON, ILLINOIS

TriQuarterly Books
Northwestern University Press
Evanston, Illinois 60208-4210

Printed in the United States of America

10 9 8 7 6 5 4 3 2 1

ISBN 0-8101-5135-9

Library of Congress Cataloging-in-Publication Data

Jackson, Jacqueline Dougan.
More stories from the round barn / Jacqueline Dougan Jackson.
p. cm.
ISBN 0-8101-5135-9 (alk. paper)
1. Farm life—Wisconsin—Beloit Area—Anecdotes. 2. Duggan family—Anecdotes. 3. Dairy farming—Wisconsin—Beloit Area—Anecdotes. 4. Family farms—Wisconsin—Beloit Area—Anecdotes. 5. Beloit Area (Wis.)—Social life and customs—Anecdotes. I. Title.
S521.5.W6 J27 2002
977.5'87—dc21 2002001618

The paper used in this publication meets the minimum requirements of the American National Standard for Information Sciences—Permanence of Paper for Printed Library Materials, ANSI Z39.48-1984.

Cover photograph: Schoolchildren visiting the Dougan farm

Again, to Grampa

CONTENTS

TO THE READERS OF *MORE STORIES FROM THE ROUND BARN*

There is a wealth of stories connected with the Dougan Dairy of Beloit, Wisconsin, through its years of activity—from my grandfather's buying of the farm in 1906 to my father's retirement in 1971. These have come from hundreds of people and sources. A number have already been published in *Stories from the Round Barn* (Northwestern University Press, 1997), and all the stories are a part of a larger work in progress, *The Round Barn*. Enough of you have wanted more stories—what happened to Esther? to Trever? to the farm?—that the Press has asked for a second book. The stories here do not exhaust the supply.

It's not possible to select out for thanks only those people who have contributed specifically to these stories, for there's too much intertwining. I need to give credit to the dead as well as the living, and I will miss some. All the following have talked or written to me or my parents, sharing their knowledge about the farm and the people who participated in its life. Many gave pictures, clippings, and other materials. My Dougan grandparents died before this work was begun in this form, but their contributions (and their lives) are the foundation of *The Round Barn*. Some of the living have critiqued parts of the manuscript, including their own sections, thus keeping a brake on my fictionalizing. I'm grateful to everyone who has helped me put together these accounts.

The family comes first: Eunice and Wesson Dougan, Ronald and Vera Dougan, Trever Dougan, Joan Dougan Schmidt, Lewis Dalvit, Pat Dougan Dalvit, Craig Dougan, Jackie Dalvit Guthrie. Eloise Marston Schnaitter has been the richest nonfamily source, and she supplied many of the details of

Esther's story. Others include Arthur Adams, Pat and Ralph Anderson, Bob Babcock, David Bartlett, Oscar Berg, Geneva Bown, Phyllis Bruyere, Georgia Clary, David Collins, Scottie Cook, Al Cox, Jean Maxworthy Davis, Robert Fey, Erv Fonda, Georgie Freitag, Dan Goldsmith, Edward Grutzner, Russell Gunderson, Jean and Phil Holmes, John Holmes, Sally Holmes, Lloyd Hornbostel, Bernard and Grace Kassilke, Charles Kellor, Mark Kellor Jr., Marie Knilans, Richard Knilans, Omer Koopman, John Kopp, Marge Kopp, Dorothy Kirk Lueken, Homer Mathews, Bob Maxworthy, Dolores McCormick, Howard Milner, Roscoe Ocker, David Orlin, Sandy Parker, Ed Pfaff, Dick Post, Lester Richardson, Lester and Mildred Stam, Russel Ullius, Fannie Veihman, Fred Veihman, Harry Vogts, and Harlan Whitmore.

A number of these stories were first published in the *Beloit Daily News,* and I thank editor Bill Behling, associate editor Larry Raymer, and Minnie Mills Enking. Others have appeared in *Brainchild,* the *Alchemist Review,* the *Writer's Barbeque,* and *TriQuarterly.* Some have been read over Wisconsin Public Radio's *Chapter-a-Day* by Karl Schmidt.

Those who have supported and critiqued during the writing process include John and Peg Knoepfle, Carol Manley, Gary Smith, Karl Schmidt, Phil Kendall, David Bartlett, Paul Doby, Walter Johnson, LaVerne and JJ Smith, Jean Ladendorf, Michele Woolsey, Sue Anders, Lloyd and Julia Hornbostel, the members of the Brainchild Writing Collective, Bill Furry, Eva and Chad Walsh, Alison Walsh Sackett, Carol Dell, Sandy Costa, Robert McElroy, Berniece Rabe, and my daughters, Damaris Jackson, Megan Ryan, Gillian Ferranto, and Elspeth DeBow. Professor Richard Dimond helped with retrieving memories. Sangamon State University (now University of Illinois at Springfield) granted me three sabbaticals. Some of the above people have helped me with the researching, transcribing of tapes, typing, word processing, and proofing, as did Wendy Baylor, Betty Bradley, Ruth Vogel, Marian Levin, Lola Lucas, Charla Stone, and Dorothy Ford. Further (and fervent) thanks go to Elle DeBow for adapting this manuscript to current technology.

I have had much help in gathering and preparing photographs from, among others, Paul Kerr of the Beloit Historical Society, Steve Larson of *Hoard's Dairyman,* James Quillen, Mitch Hopper, Wesley Nelson, Beverly Jorgenson Soper, Steve Truesdale, Jerome Dougan, Craig Dougan, Pat Dougan Dalvit, Eloise Schnaitter, Marie Knilans, Howard Milner, Cheryl Martingilio, Carol Hansen, Phyllis Bruyere, George Lentell, and Howard Reep. Very special thanks go to Mitch Hopper, who has taken apparently impossibly damaged photos and repaired them via computer (even added a small cow to an aerial view!) and who also has created and is maintaining my handsome Web site. I owe the existence of much of this book, the previous book, and the larger work to come to my grandparents and parents for creating documents, letters, photographs, and other source material and never throwing anything out. I'm also grateful for their colorful lives. And I'm indebted to my brother, Craig, for his excellent memory and for the diaries he kept throughout his teens.

Again, my appreciation goes always to my writing mentors: Chad Walsh of Beloit College; Roy Cowden, director of the Hopwood Program, University of Michigan; and William Perlmutter, of St. John's University. And again, the greatest of thanks to my unequaled editor, Reginald Gibbons, of TriQuarterly Books.

INTRODUCING THE ROUND BARN

There is the land. In the center of the land are the farm buildings. In the center of the buildings is the round barn. In the center of the barn rises a tall concrete silo. On the side of the silo are printed these words:

> THE AIMS OF THIS FARM
> 1. Good Crops
> 2. Proper Storage
> 3. Profitable Live Stock
> 4. A Stable Market
> 5. Life as well as a Living
>
> —W. J. Dougan

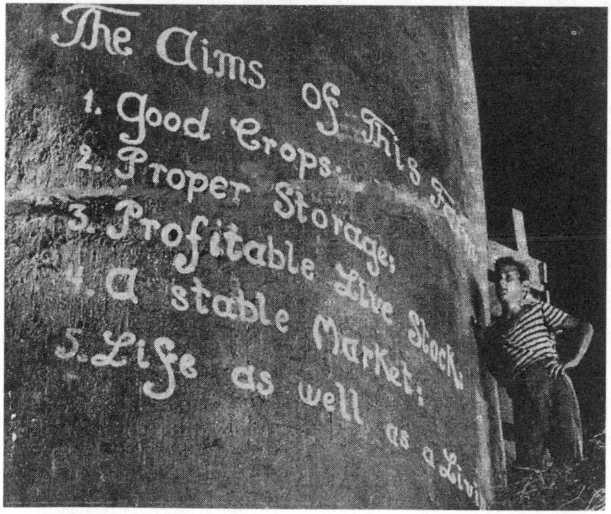

Craig and the AIMS *on the round barn's silo.*

Jackie could read these words before she could read. She said, "What do they say?" and her older sisters read them to her, or a hired man, or whoever was there. She learned them by heart without trying. She did not ask what the words meant.

W. J. Dougan is Grampa. He had the words lettered there, inside the barn on the silo, when he had just built the round barn. That was 1911, when Daddy was nine years old. Jackie sees these words every day. Sometimes twenty times, on a day when she and Craig and the others are playing hide-and-seek in the barn. Sometimes not for several days in a row. But add up the times she has seen them, and the days of her life, and they will come out even.

Jackie is fourteen. She sits on the arm of Grampa's easy chair. She rumples his thinning hair and shapes it into a Kewpie-doll twist. This is a ritual, with all the grandchildren, ever since they were little. Grampa laughs with his stomach, silently.

An idea strikes Jackie. She takes a pencil and paper. These are always near Grampa, for Grampa is deaf. They are always near Jackie, too, for Jackie writes things down. Maybe she has this habit from writing for Grampa all her life. Being his ears. She writes, "Grampa, I am going to write you a book. I am going to call it *The Round Barn*."

Grampa studies the paper. He takes a long time to ponder it. Then he nods slowly. "*The Round Barn*," he says. "Yes, the round barn will have a lot to say." He crinkles all over his face and laughs silently. He is pleased, she can tell.

"I can write," says Jackie to herself, "what the round barn sees. Not just what I know it sees. But what Grampa knows it sees. And Daddy. The milk-men. The cows. All of us! For the round barn is in the middle of us all, and it sees everything. It is the center."

Jackie thinks, Here are the circles of the book.

She draws a picture, starting with the silo and going out to the barn, and beyond.

"That's it," says Jackie, "if it were just flat. But the book isn't flat, just as the barn isn't flat."

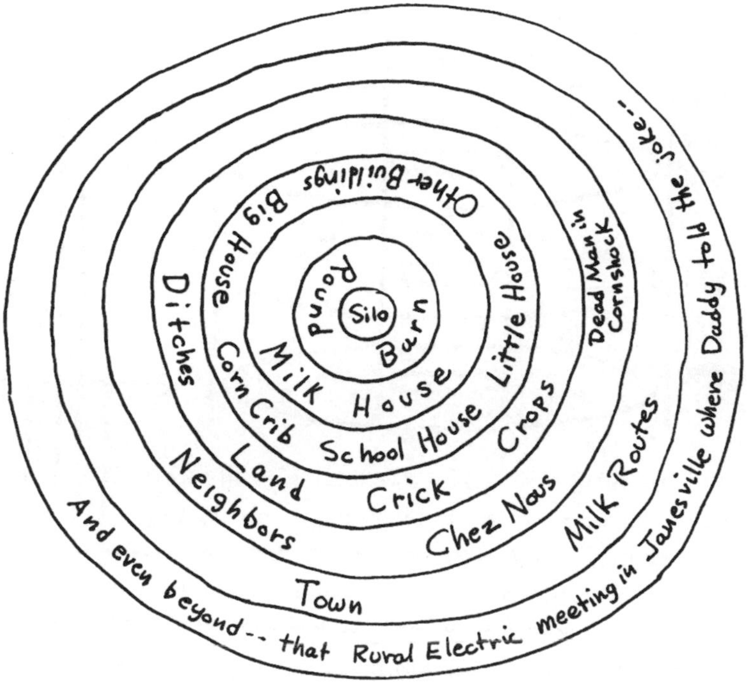

She takes another sheet of paper. She draws another picture. It looks a bit like the round barn but without any hip roof. It looks a bit like three-dimensional tic-tac-toe.

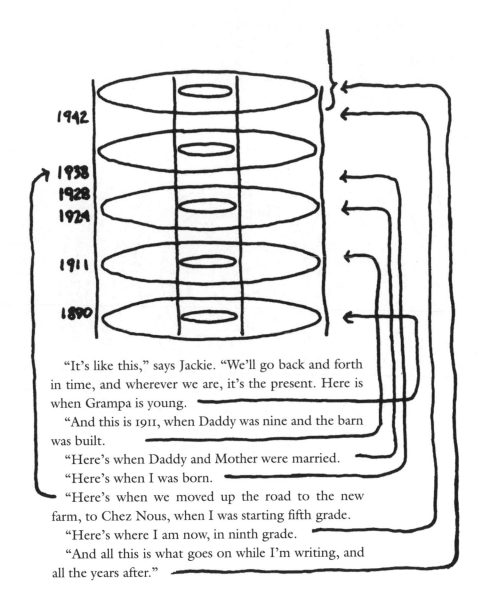

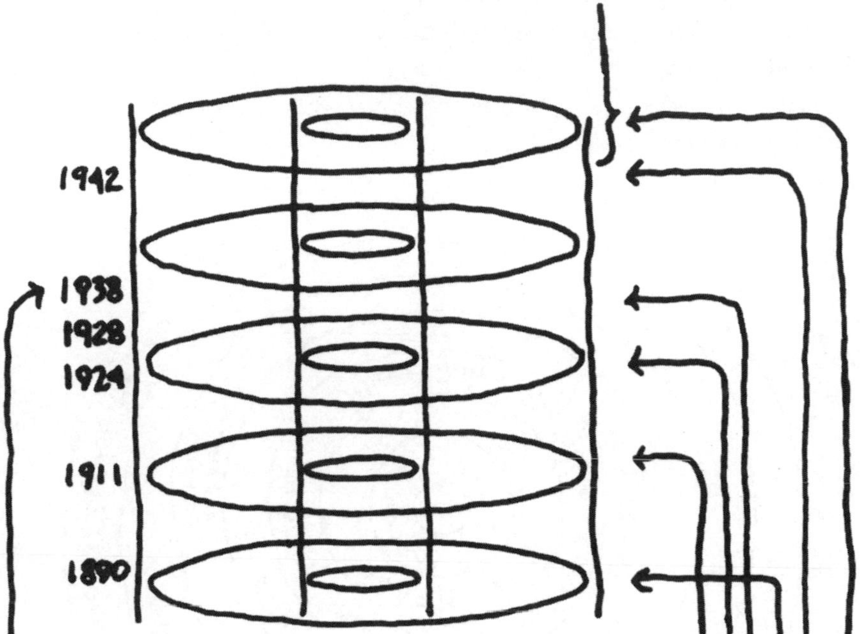

“It’s like this,” says Jackie. “We’ll go back and forth in time, and wherever we are, it’s the present. Here is when Grampa is young.

“And this is 1911, when Daddy was nine and the barn was built.

“Here’s when Daddy and Mother were married.

“Here’s when I was born.

“Here’s when we moved up the road to the new farm, to Chez Nous, when I was starting fifth grade.

“Here’s where I am now, in ninth grade.

“And all this is what goes on while I’m writing, and all the years after.”

Looking east toward the farm buildings, across a cornfield. The horse barn is on the left, then the round barn, outside silo, and side barn, and, hidden in the trees, the Big House.

For the circles go out, concentric, in space. But they also go up and down in time. Like an onion. But not like an onion completely, for onion parts are too cleanly separated. They pop apart.

It's more like elm wood. Elm logs can hardly be split, for the fibers interpenetrate, ring from ring, and bind all the circles together.

The story, the farm, Jackie decides, is like a log of elm wood. Everything, in all directions, in all dimensions, is bound together.

THE FAMILY

Here's the family you'll meet in these pages, and this list will help you keep us straight. Those names mentioned in these particular stories are capitalized here; those not are in plain type.

The Place

The Dougan farm, just east of Beloit, Wisconsin, in Turtle Township, Rock County.

Grampa: Wesson Joseph Dougan, 1868–1949

Generally called Daddy Dougan by farm people and the community. He began his career as a Methodist minister but left because of deafness. At fourteen he took over the work of the family farm full-time—his father was injured—so he was unable to start high school till his father's death and the sale of the farm in 1887. He attended Wayland Academy in Beaver Dam and the University of Wisconsin. In 1906, he bought the Colley farm, began peddling milk in Beloit in 1907, and built the round barn in 1911. His mother, DELCYETTA, bore him when she was forty-five. He had three older sisters, DELLA (of Mason City, Iowa), IDA, and LILLIAN. Ida married JAMES CROFT and lived in town; they adopted a daughter, HAZEL. After James's death, Lillian moved in with Ida. Grampa also had second cousins, JENNIE and NELLIE NEEDHAM, as well as a niece and a nephew, the BOSWORTHS, the "rich relatives" of Elgin, Illinois, the youngest of the four daughters being BETSY.

Grama: Eunice Trever Dougan, 1869–1959

Eunice came from England at six months, with eight siblings; two more were born in Wisconsin. She graduated from Lawrence College and taught for two years before marriage. Her oldest brother, GEORGE, was a conservative Methodist minister of some distinction; her youngest, Albert Augustus, became a beloved professor at Lawrence, wrote an ancient-history text still in use, and has a hall named after him. Uncle Bert was the Dougan kids' and grandkids' favorite, and Grama's sister RIA, nine when she came to the States, was the favorite among sisters. Rose, the youngest child, was epileptic and mildly retarded.

Wesson and Eunice's Children

Wesson and Eunice's first child, Esther (1900), bled to death at a botched birth (the drunk doctor cut the cord too close to the body). They had two sons, RONALD (1902–96) and TREVER (1904–83). ESTHER (1909–76) was a foster daughter. All three attended the District 12 school (with occasional stints at a town school) and Beloit High School. Ronald went to Northwestern for three years; spent a year in France and married (in 1924) VERA WARDNER (1895–1988) of Chicago, who was in France doing the same type of work; returned to Beloit and took his senior year at Beloit College; and went into business with his father. Trever went to the University of Wisconsin, married Bernice Marion (1905–94), worked for United Airlines for many years, and eventually owned a Chicago blueprint firm.

Ronald and Vera's Children

Ronald and Vera had four children. JOAN (b. 1925) married Karl Schmidt and had PETER, JEREMY, KATIE, Dan, and Tom. PATRICIA (b. 1926) married LEWIS DALVIT and had Jackie Jo and Stephanie. JACQUELINE (b. 1928) married Robert Jackson and had Damaris, Megan, Gillian, and Elspeth. CRAIG (b. 1930) married Carol Glad, who had two sons; Craig fathered Cynthia Sue and Trever. After Carol's death Craig married Barbara McDonald, who had three children, thus making a family of seven.

Trever and Binney's Children

Trever and Binney had two children. JERRY (b. 1932) married Debby Greabell and had Scott, Patrick, and Dan. KARLA (b. 1937) married John Pendexter and had Leslie, Jay, and Geoff.

Esther's Child

Esther had one son, RUSSELL (1926–51). Russell married and had sons RUSSELL and BILL.

MORE STORIES FROM THE ROUND BARN

I GRAMPA'S COURTSHIP

It is 1938. Jackie is ten. She and Patsy and Craig are in the living room at Grama and Grampa's. Patsy says, "Grama, how did you meet Grampa?"

Grama tells them. Grampa can't hear, but he knows what story is being told, by the looks and the laughs and the huge enjoyment of everybody. He enjoys it hugely, himself.

Grampa's courtship is like this. He's at the University of Wisconsin. He's intent on his studies; he's late in becoming a student, so he must apply himself seriously. He must also earn money. He supply preaches at a little church in MacFarland, near Madison. He works one summer on the shores of Lake Geneva, a place called College Camp, where people come to live in the tents and cabins, eat in the large wooden dining hall, and, under a gigantic tent, listen to lectures and concerts. It's called College Camp because it gives people education and culture while they enjoy the cool water and lake breezes. It's a little Chautauqua. College students wait on the tables and do all the work around the camp.

Another college student working there is Grama. Her name is Eunice Trever; she goes to Lawrence College in Appleton, her hometown, where she lives near her brother, the Reverend George Trever. She and Grampa wait on tables together. Grama likes the serious young divinity student.

One night after dinner, Grampa is picking a plate up off the table to put on the large tray of dishes he's balancing in the other hand. A pat of butter on the edge of the plate spills off onto the wooden floor. Grampa looks down at the butter pat, then looks around. He sees no one but Grama watching him. He gives her the merriest, most mischievous look she's ever seen; his eyes fairly disappear. With his toe he nudges the pat over and into a knothole in the floor. It vanishes.

Grampa, far right, and Grama, back row, far left, met at College Camp, Lake Geneva, Wisconsin. This picture is of the student staff.

At that instant Eunice's heart is won. She's in love, definitely, deeply, desperately. She knows that Wesson Joseph Dougan is the only one for her.

Grampa finds Grama attractive. But another young woman working at the camp has also recognized what a prize Grampa is, and she's set her cap for him.

"What does 'set her cap' mean?" asks Craig.

"Oh, the foolish thing!" Grama exclaims. "It means she did everything she could to make Wess notice her; she just made a fool of herself, she was so determined to get him!"

The unhappy situation is Grampa likes that other one, too. When he's with Eunice, she's in heaven; but when he pays attention to that other one, she suffers the pains of Hades.

The end of summer comes. Grampa is serious about his studies; he

Eunice and Wesson, college photos. They were about this age when they met.

doesn't want his work complicated by the two young women he's become fond of. He can't make up his mind between them. He's not yet ready to make up his mind. Summer is summer, but winter is a different matter. "Don't mail me any letters," he tells Eunice. He says the same thing to her rival. He needs time. He returns to the university, Grama returns to Lawrence, and that other one returns to wherever she's going to school.

By Thanksgiving, Grama can stand it no longer. She writes Grampa a love letter. She pours out her heart to him. She doesn't mail it but sends it hand delivered by a mutual acquaintance from the summer who is traveling down to Madison.

When Wesson gets that letter, he's undone. The scales are tipped; he can resist no longer. He writes back to Grama and suggests they exchange pictures. He signs the letter "Love and kisses." He hopes she can soon make a visit to Madison. Grama does, and they become engaged.

Jackie, Patsy, and Craig clap and cheer. Patsy goes and sits on the arm of Grampa's chair and kisses him on the top of his head where his hair is thin and then makes a Kewpie-doll curl out of the thin hair. Craig and Jackie scrunch on the rug over to him and each hug a leg. They want to show him how glad they are that he picked Grama and not that other one. Patsy spells on her hand, M-A-I-L A L-E-T-T-E-R, and they all laugh at Grama's cleverness. Grampa's eyes disappear.

Grama gets a little white book out of the bookcase. It's called *Our Wedding*. She turns the pages and reads out loud to them from the faded ink. She shows them the first page:

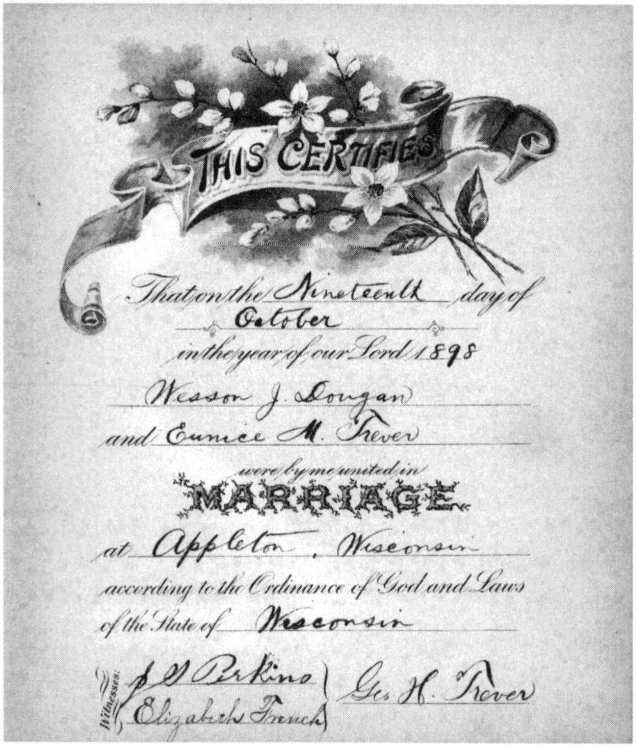
THIS CERTIFIES
That on the Nineteenth day of
October
in the year of our Lord 1898
Wesson J. Dougan
and Eunice M. Trever
were by me united in
MARRIAGE
at Appleton, Wisconsin
according to the Ordinance of God and Laws
of the State of Wisconsin
Witnesses: J. S. Perkins, Elizabeth French
Geo. H. Trever

She shows them the newspaper clipping:

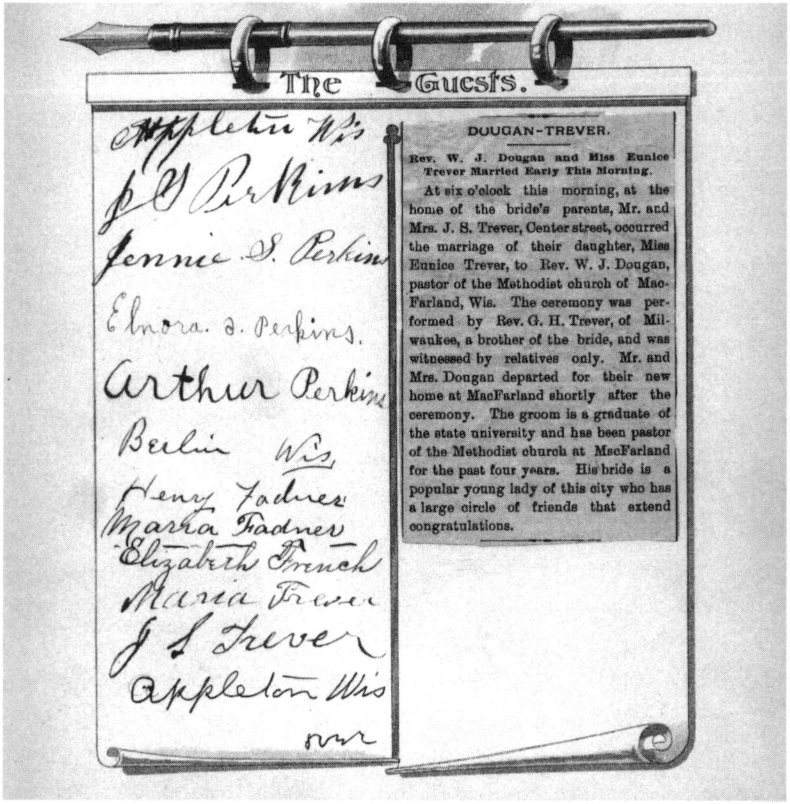

The Guests.

Appleton Wis
J S Perkins
Jennie S. Perkins
Elnora J. Perkins.
Arthur Perkins
Berlin Wis
Henry Fadner
Marha Fadner
Elizabeth French
Maria Trever
J S Trever
Appleton Wis
over

DOUGAN-TREVER.

Rev. W. J. Dougan and Miss Eunice Trever Married Early This Morning.

At six o'clock this morning, at the home of the bride's parents, Mr. and Mrs. J. S. Trever, Center street, occurred the marriage of their daughter, Miss Eunice Trever, to Rev. W. J. Dougan, pastor of the Methodist church of MacFarland, Wis. The ceremony was performed by Rev. G. H. Trever, of Milwaukee, a brother of the bride, and was witnessed by relatives only. Mr. and Mrs. Dougan departed for their new home at MacFarland shortly after the ceremony. The groom is a graduate of the state university and has been pastor of the Methodist church at MacFarland for the past four years. His bride is a popular young lady of this city who has a large circle of friends that extend congratulations.

"Six o'clock in the morning!" cries Patsy in disbelief.

"The train left at seven," says Grama. She reads from the book her own account, on the page marked "The Guests."

> We had very few guests at our wedding. We were married at six in the morning by my minister brother George. We had a wedding breakfast, then took the seven o'clock train for MacFarland. Mr. Dougan could not leave his flock for more than a day, even for his wedding. We spent

> some time in Madison buying some things, and arrived at MacFarland at four o'clock in the afternoon. When the train stopped, it seemed like all the children of the village were at the train. Their mothers were in a nearby blacksmith shop peeking out to see the new bride after having the little parsonage well equipped with good things to eat and a table loaded with goodies, besides a fire in the wood stove with a teakettle of boiling water singing away a welcome. Since that day the guests have been coming.

On a different page, called "The Wedding Journey," Grama repeats herself: "'We went right to our charge. Mr. Dougan was a very conscientious minister. We could not take time for a journey just then. We went right to MacFarland where he was a student at the university, and a minister at MacFarland.'"

There the account ends. "I was too busy to fill in the rest of the wedding book," Grama says. "And the journey didn't matter. Daddy and I have had a long, lovely journey through the years." She tells them about life as a minister's wife, how little they had to live on. She tells them about the two hundred and fifty dollars pay per year and the time a delegation of ladies of the church came to her and asked her about a Christmas present for Grampa.

"We are thinking of a nice buffalo robe, for his sleigh," they say. "It would keep him so warm when he has to drive all around the countryside, making pastoral calls. Do you think he'd like one? Do you think it would be a suitable gift?"

Grama assures them that he would, that it would.

"Do you suppose it will be all right if we take it out of his salary?" ask the ladies.

Jackie, Patsy, and Craig whoop and scrunch over to hug Grampa's legs again, this time in sympathy. B-U-F-F-A-L-O R-O-B-E, Jackie spells on her hand, and Grampa laughs silently.

Grama tells them about Grampa's going deaf and leaving the ministry.

3 PLAY HORSIE

When he was little, Daddy didn't know that boys are different from girls. He thought everybody was the same as he was. It never occurred to him that they might be different. He had no sisters. Even if he had, he wouldn't have seen them undressed. He never saw his father or mother undressed. He didn't see pictures of unclothed people, not even reproductions of the works of the Great Masters or photographs of Greek statues. That was the way it was in that generation, in the Big House, when he was little.

Jackie had always heard that Daddy ran after a little girl once when he was small and pulled down her pants because he'd heard there was a difference. One day Daddy tells her that this story is apocryphal. He tells her the true story. He'd never have been brave enough to run after a little girl and do that. What happened was just the opposite. The little girl ran after him.

Ronald is six; it's 1908. He's at school, the one-room schoolhouse in the field just beyond the corner of the East Twenty. There's a curve in the road there, at the edge of the schoolyard, and a culvert under the road. It's recess time. A little girl his age asks him to play horsie. The girl will be the horse; he'll be the driver. She holds a jump rope between her teeth and hands him the ends. Ronald twitches the reins and says, "Giddy-yap!" She gallops; he gallops behind her. She gallops under the culvert. It's hidden in the culvert. She says, "I'll show you what I have if you'll show me what you have." Ronald has only a broken harness buckle and three aggies in his pocket. He doesn't think these will interest her, but he's interested in what she has to show him. "All right," he says. She pulls down her drawers and shows him.

Ronald is appalled. Distraught, he stumbles out of the culvert while she cries, "Wait! You promised!" All afternoon he doesn't look at her. He goes home; he picks at his supper. He goes to bed. In bed, he starts to cry. He

District 12 school and pupils on the last day of school. Trever is on the left in bloomers; Ronald, beside him, has his hand on his hip. Miss Church is the teacher.

cries uncontrollably. He is terribly, terribly sorry for girls. The world contains a sadness he has never suspected.

His mother hears him weeping. She can't make him stop. She can't find out why he's shaking with sobs. Finally, she carries him to the rocking chair and holds him in her arms. She rocks and rocks and rocks and sings lullabies. She rocks him to sleep. He never tells her why he cried.

There is more to the story. It's the next day. It's recess. Ronald's little brother is four. Trever is too young to go to school but he comes anyway, almost every day. The teacher doesn't mind. Ronald watches while the same little girl and another little girl come up to Trever. "Let's play horsie," they say. They take the jump rope in their teeth and hand Trever the reins. They gallop off across the pasture. Trever gallops gaily behind them. Ronald watches them go. They disappear into a gully. Ronald wanders off and sits behind the boys' backhouse. The infinite sorrow strikes deep within him.

4 THE WEDDING

Ronald is in the third grade. His teacher, Helen Gillette, rooms at the farm. She takes her meals at the big table in the dining room with Grama and Grampa, Ronald and Trever, and all the hired men.

For Ronald, the sun rises and sets on Miss Gillette. He goes across the field with her early in the morning, carrying both lunch buckets. He helps her open the schoolhouse, get the fire going, carry in wood, fill the water pail. After school, he washes the blackboard and claps the erasers on the outside of the school building so vigorously that the clouds of chalk dust make him sneeze.

He helps sweep out and tidy up. Then he walks back across the field with her, carrying both lunch buckets, now empty. Trever, in first grade, likes Miss Gillette, too, but he can't be bothered coming early and staying late.

Miss Gillette is fond of both boys, but she's concerned about Ronald, for as soon as he gets home from school he curls up with a book. Except for his chores, he reads till suppertime. After supper, he settles down again and reads till bedtime. It pleases Miss Gillette that Ronald likes reading so much, but she worries that he doesn't get enough exercise, doesn't play outdoors. All he does is read. She makes a bargain with him. She will read to him every evening after supper for an hour, if he will play outdoors after school till suppertime. Ronald agrees. He loves reading, but even more he loves being read to, especially if the reader is Miss Gillette.

There is plenty to do outside. He and Trever go down to the crick and repair the dam that makes their swimming hole. There are still hot days in September, and any day is good for the waterwheels they construct along the banks where the current flows fastest.

They have races in the field across from the house, starting with the big tree and each following the fence in the opposite direction, passing each other on the far side of the field, then running on around and back to the tree. When Ronald gets a stitch in his side, he stops quickly and spits under a stone. This is a sure cure. Though Ronald is older and taller, Trever always wins the races. Only once does Ronald outrun him. He's mad at Trever, chasing him, and his brother runs for the horse barn. Ronald has in his hand an old, large turkey egg he has found. He throws it at Trever just as Trever reaches the horse barn entrance. It misses, hits the top of the door just ahead of him, splatters back, and in the confusion of wiping egg from his eyes, Trever falters. Ronald overtakes him. Trever whirls, and a nasty fight ensues. Ronald wins because he's stronger and can pound Trever's head on the ground. But they are both covered with rotten egg.

They have another sort of contest. In the icehouse above the granary, they each keep hidden a metal cocoa can, the brand with the picture on its side of the lady in the long dress holding a cup of Baker's Cocoa. The contest is to fill your can with pee before your brother does. They'll be down at the crick, or some other outpost, and Ronald will notice Trever edging away from him. Realizing what's up, he'll break into a run just as Trever does. Panting and gasping, they'll reach the ladder to the icehouse and scramble up it. They'll dig their cans out of the sawdust, pry off the lids, fumble with their trousers, and start to pee. Such have been their exertions, however, that they are trembling. They piddle on the sawdust, piddle on their clothes, piddle on their hands. Precious little pee goes into the cans. They conduct this contest honorably—neither one would dream of sneaking up to pee alone or pour pee from the other's can.

Out in the horse barn, they gather horse apples and keep them in special spots. Ronald's cache is in an unused horse manger. When cold weather comes, they don't have to wait for snow for snowballs; the horse apples freeze solid, and they have horse-apple fights. Ronald is usually the victor in a horse-apple fight.

Ronald, eight, when Miss Gillette was his teacher.

They find an old umbrella in the farm dump and make bows and arrows to play Indian. The long spokes form the bows; they tie bowstrings to arch them. The short spokes are the arrows. They hold the arrows to the grindstone and pump the treadle. The grindstone whirls. Sparks fly from the spoke. They grind until the spoke becomes needle sharp. Trever shoots an arrow and hits Ronald in the eye. They rush him to the hospital. The arrow has pierced only the white part, so he won't lose his sight. But he wears a patch for a month. Their father confiscates the bows and arrows.

And every night Miss Gillette reads aloud, from *St. Nicholas* magazine, or Dickens, or *The Little Shepherd of Kingdom Come*. Trever, and Ronald with his patch on, curl up on either side of her. Grama listens and knits. Sometimes Grama plays a game of chess with Grampa during the reading, for though he's glad it's going on, he can't hear it.

Miss Gillette clowning with two of the hired men.

On some nights, however, Miss Gillette doesn't read. She has a beau, whose name is Red Beaumeister. He has fiery red hair. He comes out to the farm and carries Miss Gillette away in his buggy. Ronald watches them go and feels twinges of jealousy. He wishes he were old enough to be Miss Gillette's beau.

Spring comes. Ronald pokes a bar of metal from the dump through a bob-wire fence. He turns it over and over, winding up the two strands of wire till they are taut as a spring and will turn no farther. Then he lets go. The spring unwinds in a flash, spinning the bar of metal faster than the vanes on the windmill in a high gale. At the end, the bar spins right out of the fence and strikes Trever on the chin. They rush Trever to the hospital. He has to have seven stitches.

Ronald learns that Miss Gillette is going to marry Red Beaumeister. The wedding will be on the lawn, as soon as school is out. The spirea bushes and Grama's roses will be the background. Grampa will be the minister. Grama will bake the cake and handle the reception. Everyone is invited: Ronald and Trever, the hired men, the schoolchildren and their families, people from town. It will be a gala event.

Although Ronald is sorry he can't marry Miss Gillette, he accepts the fate that has made such a difference in their ages and pitches vigorously into the wedding preparations. He helps Grama with the kitchen work, keeping the wood box full for the baking. He peels chicken off the bones of boiled hens for the chicken salad. He helps the hired men groom the lawn, he helps Miss Gillette pick flowers to put around the house. He hangs over his father's shoulder while Grampa refreshes himself on the wedding service.

On the morning of the great day, he helps carry all the chairs from the house to the front yard and arrange them in rows. Then he helps the hired men build trestles of planks laid across milk cases for the overflow guests. When there's nothing more for him to do, he goes and scrubs up thoroughly. He gets dressed in his Sunday suit, a white shirt and tie, his long black stockings, and his best shoes. He wanders into the kitchen.

His mother exclaims when she sees him. "My goodness, Ronald! It's still an hour and a half till the wedding! Don't get dirty, now!"

Ronald moseys around, keeping clean. Everybody else is still busy. He takes a book he's begun, *A Connecticut Yankee in King Arthur's Court,* and goes up to his room. He settles on his bed and starts to read.

He reads how the Yankee is transported back to King Arthur's time. He reads how he saves himself from death at the stake by predicting the exact time of an eclipse of the sun. He reads how it feels to joust, in a ludicrously hot and heavy suit of armor, and, worse yet, have a fly invade your helmet. He reads and reads, lost in the magic of Camelot. He finally reaches the last line, finishes it, and takes a moment to return to reality. The sun slants through the window.

Suddenly he remembers. The wedding! He sits up, transfixed. Things are strangely silent. He leaps off his bed, flings open the door, and races downstairs through the empty house out onto the lawn. He stops dead.

Some hired men are carrying the trestles away. Out on the road, Trever is throwing a stick for Bob to chase. There's no sign of his parents, the bride, the groom. Not a guest is in sight. Ronald stands stricken. The wedding and the reception are long over.

He crawls into the middle of the lilac bush, where no one can see him, and cries.

5 HEELS

Ronald is just twelve, in May 1914. When June comes, he graduates from the final grade, the eighth, at the district school across the field by the crick. Before being accepted at high school in town, all country-school graduates must pass examinations. These are held at the county seat. Ronald goes to Janesville and spends two exhausting days taking tests. He fails in three subjects, a rude surprise, for he's a voracious reader, did well in the district school and also in Strong School, across from Aunt Ida's on Bushnell Street, where he attended for brief periods. He'd even skipped two grades.

Grampa and Grama confer. There isn't much point in sending their son back to country school. He'd feel disgraced, and the teaching, or his application, or a combination of the two, are obviously lacking. He should be tutored and then give the exams another try. But there's no rush. He's two years younger than his classmates starting ninth grade. They decide to keep him home a year, have him study with his cousin Hazel Croft, now a teacher in Beloit, and work on the farm. He's small for his age. This plan will allow growing time for both mind and body.

Ronald is jubilant. He'll be a regular farmhand; he'll receive wages! A dollar a day! He'll have a title: Assistant Herdsman. Summer and riches spread gloriously before him. He doubts if he'll have much time for studying.

The evening before his starting day, his father calls him to his desk, has him sign his worker's contract, and gives him a solemn talk about responsibility. Ronald stands on the red rug, the spot where all new men stand to learn Daddy Dougan's expectations. Later, he knows, they are sometimes summoned there to be reprimanded or praised. He determines that he shall be one who is praised. He goes to bed before sundown.

He wakes early, filled with zeal. He hurries to the barn. It's clean and in

All the hired men. Ronald is in the middle, sans cap, his arm linked through his father's. This is on the ramp to the round barn loft, a favorite spot for pictures.

readiness; it's been scraped and limed the evening before. The cows' grain is in their mangers. He would have liked to fetch the cows, but they don't need to be fetched. They're already in the barnyard, jostling at the vestibule, stamping and lowing. Their bags are heavy with milk. They are nervous; a storm's about to break. Ronald beats the herdsman to open the doors.

Bessie, the boss cow, leads in and heads along the sidewalk to the stall she always takes. The second most important cow is next, and then the third in rank. The old cows, the timid ones, and the new milkers bring up the rear and get whatever stalls are left to them. Bessie steps across the gutter, thrusts her head through her stanchion, and starts to eat. Ronald snaps the stanchion shut and goes around the circle, snapping the others.

The men milk. Ronald does his share, but that isn't so very different; he's been milking cows regularly since he was six. What is different is the way he

The cow barn from the middle—where Ronald fell. The cows were all facing him, and duly startled. The number of Holsteins indicates this picture is from the fifties.

feels, grown up, joshing with the other men, being a real part of the group. Outside the thunder rumbles, the rain begins to pelt down. They finish the milking but leave the cows in their stanchions until the cloudburst ends.

Up in the kitchen, Ronald eats a breakfast of sausages, eggs, and a huge stack of buckwheats. He finishes first and beats everyone back to the barn. He looks around for what to do next. The cows are restless, their mangers empty. He hurries to the upper barn and climbs the ladder into the haymow. The hay level is high from the June haying; it's near the top of the chutes. He grabs a pitchfork and vigorously attacks the hay. It's hard work getting it loosened and onto his pitchfork. He wrestles forkful after forkful into a chute. But the hay refuses to fall to the cow barn floor, some thirty feet below. It lies there, sagging slightly, caught against the chute's wooden sides.

Ronald has seen a hired man fill the chute, then hang on a slat and stamp the hay to dislodge it and send it down. He's even seen one occasionally ride the load down into the lower barn. He grasps the top slat, swings into the chute, and gives the hay a stamp. It's stamping on air, there's no resistance. In his surprise he loses hold of the slat and follows the hay down with a whoosh. He hits the concrete floor. The cows in their stanchions rear back in one wild, bulgy-eyed leap. The simultaneous clank of all the stanchions is sharp punctuation to the jar through his head and neck and teeth, to the pain that rips through his feet. There is hay under him, yes, but not enough to make a real cushion. He hadn't filled the chute full enough.

He sprawls there, contorted with agony. He gasps out words it's good his father can't hear, words he didn't even know he knew. He crawls around on his hands and knees before the startled cows, blinded with pain, weeping tears of humiliation, raging at himself for being a fool.

The herdsman comes in, finds him, carries him up to the house. Grampa examines his injuries, then hitches up the buggy, and he and Grama hurry him to the hospital. The doctor says he's broken both his heels.

Ronald is on crutches half the summer. He has plenty of time to work with Hazel on his fractions, to improve his spelling, and to memorize the major rivers of the world.

6 ESTHER, PART ONE

It is May 1915. Wesson and Eunice are on their way to town to take the train to Sparta, where the Wisconsin Home for Dependent and Neglected Children is located. As they leave, they stop at Marstons', their closest neighbors down the road. Lura Marston, and her mother, Mrs. Smith, are the only ones in whom Eunice has confided about the many miscarriages she has had since Trever's birth, eleven years ago. Eunice says to the Marstons' only child, "Oh, Eloise, we're going to get you a little playmate, just your age."

Eunice and Wesson have longed for a daughter ever since their own first child died within a few hours of birth. At Sparta they sign indenture papers for a beautiful almost-six-year-old girl. She has light brown curly hair and a sweet face. Her most striking feature is her eyes, unusually large and blue. Eunice and Wesson are charmed. Her name is Agnes Groose. The papers state that Agnes is to stay with the Dougans until she is eighteen, at which time they must provide her with "two suits of good clothes" and fifty dollars, and she will be on her own. The papers also instruct that she be taught a trade at which she will be able to earn a living.

Agnes has sisters and brothers at the orphanage, but Wesson and Eunice take only her. They are not told anything about Agnes's parents.

They return on the train. At the farm Agnes meets her new brothers, Ronald and Trever, and they show her all over the house and barns. She is quiet and shy. She has her own room upstairs. Eunice arranges her few possessions in a drawer.

That night Eunice holds Agnes on her lap before bedtime. Agnes cuddles against her. Eunice says to her, "We've wanted a little girl for so long! Ever since our own baby died. We're going to change your name to Esther, after that baby, and after Esther in the Bible."

Ronald, Trever, and Esther, shortly after Esther joined the family.

Agnes's body goes stiff. She draws away from Eunice. She will not cuddle anymore. Hurt and upset, Eunice puts Esther to bed.

A few days later, Eloise Marston is invited to a tea party. She arrives, all dressed up. Esther is dressed up, too. Eunice introduces the girls and brings in the tea.

There is a small table and chairs and a cloth on the table. There is a small china tea set with a little teapot and diminutive cups. There are small sandwiches on a plate.

Esther presides at the teapot. "Won't you have some tea?" she asks politely. "Oh, *pardon* me," she says frequently, even when there isn't any need. Eloise is disappointed. Esther is so proper, so exaggerated. What sort of fun can she be?

When the party is over, Eloise says, "Goodbye, Esther."

Esther leans forward, her eyes suddenly hot and angry. "My name *isn't* Esther!" she hisses. "It's *Agnes*, the name my mother named me!"

The weeks go by, and Esther turns out to be fun to play with after all. She loses her formality. Eloise decides that that first day was the result of the new situation and the training of the orphanage.

Trever is delighted with a little sister. After all these years, he now has someone who will look up to him and listen to him, and Esther is an avid listener. He sits on the flour box in the kitchen and tells her stories while she fills the wood box for him. She follows him around and admires his ability in running and throwing and shooting pigeons with his air rifle. Ronald is glad enough to have a sister, too, but he's thirteen and busy with other things. Esther's coming doesn't particularly affect him.

On her sewing machine, Eunice stitches sturdy play clothes for her new daughter. She makes her a dress for church and enrolls her in Eloise's primary class at Sunday School. She shows off her pretty little girl to all the other mothers. Esther smiles shyly at the attention.

Esther's new father takes her with him to see the piglets and to watch the calves being fed. At night, he sometimes holds her in his lap and they look at a picture book together.

Esther settles so well into life on the farm that it isn't long before it seems as though she has always lived there. She and Eloise are best friends and share a desk at school.

Esther (on left) and Eloise playing dress up.

When Christmas comes, Esther receives a large and beautiful doll from her foster parents.

She names the doll Agnes.

She also receives, from Wesson's sister Lillian, a little silver spoon with AGNES GROOSE engraved on it. Neither Lillian nor anybody has been told Esther's former name, but Aunt Lillian rummaged through her brother's private papers and ferreted it out. The spoon is her way to remind Esther that she is not really a Dougan. Grama and Grampa are furious; Grama confiscates the spoon and hides it away in her own dresser drawer. "'Agnes!'"

she exclaims as she crumples the tissue paper around the slender object and shoves it underneath her handkerchiefs.

Esther and Eloise are chums during their childhood. They play dress up together. Eloise's Grandmother Smith keeps, on an old iron bedstead in the attic, a number of basic hat forms of both felt and straw and one of velvet. At each change of season, she selects a suitable form from the "hat bed," buys ribbon or feathers or flowers or a little veil, and decorates her hat. The girls take the old ribbons and feathers and flowers and veils and decorate hats for dress up. Eunice lets Esther have her old hats for play, too, and long dresses, purses, and gloves. They keep Cracker Jack prizes and other small treasures in the purses.

The girls make elegant mud pies. Ronald and Trever made mud pies when they were younger, but theirs were rude affairs compared to the girls' confections. They carry down from the barn buckets of ground grain and make golden fillings for their chocolate layer cakes. They sprinkle white lime from the slack lime bin for frosting. They decorate cookies with fat brown velvetweed seeds for raisins and whole corn kernels. They carry off so much oil meal that the herdsman, passing them, says, "Hey, how much of that cattle feed are you using here, anyway?" But when Wesson passes he pauses, laughs till his eyes crinkle, admires the cakes, pats the playmates on their heads, and exclaims to the world in general, "Little gellies having fun!" "Gellies" is the way he always pronounces "girlies." The girlies smile up at him but don't speak.

The two listen in on club meetings in the living room of the Big House, or at the Marston house, and form their own club, the Cicero Club. Its elegant name comes from the writer whom Ronald is translating in his Latin class. Esther is president, and Eloise keeps the minutes.

The girls continue to attend school together, in the one-room district schoolhouse on the edge of the Dougan East Twenty. They go to Sunday School together and are in Mrs. Frey's class. When Mrs. Frey passes the collection basket, Eloise usually puts in three cents. Sometimes, if she's lucky, it's a nickel. The other children also put in small amounts. All except Esther Dougan—Esther usually puts in fifty cents. Mrs. Frey exclaims, "Oh, look, children, what Esther has put in! Fifty cents to go to the missionaries! Isn't that splendid, children? Esther, dear, you must save all your money, you have so much to give. What a generous girl! Don't you think so, children?"

Esther smiles and blushes. "I get paid for my chores," she says.

At one point Mrs. Frey says to Eloise, "Don't feel bad, Eloise. Esther's a Dougan, and she can afford it." But Eloise is aware of Daddy Dougan's desk and the cashbox. Wesson's office is at the end of the living room, a large rolltop desk against the north wall. The cashbox is on a shelf in a drawer. When the drawer opens, the cashbox can be swung out. Every day the milkmen come in after noon dinner and check in from their routes. They have lots of change in their change makers, for many people pay for their milk by leaving pennies and nickels and dimes in the returning empty bottles. The routemen count their money and put it in the cashbox.

W. J. isn't careful about the cashbox. When there's a sudden call, an emergency in the barn or field or milkhouse, he leaps up as if he's killing snakes and is off running, leaving the cashbox unlocked, and sometimes even open. Eloise has seen this happen several times. She knows Esther has, too. And she knows that Esther sometimes helps her father stack the pennies, the nickels, and the dimes and slide the stacks into little dusky rose or green or blue sleeves, making fat heavy cylinders to take to the bank.

When the wartime flu epidemic strikes, the farm is hard hit. Eunice is ill; the help are ill; Ronald and Trever are ill. Aunt Lillian moves out from town, and she and her brother, Wesson, put in twenty-hour days doing all the barn and the milkhouse work alone. Esther, who doesn't become ill, is shipped to town. She lives at Aunt Ida's and goes to Strong School across the street for several months.

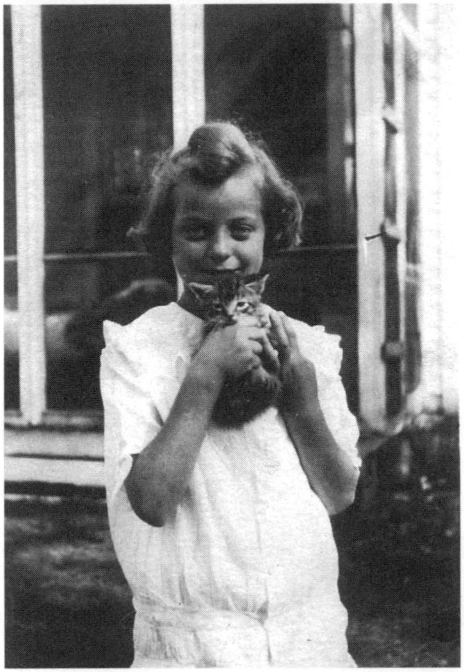

Esther with a kitten.

Albert Marston, Eloise's father, is returning with his team and wagon from the grist mill on the west side of town one day when he spots Esther wandering through a vacant lot several blocks from Strong School. It's during class hours. Esther spots him, too, and immediately drops into the tall weeds, where she can't be seen. Albert stops and calls to her, but she doesn't respond. He tells his wife; Lura reports the incident to Wesson and Eunice. She feels they ought to know, to nip such behavior in the bud. Her parents ask Esther about her truancy. She is entirely innocent. She was in school the whole day. Mr. Marston couldn't have seen her. They believe Esther. They don't check with the school. Eunice tells Lura in the Marston kitchen that

Albert is wrong, that he must have mistaken some other little girl for Esther. But Albert knows whom he saw. Thereafter, whenever Eloise tells her parents of Esther's deceptions, they don't tell the Dougans and instruct Eloise to stay quiet. "Her folks believe Esther in preference to anyone else," says Lura. Albert says, "We won't get mixed up in it again."

They try not to get mixed up in other ways. Esther often wants Eloise to stay overnight, but Eloise is reluctant. Esther has to get up very early; she's on the job by 5:30. Eloise feels uncomfortable staying in bed while her friend is working. She always gets up and helps, too.

"Then don't stay over," her grandmother Smith advises. "Say you're needed at home. That's true enough." She adds, "The Dougans are too hard on Esther. They order her about."

Lura mimics Eunice Dougan's sharp voice. "'Esta—get Ronald some more milk.' 'Esta—Trever hasn't had his pie yet.' 'Esta!' 'Esta!' 'Esta!'"

"I don't think Wesson realizes how hard Eunice is on Esther," Mrs. Smith says. "He can't hear."

Lura sniffs. "He has eyes, hasn't he?"

"Eyes can't smell trouble," Mrs. Smith replies.

7 PAGEANT

It is 1916. Ronald has just turned fourteen and is finishing ninth grade at Beloit High School. He's young for his grade and small for his age. His English teacher is Miss Annie McLenegan. She is a stern taskmaster, but he's learned more from her than from any teacher yet. Lately he's been learning history as well as English, the history of Beloit, for everyone is caught up in pageant fever. And Miss McLenegan most of all.

It's now eighty years since Caleb Blodgett came from the East and built his hostelry between the banks of Turtle Creek and Rock River, founding what was first called New Albany, then four years later changed to Beloit. Some myopia of the city fathers allowed Beloit's seventy-fifth anniversary, in 1911, to slip by without notice. But Annie McLenegan, in her capacity as director of the Beloit New Drama Society, determined to rectify the error. She spoke to the mayor, Harry Adams; she spoke to Professor Theodore Lyman Wright; she spoke to a woman in Madison experienced in putting on municipal pageants. The result is a massive event that will glorify Beloit's past and prophecy its future. The pageant itself, by the pride it engenders in Beloiters, will help bring that future to pass. The town will sponsor it; Professor Wright, with the help of a fellow professor, will write it; the Madison woman will direct it; and any Beloit resident may take part. Annie McLenegan and the New Drama Society are the organizers and indefatigable workers. The site is a natural amphitheater on Rock River, north of the Fairbanks Morse factory, known as the Frog Pond. It is rechristened "Pageant Park." The dates are Friday and Saturday, June 1 and 2, with performances both days at two and seven. The project, begun almost a year ago, is nearing fruition.

The ninth- and tenth-grade boys are Indians. Technically, Ronald isn't a Beloit resident, but he's included because he goes to Beloit High. Trever is in the pageant, too; he's been attending Strong School off and on this year. He's not happy about being a blade of grass, but all the Royce and Wright and Strong School students are grass or prairie flowers. He wishes he were going to Merrill. It's the Merrill School boys who get to be Turtle Creek and bullfrogs.

None of the country schools are invited to participate. Esther's and Eloise's hearts are bitter. They would be willing to be anything. Mainly, they ache to wear the long calico dresses and carry the lunch buckets that some of the girls in their Sunday School class get to. They yearn to portray little pioneer girls and to be in on the heady excitement of the pageant.

And exciting it is. The main actors have been rehearsing for months; Ronald and Trever's rehearsals began mid-March. His mother sews Ronald soft leather shorts with fringes at the sides, and a bright red breechclout. She cuts out and stitches up moccasins. He won't wear a shirt but will have ropes of beads looped around his neck and down his chest. All his skin that shows will be painted red. He painstakingly makes and decorates his own headband and sews a large turkey feather into the back. Esther and Eloise hang on his table. Grama makes Trever's grass blade costume, too, from a pattern all the grass blades' mothers have been given. Esther and Eloise loiter by the sewing machine, fingering bits of coarse green fabric. They try on Trever's hat, which extends to a long point and has a flexible rod sewed into the length of it so that it will bend a little yet not flop over. They are consumed with envy.

W. J., eligible as a Beloit businessman, is in the pageant, too. He will be among the early settlers and lead a heifer across the stage. His costume is nothing to covet, just a simple shirt and pants. He doesn't need to go to practices, either, only to the dress rehearsal.

The night before the pageant is dress rehearsal for just the national groups. An international procession in full dress will form an elaborate and colorful finale and show all the nationalities contributing to Beloit's culture,

The Blackfoot Indians. It's hard to be sure, but Ronald is probably the slim boy kneeling, left center.

education, and industry—the Swiss, the Greek, the Norwegian, the Lithuanian, and sixteen more. The main dress rehearsal was the night before that. Ronald found it thrilling to be covered with war paint and to race whooping out of the trees onto the spotlighted stage with the other Blackfoot Indians. Trever complains that his part is not as much fun. The grass mainly sways until it gets mowed down by the newly invented reaper.

At supper the night before, Ronald's face and ears, still somewhat ruddy from the grease paint, and Trever's skin with its greenish tinge, are visual reminders of the pageant. But no one needs to be reminded. The talk is of nothing else. The newspaper has been building to it for weeks. Huge crowds are expected; Beloiters are urged to get their tickets ahead of time to cut down the pressure and delay at the ticket booths. The newspaper shows where private conveyances can park in a well-lit, policed area. It gives the

The blades of grass (boys) are on the left, the meadow flowers (girls) on the right. Trever, one of the grass blades, cannot be identified.

route of the Interurban that will be bringing at least twenty-five hundred people up from town for each performance. People can come in motorboats only to landing sites north and south of the park. No motorboats will be allowed on the river during performances. River Road will also be blocked off, to prevent accidents to pedestrians and eliminate traffic noise. To assist in keeping order, the soldiers of Militia L have been sworn in as additional policemen, able to make arrests.

W. J. skips the after-supper Bible reading and instead reads aloud the synopsis of the pageant, printed in the *Daily News* as an aid to appreciating the city-drama. The whole family and all the hired men listen. They will all attend. Grampa, of course, won't be able to hear the actors or music, even during his own part, so the synopsis is especially useful to him.

" 'When the Pageant unfolds its ponderous beauty before the eyes of thousands,' " reads W. J., " 'there will be scenes that will stir one's blood, excite pity, wring laughter from the stubbornest throat, open the dry ducts of sentiment, and start old memories surging in the stiffened brain.' "

Grampa pauses, looks all around the table, rubs his head, and laughs. Then he continues. " 'There will be something for everybody in that dramatized history of Beloit life. Imagine you are already seated on the hillside waiting for the performance to begin. The audience is still, there's the signal. Coming down out of the green background figures appear.' "

Grampa reads how the ice that buries the great Northwest is symbolized by Father Time, and how he also foreshadows the coming centuries, the ultimate founding of Beloit, and its manufacturing preeminence. "The paper says that," and Grampa reads, " 'this will be a mighty pretty scene, and should put the spectator in the mood to receive all of the great drama. But it is really only a preliminary. Take a long breath after its beauty is past, for the real drama is about to begin.' "

Ronald, who not only has watched rehearsals but has also had to memorize the beginning of the pageant in English class, interrupts his father to expand on just how pretty it will be. Father Time is supposed to be the glacier, and he has with him a horde of snowboys dressed in white. Two tall men—professors from the college—are in robes with turtles on them, and they are East Wilderness and West Wilderness; they are surrounded by Father Time and the snowboys.

" My cold! My cold prepares the Hill for heat," Ronald declaims, deepening his voice.

> These icy shufflings of my frozen feet
> Shall carve a valley for the future home
> Of all the flaming energies to come,
> When toil shall shape a City-life complete
> Beside Rock River, 'neath the sun's sky-dome.

"Then the snowboys hail the sun and the end of the Ice Age, and they peel off their white robes and they all have red jackets underneath; the stage changes from white to red like magic! The snowboys turn into sunboys! And they drive the glacier from the stage with little daggers of flame. Then the college girls come on and dance with blue balloons; they're supposed to be the Zodiac and planets and months and years."

Ronald signals to his father to continue reading, and he does, about the coming of the mound builders, who create the outline of a turtle mound on stage, carrying the sacred earth in earthenware vessels, and hold a solemn burial of their chief. The migrating Winnebagos disperse the mound builders and settle next, and there's a scene of Indian life, with bark wigwam building and fires and cooking and children playing lacrosse.

"Mr. Perrigo is Chief Walking Turtle," says Grama. "My, you should see his costume!"

Then from the river comes a burst of robust song, and the first French traders beach their canoes and cross the road singing. They trade with the Indians and leave behind the first white settler in the Rock Valley, Thibeault, and his two squaw wives.

The next scene is of Steven Mack and Ho-no-ne-gah, the Indian princess who frees his bonds, and he marries her. These are familiar names to everyone—Hononegah and Macktown are small towns nearby.

Soon comes Chief Black Hawk, seeking alliance in war against the white man, but the peaceful Winnebago refuse, and their village is destroyed by Black Hawk's Indians.

Ronald gives a quiet whoop.

"That's where Ronald comes in," Grama supplies, unnecessarily.

In pursuit of the marauders comes a troop of rangers and backwoods soldiers. One is Captain Abraham Lincoln, who is beaten in a wrestling match, as actually happened; he tells one of his stories; wins in a feat of strength; and gives the first antiliquor address in the Beloit area.

"I don't imagine drink had anything to do with Lincoln's losing the wrestling," W. J. says gravely, but his eyes twinkle.

The Parade of Agriculture. Grampa, in white coveralls, is leading a heifer.

And then, in 1836, Caleb Blodgett and his family arrive, in their prairie schooner. This scene is of special interest to all the farm, for not only is it where W. J. walks across with the heifer, but actual Blodgett descendants play the Blodgett parts. One of these is Mr. Sid Blodgett, whose fields adjoin the farm.

"Actually, lots of descendants are playing the parts of their ancestors," says Grama, who knows the pageant as well as Ronald does. "Professor Lucius Porter plays his grandfather in the founding of the college, and Mr. Wheeler plays his, who invented the Eclipse windmill, and the very great-grandchildren will portray the settlers' first wedding; they're using the actual dress. Oh, it's going to be grand!"

Grampa reads on: the establishment of the college, with people giving up their lots so that the college will have a central place in town, on top of the hill beside the river. Horace White's gift of the large city park. In a symbolic interlude, the river's bluffs and Big Hill are shown by YMCA tumblers and a troop of gymnasts. Flowing between the hills, a large group of college and high-school girls interpret the Sinnissippi, which is Rock River by its Indian name. In parody of that dance, the boys who represent Turtle Creek and its envied bullfrogs caper and leap. Then Father Time leads industry into Beloit, with girls doing wind dances, followed by Wheeler and the harnessing of the wind by his Eclipse windmill; the dance of the prairie grasses and flowers—

"Trever's part," inserts Grama, and Trever makes a face.

—reaped by the twine binder invented by John Appleby; followed by the damming of the river and the laying down of railroads by laborers doing a mechanical drill; the coming again of Abraham Lincoln on a campaign tour; the start of the Civil War, with the departure of the soldiers and then their glad and sad return; and Lincoln's death. There follows the threefold dance of Industry: Smoke, Steam, and Electricity, using hundreds of college and city girls—

"There's pipes buried in the ground," Ronald interrupts, "and in the middle of the dance, they puff out steam and smoke, and the girls dance behind, like they're in clouds. But not too close."

—and the grand finale, which is the International Procession of Education and Industry, with a solo dance by Miss Farman of the college, the director of all the dancing. She interprets the pageant flag, just voted Beloit's official municipal flag, the Flaming Wheel, designed by Professor Wright.

"Two thousand Beloiters are acting in the pageant—one tenth of the city's population!" concludes W. J., shaking his head in amazement, and scanning the rest of the article. "They say this is the greatest endeavor the town has ever undertaken and the second largest pageant ever in Wisconsin.

Trever and his bicycle, at the age when he was tempted by the Perrigo job.

Trever is ecstatic. Fifteen dollars a day and quitting school besides!

"But . . . ," says his father.

Trever checks his rejoicing. He'd forgotten that almost everything has a "but."

"You'll have to pay me for the team and the use of the scoop. I'll need about half your pay, seven dollars and fifty cents a day."

Trever is daunted for only a moment. Fifteen dollars would make him a millionaire, but seven dollars and fifty cents is still an unheard-of salary. He nods vigorously.

"There are some other things you need to find out before you accept," W. J. goes on. "Go to your future employer and find out how long the working day is. Ask him how long the job is going to last and if you will have the stigma of being laid off."

The next day Trever returns with his tail between his legs. The day is from sunup to sundown. The job will last maybe a week, maybe a month. He tells his father he's decided not to take it.

The Perrigo place continues to bustle with activity, and Trever continues to trudge past it, morning and night. In a few months, the whole project fizzles when the seam of fine sand runs out. Left behind are the narrow-gauge tracks, a rusting steam shovel, and several deeply scarred acres which look like the savage scratches made by some monstrous creature in its death throes.

9 WHATEVER WILL HAPPEN . . .

It's January 1917. A glaze ice covers the roads and fields, making every twig on every tree, every stiff weed in the fencerows, swollen and glittering with a million stars.

The phone rings at the Big House. Grama answers it. She listens, gasps, shrieks, "Oh, no, no! I'll send Wess up right away, and the men!"

She hangs up. She spells rapidly to Grampa. Grampa doesn't catch it right away. His face is heavy with concentration on Grama's flashing fingers. She spells again, impatiently, crying aloud, "Shot! The little girl is shot! The Diderich girl! They have to have help!"

Grampa's face clears to register alarm and concern. "Tell the men to follow me!" he orders. He rushes out of the house without even a coat. A moment later he gallops by on Kit. Kit is a rotund little horse, and Grampa is riding her bareback with nothing but a bridle. He swerves onto Colley Road and heads for the second farm up.

Ronald and Trever rush to tell the men. They hastily hitch up a wagon. They all follow Grampa, some on foot, skidding and slipping on the ice, some riding on the wagon. At the second corner on Colley Road, by the schoolhouse, they find Grampa lying on the ice. Kit is standing nearby, her reins trailing.

"Leave me, help the little gelly!" Grampa gasps. "We took the corner too fast! Kit fell on the ice. I've broken my leg!"

Most of the men rush on. Two make a stretcher from a canvas in the wagon. They load Grampa on and bring him back to the Big House. They carry him in.

"Dearie," says Grampa to Grama, "I've broken my leg."

"Oh! Oh!" Grama wails. "Whatever will happen to me next?"

10 GRANITE

The little Diderich girl is dead. The accident happened like this. Mr. Diderich kept a loaded shotgun on two nails over the back door. Leona, who was nine, had to go to the outhouse. She jumped up to get her sweater off a nail. She dislodged the shotgun. It fell and discharged into her stomach. She lived till the next day.

The whole community grieves. Grampa and Grama grieve, and the hired men, and the neighbors. Trever grieves. Esther grieves, and Eloise. The girls are Leona's age, and Eloise was Leona's seatmate at school. Ronald grieves; he's a good friend of Leona's older sister Mary. He had always liked Leona, her thick auburn braids and freckles and the pert way about her.

When the hearse comes out Colley Road bringing Leona home from the undertaker's, Eloise stands at the living room window of the Marston farmhouse and watches it go by. She watches till it's out of sight around the bend beyond the dairy. Esther, Trever, and Ronald also watch, from the bay window of the living room of the Big House. A little later, word comes back that on the same corner where Grampa fell on Kit, the hearse tipped over and Leona's small white casket slid out and skidded across the ice.

Ronald and Trever and Esther don't go to the wake. Their parents do. Grama has been taking up food: cakes and pies and chicken salad and fresh bread. They hear from Grama that Leona lies in the little white enamel casket, in a soft white nightgown with lace, and that the doll she got at the schoolhouse Christmas party is cradled in her arms.

"She got that doll only three weeks ago," says Grama. "Who'd have thought that she'd be buried with it?"

There is no school the day of Leona's funeral. All her classmates attend, along with their parents. The whole neighborhood attends. The Diderich house is hard pressed to hold everybody. There are rows of wooden folding chairs from Rosman and Kinzer Funeral Parlor set up in the dining room. Grama, with Ronald, Trever, and Esther, sits there, beside Eloise and all the Marston household. In the living room the small white casket, now closed, rests on a table. Grampa, on crutches, is behind the table, conducting the service. The Diderich family is seated in the living room, a little apart from the others. From his spot, Ronald can see the casket, and his father, and the Diderich family faces.

"'Let the little children come unto me,'" quotes Grampa, "'and forbid them not, for of such is the Kingdom of Heaven.'"

"Oh, my baby, my Leona, my poor, poor, baby!" All through the service Mrs. Diderich sobs, keeping up a broken counterpoint to Grampa's strong theme of comfort. Mary keeps her arm around her mother.

Mr. Diderich stares straight ahead. He never looks at the casket. Not a muscle in his face moves.

Ronald is shaken. His eyes keep being drawn from the casket to the mother's wet and mottled face, to the father's granite one. He keeps picturing Leona's face and the soft white nightgown and the doll. He keeps picturing the two empty nails over the back door. He tries not to picture the wound or to imagine what it must have felt like.

When the service ends, the undertaker steps forward. But Mrs. Diderich is ahead of him. She staggers from her chair and flings herself onto the casket. She weeps hysterically. Grampa speaks to her with compassion, but she's beyond hearing. Mr. Diderich sits like a statue.

Nobody knows what to do. Finally, several men break her embrace. They wheel the small casket out the south door, to take it to the cemetery. Mr. Diderich walks behind it, looking straight ahead. Mrs. Diderich, now in a plush coat with a fur collar, follows. She's supported by Mary and two neighbors. "I can't go! Don't make me go!" she wails. Ronald hears Sally Holmes, his former first-grade teacher, say softly, "If she doesn't go, she'll always regret it."

The Dougan family is the last to join the procession. They wait for Grampa. He comes from the living room on his crutches. He shakes and shakes his head.

"I ache for the mother," says Grampa, "but I ache even more for the father. That poor man has an iron fist gripped around his heart."

II FINALITY

It is a few weeks after Leona Diderich dies from a gunshot blast into her stomach. She was Eloise's seatmate at school. Eloise misses her keenly. The teacher, Blanche Carpenter, has moved another student into Leona's empty space.

Today, Eloise has stayed after school, helping tidy up. Then she will walk home with Miss Carpenter, for the teacher rooms and boards with the Marstons.

In a large ledger, Miss Carpenter is filling out the attendance record for the end of the month. Eloise stands by her desk, watching. The teacher comes to Leona Diderich's name and draws a line through it. In the space following it she writes, "Deceased."

It is at this moment that Eloise first realizes the finality of death.

12 AUNT LILLIAN

Aunt Lillian, Grampa's third sister, is a trial to Ronald and Trever when they are boys. She oversees her nephews' language, manners, and play. She objects to their stockpiling frozen horse apples, which they use for ammunition in fights. She calls the droppings "choaties" and feels they should be swept up, left on the manure pile, and ignored as a by-product of existence.

"Even people make choaties," Trever objects, but Aunt Lillian lifts her chin sharply and looks in the other direction.

It's because of Aunt Lillian's nosiness and barbed tongue that W. J. suggests to Vera and Ron, when they come from France in 1924, married, that Vera trim three years from her age so that she'll appear to be only four years older than her husband. It's because of Aunt Lillian that Vera burns all her diaries just before Joan is born, so that if anything happens to her—she and Ron are living in the same house with Aunt Lillian, Aunt Ida, and Hazel—her most intimate thoughts won't be revealed to Lillian's prying eyes.

Joan is small when Aunt Lillian says to her, "Why are you looking at me like that? Why do you keep looking at my nose?"

Joan answers, "Because Mommy says you poke it into everything!"

Joan and her sisters and brother are older when Aunt Lillian objects to the words of the comic books they are reading out loud to one another. For "gosh" and "golly" and "gee whiz" Aunt Lillian makes them substitute "blank."

"They aren't even *swear* words," objects Craig. "They're only *slang!*"

Aunt Lillian sniffs. "In this house, I will not listen to such language!" "This house" is Aunt Ida's house, across the street from Strong School, on Bushnell. Lillian has long lived there with her widowed sister and pays room and board. The two sisters do not get along. After Ida dies, Lillian goes on living there with Ida's adopted daughter, Hazel.

Lillian comes to a family Sunday dinner at the Little House and investigates the ice box. "Who will drink the skim milk?" she calls into the dining room where everyone is seated.

"Nobody needs to drink the skim milk," Patsy calls back. "We just use that for the dog and cats."

Aunt Lillian rejoins the table carrying a glass of blue-tinged milk. "Then *I'll* drink the skim milk," she says. Forever after, when anyone is being a needless martyr, someone will remark, "Then *I'll* drink the skim milk."

Over the years, Lillian is a thorn in the flesh of her sister-in-law, too. Whenever Eunice accompanies Wesson on a speaking trip where they are away a few days, Aunt Lillian comes out to the farm. This is so that there will be someone in charge of the Big House, her brother says, but everyone knows it's primarily to separate her and Aunt Ida for a while and at a time when no one else—that is, Eunice—will have to put up with her. But Eunice always returns to something Lillian has done in the house—rearranged furniture, or altered schedules and menus, or made repairs on something that was working well enough before Eunice left. One time she proudly shows how she has "renovated" all the pillows. She'd taken the ticks off; laundered them; laundered the feathers, too; restuffed them; and sewed them back up. "They are like new," she boasts, but Grama fumes. "Those pillows didn't need cleaning!" she says. "Why doesn't Ida keep her home?"

She is sometimes a nuisance to the hired men. When she's at the farm, she insists on washing and salving the minor cuts and scratches they get on their hands. When it's a hot day and they come in, all sweaty, she sticks her head into the washroom off the kitchen and orders, "Now, before you splash that cold water all over your face, you soak your wrists real good until you cool off." Outside, she bosses the men and her brother, too, until W. J. gets exas-

Aunt Lillian in her thirties.

perated and exclaims, "*Oh,* go inside!" He can't hear his big sister calling him "Wessie," but the men can, and they smile.

Vexing as Aunt Lillian is, she has had moments of glory. She's the only one of Grampa's sisters not to marry. Aunt Della marries a rich man much her senior. When he dies she marries again. Her husbands provide her with fashionable dresses, elegant carriages, purebred riding horses, and many acres of land.

Aunt Ida also marries a much older man, James Croft, who drops dead crossing Horace White Park when Ronald and Trever are boys. Daddy's story of Uncle Jim is complete with quotes. He was an agent for the St. Paul railroad, and every morning he'd walk downtown and stop at Murray and Frank Johnson's grocery store. "He'd go in," says Daddy, "look around, take a dried apricot, maybe fish a pickle out of the barrel, and say, 'Dammit, your store smells just like a high-holer's nest, dammit, Frank!'—meaning a flicker nest; flicker nests smell particularly bad, worse than an owl's."

Facing the park was a livery stable. "I had a friend who lived next door," Daddy goes on, "and we'd build fires in his backyard, and the smoke would blow over the fence and make the stable owner mad. He had one of his outfits tied outside that day, and when he saw a man collapse in the park, he drove across, picked him up, saw it was Jim Croft, and drove him home, but he was already dead."

Uncle Jim was a difficult man, to believe Lillian, who writes in 1895, "Mother, don't mind Jim, he treats me that way too, he don't think how it hurts. . . . There are no hard feelings between any of us, Mother. Be good to Ida for she needs our help and council, she has her social duties to attend to but I fear she is almost a slave to them, I would free her if I could but she is happier that way." Lillian is perhaps referring obliquely to Jim's drinking; later, at Lillian's expense, he "takes the cure." The "cure" is a town one goes to that dries out alcoholics. But with Uncle Jim, the cure doesn't take.

Ida is left reasonably well provided for in the Bushnell Street house, though she sometimes takes in a roomer or two, to augment her income. Her daughter, Hazel, has a beau at one point. He smokes cigars; Aunt Ida doesn't approve of him. When he moves from Beloit, he writes Hazel letters. Her mother intercepts and destroys them. Hazel feels abandoned, and no doubt the young man thinks Hazel doesn't reciprocate his love enough to reply. The missives taper off and stop. No one ever tells Hazel of the deception, and she grows old and crabbed taking care of her mother. The one time she tries living in another city, Ida becomes so ill that Hazel has to return home.

But the third sister, Lillian, never marries. She becomes a telegraph operator. She has a job as station master and train dispatcher at the Elba station, a little office at a lonely country switching near Beaver Dam. She is the only woman in all the Chicago, Milwaukee, & St. Paul Railway system and has the responsibility of arranging thirty-four trains every twenty-four hours. She writes her mother, in the same 1895 letter where she commiserates about

Jim Croft, "Your letter received this morning and I could see how every line was filled with love and anxiety for my welfare. No, Mother, I promise you I will never, *never* marry anyone and especially an *old* man, so do not worry and in just one year I will quit office work and come home to stay. We will have a piano and some few pieces of nice furniture and you shall have *your home* as long as you live and I will do all in my power to make you happy and I intend to have a home of my own somewhere sometime and somehow if there is only one room in it but it will be all mine and a home. When I get it—the piano—you may give one hundred dollars toward it."

She goes on to say she's been poorly for several days, a severe time with bowel trouble, but is improving. She's taking a cinnamon medicine, also hemlock in water. Her mother isn't to worry; she lies down a lot and doesn't lift a pound or even sweep the office. She advises her not to get the cape, for capes are cold, and her cloak looks far better. She tells her not to worry that Wesson won't let anyone help him make the move, by team, to the MacFarland parsonage, but to please him by letting him get everything ready before she moves in. She finishes, "Mother dear cheer up as there are better times in store for both of us I am sure. . . . Be very careful to keep well, Mother, for I want you to live a long time that I yet may make you happy."

Lillian's office is equipped with a stove and benches and serves as a rest house where train crews can sit while their engines are watering. There is usually no one there but herself. For company she keeps a pet blue jay and a dog, Joe.

The blue jay is a nuisance. He jumps up and down on the open telegraph key and sends out garbled messages. Lillian stops him by throwing a handful of straight pins on the floor. The jay hops down and with his strong bill bends every one. He's also a nuisance to Joe. He waits till the dog is gently snoring, spread out on the floor with his underbelly exposed, then steps up and pecks him in a tender place.

One bitter cold night Lillian is at her post when the door opens, and men

Aunt Lillian at fifty-five, her age when she and Grampa ran the farm during the flu epidemic. She's with the collie, Bob. The small dog is Vic.

who are not railroad men start filing in. She grasps a stick of wood under her telegraph table but keeps her weapon hidden. Joe raises his head from his paws and watches. He shows no alarm. The men come and come, until there are fourteen in the small office. Each man raises his hat as he passes her and says, "Evening, ma'am." They are hobos. They sit down on the wooden benches. Lillian relaxes her grip on the kindling and returns to her work.

All night long the men sit there, not speaking among themselves or to Lillian. The first time Lillian lifts a log from the wood box to feed into the red-hot iron stove, one of the men takes it from her and performs the task. From then on, one or another refuels the stove when it needs it. The only voice heard is the blue jay's. When morning comes, the men stand up and file out. As each one passes her he tips his hat and says, "Thank you, ma'am."

It's often boring in the little office. Though it's against the rules, Lillian leaves her key open half the time and listens to people talking up and down the line. One day she hears an operator direct a freight down the track. She knows that just twenty minutes before, another operator from the opposite direction has sent a passenger train down the same track. She figures quickly and sees that the two trains will meet right outside her station. She rushes out, flags down the freight, and makes a very angry engineer pull onto the siding. He no sooner has gotten his long train off the main track than the passenger train whips by from the other direction. The engineer is subdued. Lillian is a true hero, but because of the reluctance of those who made the mistake to draw attention to it, and because Lillian was eavesdropping when she shouldn't have been (no matter how fortunately), she is not singled out for special notice.

All this is when Lillian is a young woman, before she comes to Beloit to live at Aunt Ida's after James Croft dies and to be a vexation to her young nephews.

Ronald and Trever are often at the house on Bushnell Street. It's a convenient place to stay when in town, or to be sent when guests overflow the Big House, or to be nursed when one is sick—for their mother, with all the work at the farm, has little time to spend on illness, while Aunt Ida's time is almost unlimited. They like to build castles on the tablecloth, using the sugar cubes Aunt Ida keeps in a lidded dish. Ronald, and once in a while Trever, get to go around with a wax taper and light the gas lamps; at the farm, there are only kerosene lamps in the house and lanterns for the barn. Aunt Ida's is their second home.

They sometimes attend Strong School across the street, and when he's in high school, Ronald rides his bike to Aunt Ida's for lunch. He plays marbles with the boys in the schoolyard and is late to his classes in the afternoon. He and Trever know all the children in the neighborhood. They spend many a soft summer evening playing Capture the Flag or Kick the Can or Duck on the Rock. Sometimes they are knights jousting with long poles underneath the moth-circled streetlamp, with bicycles for horses. One of the boys

Ronald jousts with is Lowell Putney. He lives right around the corner on Harrison Avenue.

In 1918, near the end of the Great War, an epidemic of flu sweeps the world. The strain is a killer. It's estimated, before the end, that twenty million people die; twice as many as soldiers and civilians killed in the war. Populations are decimated; whole families perish. In Beloit, one of these families is Lowell Putney's. He, his parents, and all his brothers and sisters die of the flu. Lura Marston, at the next farm to the dairy, sobs, "Oh, it's a bitter, bitter pill!" and because there is no family to mourn them, she and other friends gather in the Marston living room to pray and to recall together all they can of the Putney family.

Out on the farm, nobody is able to attend, for almost everybody is sick. Esther isn't; she's been shipped down to Aunt Ida's. But Ronald and Trever are sick. Grama is sick. Most of the hired men are sick. Every day a nurse comes out from town for a few hours, to tend everyone.

In the kitchen of the Big House, Hilda stays well. There is nobody in the milkhouse, nobody in the barn. One routeman, Charlie Kellor, doesn't get sick; he works a double shift. In the morning he peddles the east side. When he's done, he telephones Grampa, who meets him with a fresh team and loaded wagon where Colley Road ends at the edge of Beloit. Grampa takes Charlie's team and empty wagon back to the farm, and Charlie delivers the west side. The next day he reverses it. When he gets his second wagon back to the farm, Grampa has the bottles washed from the first load. Then Charlie washes the bottles from the second load.

Grampa doesn't get the flu. Neither does Aunt Lillian. She moves out to the farm and dons overalls, apron, and rubber boots. Day after day, side by side, she and her brother do all the barn work. Lillian washes udders. She milks. She pitches hay and grinds feed. She shovels manure into the manure trolley and hoses gutters. She carries buckets of warm milk to the calves. She tends the horses. And when there's a pause in the barn work,

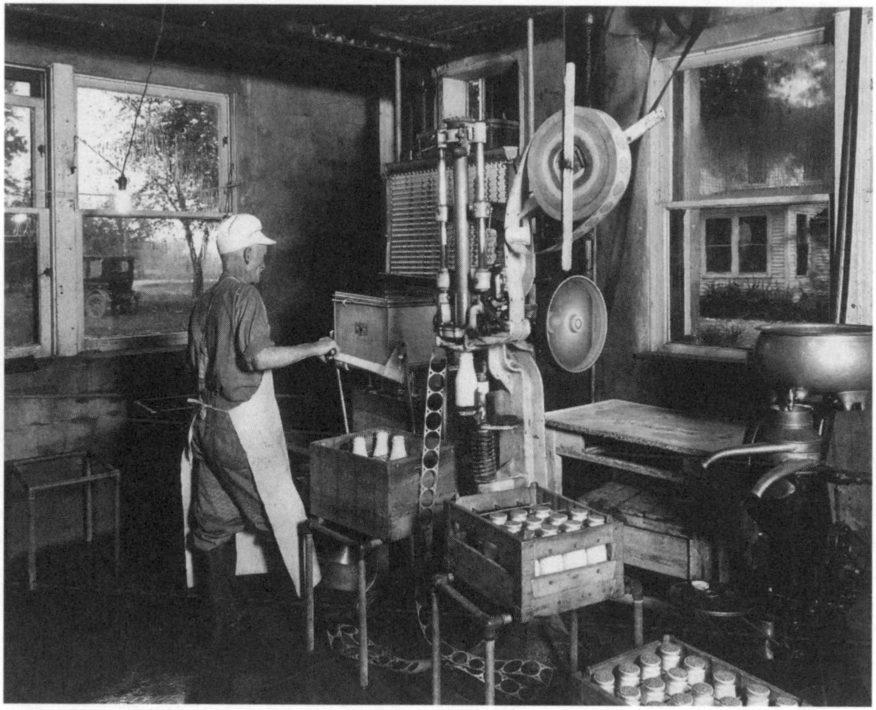

The milkhouse about the time of the flu, Pa Stam bottling. You can see a car and Colley Road out one window, the Big House out the other. The cream separator is on the right.

before it all starts over again, she and W. J. rush to the milkhouse, washing bottles and cans, separating cream, bottling the milk. "We'll fetch it!" Grampa keeps repeating. It is his battle cry.

It's a grueling, exhausting time. Aside from a few hours, there is no sleep. There's scarcely time to eat. And the work is accompanied with knowledge of death all over Beloit, all over the world, and especially anxiety for those of the household who are struggling to survive and those up and down Colley Road. Before the crisis is over and people begin trickling back to work, Grampa and Lillian are stumbling zombies, haggard shells.

But no one connected with the farm dies. None of the neighbors die. Every day the essential farmwork has gotten done and milk been processed and delivered to all Dougan customers. It's a triumph. The credit goes to the wills and stamina of Grampa, now fifty, and Aunt Lillian, fifty-five, and those few others who stayed well enough to work around the clock. Throughout the ordeal they've been upheld by Grampa's ringing "We'll fetch it!" and the glint in his eye. But there's no energy left for celebration.

Grampa does give a special blessing of thanksgiving when all the household is finally reassembled at the dinner table. By then, Lillian is back in town.

The Dougan children grow up unaware of Aunt Lillian's past except in casual mention. To them she's a fussy, forgetful, and difficult old lady. Jackie doesn't hear about the blue jay and the telegraph office, the hobos and the flu, until years after Aunt Lillian is dead.

13 FLY DOPE

It's the summer of 1923, and Grampa is looking forward to Trever's working full-time on the farm between his high-school graduation and starting at the University of Wisconsin in the fall. Ronald will not be home to assist; he is working in France for the year. Grampa needs Trever rather badly. He is also hungry for his companionship. But Trever has never been fond of farmwork and has other ideas. He's solicited to be a salesman for fly dope and takes the job. It involves driving. This is no problem, for he has managed to save enough from various jobs to buy a jalopy.

His father isn't happy at this turn of events, but because there's nothing he can do, he buys some of the product as Trever's first customer and applies it to the herd. The smallest amount comes in a five-gallon container. There's a special large sprayer that turns the liquid into a fine mist. The sprayer costs more than the five gallons do.

Trever peddles his wares up and down the roads of Turtle Township. He solicits all his father's friends and gets commissions, then goes farther afield to farms of farmers he doesn't know, in adjacent townships. He's a handsome young man and a personable one, with his sharp blue eyes, his wavy brown hair, his athletic frame. His manners are easy. He speaks well on any subject. Scarcely a farmer doesn't take time from his work to stand and chat.

When he gets around to his sales pitch, Trever is especially eloquent about the virtues of the fly dope. He explains how to apply it and shows the atomizer he says is important to use with the spray. Most of the farmers have some sort of small hand pump that they've always used; they don't need the atomizer. But they do buy the spray. Trever is a highly successful salesman. The work is not taxing, and he enjoys it.

About a month after Grampa starts using the fly dope on his cows, he

Trever with a milk truck, the summer he sold fly dope. The round barn is on the left.

begins getting complaints from customers about the taste of the milk. He himself can detect that the flavor is off, a little unpleasant and oily. There's even a bit of a smell. Everyone on the place sniffs, tastes, wrinkles a nose. W. J. rushes samples to the university, and after a while the trouble is traced to fly spray. Because Trever's is the only spray his father has used, it must be the cause. Grampa quits using the product and warns Trever.

Trever, however, is flying high. It doesn't seem likely to him that his spray can be the cause of the taste, and anyway, what's a little off flavor? There are only a few weeks of the summer left. He needs money for the university in the fall. He doesn't quit his lucrative business.

The Dougan milk shortly regains its usual excellent bouquet. Trever goes off to Ag School at Madison. The next summer, although his father again earnestly urges him to work on the farm, he signs up with the fly dope company once more. He starts down the road to revisit his old customers. His heart is light, his whistle jaunty. He's anticipating all the friendly, easy encounters. He's anticipating money in his wallet.

He is nearly tarred and feathered and run out of the township. Not only did the fly spray taint the milk but it took the hair right off the cows and blistered their skin. Trever tries to explain to the farmers that they used it wrong; they sprayed it on with a hand pump, which made large droplets, and also used far too much. But the farmers aren't about to listen. They want Trever and his fly dope off the place, and in a hurry.

Trever returns to the farm. W. J. puts him to work. When he's glumly driving a load of manure out of the barnyard, one of the hired men yells after him, "Hey, Trev! I see you got your old job back!"

Trever is not amused.

14 ESTHER, PART TWO

When Esther is ten, and back at country school, the teacher, Mrs. Ernie Smith, becomes pregnant and therefore has to resign. Esther's brother Ronald is now seventeen and waiting out a year before starting college. He's appointed teacher to finish the year. His sister and Eloise are two of his pupils. When he leaves, Mrs. Hugel comes, but she's not much interested in the job and often sends her father in her place. He leans back in his chair and poses the students mental arithmetic problems all day. Though they learn little else, they all become whizzes at adding long columns in their heads, especially one student, Robert Mackie. Then the school district is consolidated and all the students are driven in to town schools. Eloise and Esther, both eleven, go to Merrill School.

Ronald, a freshman now at Northwestern, hears frequently from his parents. While his mother's letters are full of worry about the state of his soul, the state of the laundry he sends home weekly, the state of the farm finances, and accounts of Trever's doings, she never mentions her daughter unless there is trouble. In February, she writes:

> We have been having another time about Esther. She took my watch to school, and when I went to get it, it was gone. I hunted all over and when Esther came home from school I told her to hunt. She went up and soon came down with it and said it was under a box on my dresser. I asked her if she had taken it to school and she said no, and repeated she had never had it, so I let it go. Ida was at Smiths Sunday and asked Eloise if Esther ever wore my watch at school. She said yes, one day, and Esther said she brought it downstairs and forgot to give it to me. (See her deceit?) Well Tuesday night we were alone setting supper table and I said, "Esther did you ever wear my watch to school?" She said, "No." I repeated and she declared no. I knew of course that she did, so I asked

> her if she had anybody's watch and she said yes, she wore a girl's watch. I took hold of her arm and looked into her eye and told her if she told me one lie more I would punish her severely. Then I repeated, "Did you ever wear my watch to school?" and she said, "Yes." Just think of the plight we are in. What can I do with her.
>
> I tell Papa with my help problem, by the way these new Swiss girls can't talk or understand English, and Esther, and Trever with his school and social problems, and his athletic ambitions and can't get in, and his underestimate of himself which makes him blue instead of happy and cheerful, and my anxiety about my beautiful oldest boy—all these are enough to give me nervous prostration. The only thing that helps me is the fact that God knows it all and I pray to him to guide and direct you all and I know he will.

At school, Esther always has money. At noon, she'll take Eloise and five or six other girls who carry their lunches down to a little grocery store on the corner of Porter and Copeland, just north of the railroad tracks. They will all select penny candy—jawbreakers and licorice whips and lemon drops—and Esther will pay. She's warm and generous and popular with the girls.

Later that spring, Grama learns that money is missing. She suspects Esther, and wrings the truth from her. She once more unburdens herself to Ronald:

> We are going through a bad time with Esther again. She is up to her old tricks. Ed came to me and told me he had missed a box of wafers and two dollars out of his room. I could not believe Esther had done it but yet could not see any other way. I got her up in her room and asked her if she knew anything about it. She said no—not a thing. Never had been in Ed's room, etc. etc. I said all right if you have Esther God knows it and he will tell me. Go to school and tonight be prepared to tell me the truth or it will go hard with you. When she came home she was full of plans to go to an entertainment and said she was in it. I said never mind that, we will straighten out that business about which I was talking this morning. She began to cry a little and said, "Well, I did take the wafers but I had nothing to do with the money and nobody can say I did." I made her look right into my eyes and tell me again and again. Then I let it drop awhile. Finally I came at her at a different angle and said,

> "Esther, what did you do with the money you took from Ed's pocket?" She looked at me in amazement that I should know and said, "I paid my debts with it." So after all of these terrible lies she confesses. "Debts!" I said. "What debts?" She said at the little store she had got things without paying for them. So you see the next thing was to get money somewhere. Just think of the hard boiled wickedness. I don't know what we will ever do with her. She acts as bold as if she had not done a thing.

In her next letter, Grama continues the sorry story:

> I told you last week about Esther. Monday morning I thought I would search her pockets just to be sure. I told her I hated to do it. She stood still without a change of color even. I felt in one pocket of her sweater and nothing but apple and handkerchief. I felt in the other and there was 16 cents. I nearly fell. I said, "Look, Esther, where did you get this?" Not a word. Again and again I repeated it and she finally put her hand in the drawer and pulled out the "Kings Heralds" envelope and said she took half of that. Imagine my feelings. I asked her what she could do with it when I had forbidden her to go to any store and forbidden the man to sell to her. She said she was going to buy candy of the teacher. It is a long story and I will not write more but what to do we do not know. I made her learn a prayer and say it every morning and night and learn verses from the Bible. "Be sure your sins will find you out" and "Thou shalt not steal." "Children obey your parents," and "Honor thy father and thy mother," and "A lie is an abomination unto the Lord," and "Thou God seest me" etc. etc. She can say any of them when I ask her. It is an awful thing.

Esther, increasingly beautiful as she grows into her teens, is also popular with the boys. So popular that Eloise, when they are in ninth grade at Roosevelt Junior High School, hears the rumor that Esther is pregnant. She tells Esther, who laughs and laughs at the ridiculousness of the idea.

At the Big House, there are usually six to eight hired men. These men are single, like Ed, whose wafers and money Esther stole, and for the most part young. They take their meals with the family, and read or play checkers or listen to the Victrola in the men's sitting room, off the dining room. They

Esther, about eleven.

wash up at a long sink in the washroom behind the kitchen. They have shower and toilet facilities closed off at the end of the washroom. The men use the back stairs and sleep, dormitory fashion, in several rooms opening off a long corridor. Where the corridor connects to the front part of the upstairs, the family area, there's a closed door. The men's sleeping quarters are strictly off-limits to Esther, except when on washday she helps change sheets and pillowcases on the bunk beds or when at mealtime she's sent to fetch a jar of beans or applesauce from the canning shelves that line the wall at the top of the back stairs.

The hired men—called "boys" by Eunice and Wesson and everyone—have always been of interest to Esther, sharing so closely as they do the family space. Back when she was nine, she wrote in a letter to Demice, a teenage Dougan cousin, after telling of a ride to town for her music lesson with Eloise and her mother, and of Trever's broken arm,

> We have four men that you don't know, I ges you know Richard or Dix for a nickname. If you don't know Dix it will make five boys you don't know. We have a new highered lady and her name is Ida and her last name is Kester and we all call her Miss Kester, and her brother works here too. And his name is Gie. I don't know how to write his name but the e is silent and the i is a long i like in the word, like, the i is a long one. The new boys names are Lynn, Lenard, Harry, and Gie. Our old Harry has left for good. I mean Harry Kristofson.

Eloise is in the family bathroom with Esther one day while Esther is cleaning it. The bathroom is the last room before the closed door in the corridor and shares a wall with a dormitory room. It's early afternoon, when the barn hands, who were up before four for milking, take a few hours' rest in their rooms after dinner.

"Listen," says Esther with a mischievous glance. She taps a light tattoo on the wall. There's a pause; then, from the adjacent room, the tattoo is answered. Esther taps again, a different rhythm. The rhythm is tapped back. Esther taps a third rhythm, and again it's returned through the wall.

"You shouldn't be doing that," says Eloise. "Which boy is it?"

"Oh, I don't know," Esther laughs. "Just one of them. It's a silly game we play."

Grama is not unaware of Esther's interest in the hired men. She writes to Ronald at college, "Esther is getting so crazy acting with the boys. They even tell her about it and tell her not to be so forward," and in another letter, "I am glad you went to Kohlstedts. I knew you would find Mildred a nice girl. She may be quiet. I wish Esther had more quiet reserve and modesty. I bet Mildred has character anyway."

Esther and Eloise go into high school. Eloise becomes ill and loses her fourteenth year, and almost her life, to scarlet fever and pneumonia. Every few days Eunice sends down a dish of the vanilla cornstarch pudding that Eloise likes. But Esther rarely visits her friend, and then only to stand outside and call through the window, for Eunice is afraid that Esther might catch something. So Eloise doesn't see Esther start off to school in the serviceable dresses that Eunice has sewn large for her to grow into, only to emerge later from the girls' washroom in gauzy, skimpy, stylish dresses; silk stockings; and dainty shoes.

Ronald, having finished his junior year, is now working in France. He writes home frequently. In a late summer letter in 1923, he muses about French customs:

> Take the matter of bringing up girls for instance. At home boys and girls play together in theoretically perfect comradeship. Here they never get together. A girl is always shielded by an older person—girls are taught to fear boys for the most part, marriages are arranged on a purely commercial basis, and there is no social life whatsoever. The only thing is, when the protection breaks down it is liable to be a sorry affair for the girl. At home girls are given practical freedom, they get a few knocks, I expect, but when they do come through they are better off—stronger, I guess. I'd hate to have the responsibility of being a parent in either country.

He goes on about his little sister and ends up giving a great deal of advice to his parents:

> I have been thinking about Esther a bit lately. She is practically grown up, even if she is only fourteen years old. She is probably having all sorts of dreams about glittering Sir Galahads and what not, that we can't know anything about. . . . I can remember the wonderings and all that I had only a few years ago. We aren't so far apart as I developed so much slower. I don't know, but I don't think she is exactly inclined to be the confiding sort, do you? It must take all kinds of tact to keep her confidence. Wish I were home to talk to her about the boys and girls she knows, and give her my ideas about conduct, and what not. It would never do to lecture to her. I think she rather looks up to me and if I gave her a picture of the kind of girls that likeable, decent fellows like, it might give her some ideas.
>
> She is just a normal, impressionable little kid, but with ideas years older than you had when you were her age, and much older than even I had. It surely won't do to blind ourselves to the fact that she is growing

up, and can't be disciplined much longer with lectures and "thou shalt nots."

All that I have said is so abstract—do you mind if I make a few more or less definite suggestions—things that I would do if I were with her.

In the first place I would recognize that she is going to have her masculine idols, and I would talk to her about them, never letting my ideas run away with the conversation, or never allowing myself to condemn them or become startled at her adoration. If she finds that one is more an interested individual who likes to exchange ideas without urging too strongly, the ideas will mean more to her than a thousand lectures. . . .

Then I would accept her ideas of her schoolmates pretty much on her say so, and talk about them with her. I would try to get to know them as much as possible, and that leads to another thing. She will never bring great carloads of them out to the house if she feels that they will be made to feel too uncomfortable by our scruples. For instance, if dancing is entirely in disfavor, she will hesitate to act as hostess because, I tell you mother, dancing is the chief amusement of the whole set, and when you take that prop away from a crowd that is too old for sliding down the straw stack, and too young to get a big kick out of prolonged conversations, you drive them away. Esther is bound to dance and play bridge. Wouldn't it be better if she did those things in her own home, with a good crowd of kids that you know, and in their homes, than with much the same crowd, but away from home where it would be impossible for you to know the crowd?

Then there is another thing—she will be asked to go out on dates very soon, if not already. You really must know the boys, and how are you going to do it if they haven't the courage to come around?

There are all sorts of things she will say if her confidence is gained that will be no end surprising to you, and that you can't imagine a little girl thinking or saying. The thing to do is keep the startled look off your face, take it as a matter of course, and by a subtly dropped word, attempt to give her your ideas. But don't think you can fit her exactly into the mold of little girls thirty five years ago—superficially, perhaps, but fundamentally, never.

Then about clothes—I know she is always well dressed, but I don't think her taste is far wrong, and she would get an awful kick out of planning the things she is to wear and all. Probably you do that with her already.

> About Trever, I know that after bumping around for a while as I am still doing, he will get things straightened out for himself. It is too bad you don't know more of his friends in Beloit, because he has lots of them; and thinks something of my judgment on them. He is striving for what is best in life—therefore his occasional discontent with himself when he finds out how little he really knows, or can do. I do think, though, you would have known more of his friends if the house had been open to what I deem innocent amusements, and which he has done anyway, but not at home. You say by not sanctioning it, you stand as a continual protest as to the state of things. I think there is another side to that. By condemning dancing, for instance, which is innocent of itself, when he does it, he can't help but think he is sinning, and because he does sin in that respect, other things are less of a step. Oh, I express it all so badly—but this is what I mean—open up the house to Esther's friends—let them play bridge, dance, let the boys smoke if they are used to it. It seems to me that that is the only way to keep the confidence of the girl. I surely am all for her. Forget that you are breaking your resolutions and are giving the neighbors a chance to wisely wag their heads at your seeming change of front—it doesn't really mean much anyway, if it is going to mean a greater comradeship with Esther. . . . I surely have been popping off. Forgive me if I have said too much—I do think once in a while, and then maybe twenty-one is pretty close to fourteen. I think so.

Eunice uses Ronald's letter as ammunition against Trever, who has just left home for the University of Wisconsin:

> Ronald wrote a long letter this week, mostly about Esther. That she is older than her years and is really a young woman. He hopes she will not be frivolous and foolish, but a fine type, etc. Hopes she will pick the right kind of friends among the boys and girls, etc., etc. I thought I would quiz her about her friends one day and asked her if she went with Margaret Branthaver at high school and she said, "No, she is foolish and paints and is silly with the boys. I won't go with such girls for I don't want to lose my rep. I tell you if you once lose it it is hard to get it back again." My that is the truth. After receiving Ron's letter I thought I would feel of her and see how she felt regarding the boys. I asked her what kind of boys she admired and she said, "Oh, I have my ideas about

Esther at fourteen, the picture Ronald received in France.

> them." I said, yes, but what are they? What "kind" of boy would you like to go with when you are old enough? and she said, "Well I will tell you. Ronald is the kind I admire, I bet he never does that petting stuff." I said what about Trever, you always seem to like him as well and be so proud of him and she said, "Yes, I did—he is a good kid but I don't like his ways this summer. When I saw him and cousin Helen acting so nutty he went down in my estimation."

Eunice goes on to exhort Trever, whose smoking has been giving her the deepest distress:

> You see you are read and judged where you least expect it. Oh, Trever, you can't afford to make yourself seem less than you really are. You are naturally a fine boy and have high ideals and good principles, but one sin

> leads to another and it does not take long to slide downhill. I want to look in your eye and know it is as clear and true as it was two years ago. We used to be so near to each other, don't let a nasty little cigarette separate you from your best love.

The sound advice from her elder son about his foster sister goes largely unheeded.

15 MISS EGAN

It's 1928. In the same mail, Grampa gets two letters. He reads them several times, then goes to the kitchen, holding them in his hand. Grama is punching down bread.

"Dearie," says Grampa, "I'm thinking of taking on a new barn hand, but first I need your approval."

"Whatever for?" exclaims Grama, and spells on her floury hand, "If there's a problem, don't take him!"

Grampa twinkles. "It isn't a him, it's a her!"

"Land sakes!" Grama snatches one of the letters and reads it with little exclamations of surprise while Grampa explains.

Miss Mary Josephine Egan is a maiden lady who has been teaching school for more than twenty years. She's recently inherited her parents' farm at Amboy, Illinois. She wants to make it into a stock farm, perhaps dairy. She wants to run it herself, but she knows little about modern scientific dairying. She inquired at the University of Wisconsin and subsequently enrolled in their short course in agriculture. However, Professor George C. Humphrey, animal husbandry, has recommended that the best all-round education in practical dairy farming would be gained by spending a six-month apprenticeship under W. J. Dougan on his farm near Beloit. Therefore, she has written to see whether there might be an opening.

Grama reads aloud,

> This may seem rather foolish to you but I am willing to do any kind of work that you think I could do in connection with the dairy. And as I am fond of housework and cooking I would be glad to do that in any free time. Though I am middle aged I am very strong and well and, I think, used to hard work. Of course I understand how the introduction

> of an additional worker might be more of an inconvenience than a help but I am so anxious to try it that I am risking asking you. Very truly yours, Miss Mary Josephine Egan.

"Well, I never heard tell of such a thing!" Grama says, wonderingly. She reads the other letter:

> I take this opportunity to say that Miss M. J. Egan, Amboy, Illinois, would like to have an opportunity to visit and work on a farm where she could observe and learn many things pertaining to the dairy business. Miss Egan was formerly a member of our short course in agriculture. She is concerned with a 350-acre farm, a part of which she feels might be utilized to good advantage for dairy purposes. She hesitates, however, to make the necessary investment in a herd and the equipment with her limited knowledge of dairy herd management. Miss Egan is a lady of mature judgment and apparently very nice in all her actions and attitude of mind. If you are in a position to have her come and learn something of the management of your farm and herd I would appreciate hearing from you or having you write her directly. I have taken the liberty of giving her your address, and trust you may be hearing from her soon.
>
> Very truly yours,
>
> George C. Humphrey
> Animal Husbandman

"Well, I never!" Grama repeats. She pummels the mound of bread vigorously for a moment or two. "Well, we can't have her upstairs back there with all the men—she'll have to have the front bedroom!"

Grampa and Grama meet Miss Egan at the train. She's a stately, handsome woman with very pink cheeks. She's wearing a plain blue coat and a silk dress with tiny flowers. Her hair, visible under her flat blue hat, is pinned in a coil around her head. It's just beginning to gray. She's courteous, friendly, and reserved. She's definitely a lady of breeding. She and Grama take to each other immediately.

At the farm Grama shows her her bedroom, and Miss Egan makes short work of settling. She comes down to the noon meal dressed for the job, in overalls, blue work shirt, and men's over-the-ankle work boots. Grampa seats her to his left and introduces her to all the help. They are speechless. The conversation, that first meal, is all between Grampa, Grama, and Miss Egan.

For a few days, the talk of the neighborhood is the new hand in the round barn. Then everyone, including the men she works with, forgets that this is anything unusual. Miss Egan, in black rubber boots and white apron, learns rapidly how to curry the cows, wash udders, run the milking machines. She learns to milk by hand. She shovels manure, swills out the gutters, pitches down hay and silage. There's nothing the barn men do that she does not.

Grampa takes special pains with her, and she's curious and eager to learn. He has her assist at breeding, calving, and dehorning. He sees that she's at hand when the vet comes, and she asks Dr. Russell about heel flies and milk fever, mastitis and Bang's disease, conjunctivitis and swallowing foreign objects, and all other maladies large and small that cattle are subject to. When the schedule permits, she's assigned farm chores—haying, silo filling. She learns to service and drive a tractor. She learns to manage the side delivery that rolls the dried hay into a windrow to be collected by the hay loader. She learns to pull the hay loader and to balance a load. Grampa gives her time in the milkhouse, to learn the processing end of the business.

On the job, she mainly learns the hows. At night, in the family parlor, where Miss Egan always sits, rather than in the hired men's sitting room, Grampa explains the whys. They talk about the merits of the various breeds of cattle and what makes a good cow. They talk crops and soils and machinery. They go over records and ledgers, and Grampa shows her how he enters every detail of farm care. They discuss government regulations and taxes.

Miss Egan doesn't neglect Grama. While they both knit, they discuss church missions, or the latest books, or, if it's Sunday, the morning's sermon. Miss Egan lived in foreign lands in her girlhood, and she tells her adventures. Sometimes all three play a game of anagrams. Grama is delighted that Miss Egan can play the piano. Miss Egan sings in a powerful soprano, and Grama joins in, in her strong alto. The room fairly quivers.

During Miss Egan's tenure as a hired man, there's at least one incident that everyone hears about. A salesman comes to demonstrate a new milking machine. He's on the walk behind the cows with the herdsman while Miss Egan is in the center section of the barn, shoveling silage from the cart into the mangers of the waiting cattle. He doesn't pay any attention to the tall barn hand as he goes about his demonstration. Midway, he interrupts his sales pitch.

"I know that Daddy Dougan can't hear this," he prefaces, "and so I'll just tell you this little joke I—"

The herdsman, aware by look and tone the direction the joke is going to take, protests and gestures toward the center of the barn, but the salesman is heedless. He charges headlong into a vulgar story as the herdsman becomes more frantic in his efforts to silence him. At that point Miss Egan takes matters into her own hands. "What—a friend we have in Jee-sus," she sings out in her rich voice and between the cows glimpses the salesman's astonished face. He abruptly terminates his demonstration and has slunk away before Miss Egan rolls into the second verse. She and the herdsman, and soon everyone in the neighborhood, have a huge laugh.

After six months, Miss Egan returns to her farm at Amboy. With Grampa's advice and assistance, she buys shorthorns and sets up a combined beef and dairy industry. Over the years, it prospers. Grampa and Grama speak warmly and often of Miss Egan. They correspond. Miss Egan's letters are a combination of personal news, reports on how things are going, and questions. In February 1931, she writes:

> I spoke to those new heifers about how much they cost, but they looked more depressed than ever. They are having a nice time eating and I occasionally see one that looks as if she had just swallowed a balloon. . . . There are a couple of things about which I need a little advice if you

> have any to spare. Two men came to the farm Saturday looking at bull calves and wanted a price on A-3's calf, intending to raise him and use him in their herd. We told them he was a grade but they did not seem to care. Do you think we should sell one for breeding and how much would he be worth—he is almost six months old. . . . The second question is about one of the Derwent heifers. Roy says she has been bred twice. Saturday the bull broke out and she was bred again. Roy wants to know if the breeding isn't successful this time, should we have Dr. Barth treat her? . . . The third question is one which I am afraid you will think I have a lot of nerve to ask. Is there any special account book you wish me to use this year? I suppose you think I am hopeless on accounts but I can at least make another effort to do them correctly.

Sometimes Grampa and Grama go to visit Miss Egan, and then she and Grampa confer on farm problems face-to-face. On one such visit, in going over the account books, Grampa discovers something he didn't teach well enough during Miss Egan's apprenticeship. In her tax records, he sees a tractor being regularly depreciated. He hasn't noticed this tractor among the farm machinery.

"Show me the Case tractor," he says.

Miss Egan leads him out behind the barn, where a tractor, overgrown with weeds, is rusting beside a fence post. It can't have been used in ten years.

"But Miss Egan," says Grampa. "You've depreciated this tractor several times over its value!"

"My, my!" exclaims Miss Egan. "Think of that!" She looks contemplatively at the wreck and runs a finger up and over a corroded lug. Then she turns to Grampa.

"Who can put a value on an old friend?" she asks.

16 THE SHOWER

Jackie attends her first wedding shower when she's seven. It's held at Aunt Ida's, and all the women of the farm go. Moo-Moo Stam is there, as are the wives of some of the other milkmen and married farmhands. Aunt Lillian and Hazel, of course; it's their house, too. And Grama and Mother and a few women Jackie doesn't know. The dining room table, where refreshments will be served, has a party cake on it, and flowers, and frilled nut-and-candy cups, each with a miniature Japanese umbrella that really opens and shuts. The adjoining living room is decorated with crepe-paper streamers. A low table is piled with the wrapped and ribboned gifts.

Jackie feels quite grown up to be considered a woman, along with Joan and Patsy. Their presents are on the table—they went shopping with Mother, and Joan bought a red mixing bowl; Patsy, a flour sifter; and Jackie, measuring spoons and cup. It's not specifically a kitchen shower, but these are appropriate gifts because the shower is for Josie, and Josie has worked for Grama in the Big House for a long time, doing lots of the cooking.

Mother's present for Josie is a soft satiny slip and a sheer white blouse with pearl buttons. "A bride needs some pretty things," Mother had said.

Till today, Jackie has never seen Josie in anything pretty. At the Big House, she wears cotton housedresses and feed-sack aprons. Her beige stockings are thick, and her flat black shoes don't lace but have narrow straps. She wears her glossy black hair pulled tight across her head and fastened in a bun behind. Her eyes are black as buttons, and she has heavy eyebrows that nearly meet in the middle. She has a wide mouth. She is often perspiry, and even when her face isn't sweating, her cheeks and forehead shine bright enough to reflect the overhead lights. She's not a pretty woman. But she giggles a lot and is cheerful at the Big House table.

Jackie is surprised that Josie is getting married. She is so old! Old and not pretty—she doesn't fit Jackie's storybook princesses who wed the prince and live happily ever after. But then, Mr. Griffiths is hardly a prince. He is thin and has a stringy neck, and he is a lot older even than Josie. He has worked on the farm since before Jackie was born. He isn't an ordinary hired man—he's more like the head hired man, a foreman. He sometimes tells Jackie and her sisters and brother what they can or can't do, as if he's a parent or grandparent, and this annoys them. But he plows a straighter furrow than anyone on the farm, and Grampa entrusts him with all the planting. Jackie remembers, when she was smaller, Mr. Griffiths sitting in the spring sunshine at the entrance to the loft of the round barn and cutting up wizened seed potatoes. He told her that in order to grow, every potato piece had to have an eye.

Mr. Griffiths had a wife once, before Jackie was born, and two daughters. But the daughters grew up and married and moved out west, and before

Aunt Ria (Grama's visiting sister) and Josie. The Little House is in the background.

that, something happened to the wife. Nobody tells Jackie, but she listens in to grown-up talk when they lower their voices, and she learns that Mrs. Griffiths committed suicide. She did it because she thought she had committed the unforgivable sin. Jackie is curious as to what the unforgivable sin is, and whether Mrs. Griffiths really did commit it, but she never overhears the answer to either of these wonderings. And because she's not supposed to be listening, of course, she can't ask.

She gathers more bits by eavesdropping. Usually, seven or eight hired men live at the Big House, and these men are single. Jackie knows and likes them all. Ernie Capps with the rotten ear, who sometimes stays with them when Mother and Daddy go out. Handsome Kenneth Liddle. Al Lasse, who is even handsomer. Ockie Berg. Russel Ullius, who plays croquet with them in the evenings and calls Joan "Punky." Mr. Griffiths doesn't live at the Big House but in his own brown stucco house, right at the head of Colley Road where it leaves Beloit. But he often takes his noon meal at the communal table.

Josie, Jackie overhears, first made eyes at Al Lasse, but Al never gave her the time of day. "In that way," Grama says significantly. And so, after a while, she started making eyes at Mr. Griffiths. The first Jackie hears about any of Josie's amorous intentions is through a near accident of Daddy's.

"Coming back from the Hill Farm just now," he reports to Mother at the Little House, "I was coming up on one side of that little thank-you-ma'am there by Blodgetts', and coming up on the other side, driving right in the middle of the road, were guess who? Griffiths and Josie, and he had his arm around her! I swerved and missed them, nearly drove into the ditch. I don't think they even saw me."

This is when Jackie begins tuning her ears to Josie's conversations and learns about Al Lasse, Mrs. Griffiths, and the enigmatic, unforgivable sin. She happens to be in the Big House when Mr. Griffiths is in the kitchen helping Josie with the dishes, a remarkable occurrence in itself, and the men

And then it's time to open the presents. Josie sits on the floor beside the low table and carefully undoes the paper and ribbons. She thanks Jackie and Patsy and Joan for the cup and sifter and bowl. She gives a little gasp at Mother's slip and blouse and holds the blouse to her while everyone tells her how lovely she will look in it. She appreciates Grama's embroidered tea towels, Aunt Ida's little spoon set from the World's Fair, Moo-Moo's crochet-edged pillow cases. She thanks each giver profusely.

Near the bottom of the pile she finds a small package wrapped in tissue paper. She turns it over and over. There is no card.

"Who is this from?" asks Josie.

No one responds.

She peels off the paper. There is a brown paper bag inside but still no card. Jackie watches as she puts her hand into the bag and is startled to see Josie startle. And then Josie begins to blush. It is a blush that rises up her neck and spreads rapidly over her face, deepening and deepening and deepening, until her shiny skin is a more livid crimson than Jackie ever dreamed skin could be.

"What is it? What is it?" the guests clamor. Someone on the edge of the circle begins to laugh, and a few others pick up the laughter. Someone tugs on Josie's arm, and someone else snatches away the bag. Josie is left clutching a pair of rubber baby pants.

Now everybody is laughing, hooting, whooping. All but Josie. She sits there a scarlet statue, her chest heaving as if she can't get her breath. After a moment she grabs for the tissue paper and buries the rubber pants in it. Then she starts laughing, too. Her face remains red.

There are one or two more presents to open and then refreshments. Josie is still unnaturally florid when they go to the dining room.

The wedding comes, and Grampa performs the ceremony. Josie moves into the brown stucco house with Mr. Griffiths. Grama has to get someone new to help in the kitchen. She finds a woman named, interestingly enough,

Mr. Griffiths, silo filling.

in the sitting room turn the radio way up when the song comes on, “Get Away, Old Man, Get Away.” Veiled talk about the courtship becomes open once Josie has a ring on her finger. The teasing subsides somewhat. Now, with a wedding date set, is the shower.

Josie doesn’t look like she does in the Big House kitchen. She has on a Sunday dress Jackie has never seen, with beads and a brooch. She’s put a ribbon around her bun. But she is still the same Josie for laughing and giggling. She cannot stop her laughing and giggling.

They play the games Mother leads them in, matching up famous couples, and finishing proverbs about love and marriage. Hazel plays the piano while one of the women sings a medley of old-fashioned love songs: “Let Me Call You Sweetheart,” and “I Love You Truly,” and “A Bicycle Built for Two.” They all sing along with the ones they know. Jackie knows the one she calls “Daisy, Daisy.” Joan and Patsy, surprisingly, know some of the others.

Daisy, and Jackie and Craig sometimes sing "Daisy, Daisy" to her. She's younger than Josie and not so plain, but though Jackie watches closely, she doesn't spot her making eyes at any of the men. They still see Josie once in a while, when she and Mr. Griffiths come out to the Big House for Sunday dinner.

The pair lives happily ever after, until Mr. Griffiths dies from cancer in 1947. Till then, he continues working on the farm. After his death, Josie goes back to the small town upstate where her family hails from.

She and Mr. Griffiths never have a use for the rubber pants. Jackie wonders sometimes if Josie threw them out or kept them still in the tissue paper in her bureau drawer. She wonders if Josie ever showed them to her bridegroom. She suspects not.

17 HIDE-AND-SEEK

It is 1936. Jackie is eight. She races up the ramp of the round barn to the barn floor, springs onto an extended ladder placed against a cliff of hay, and scrambles up. From the top rung, she carefully squirms over the sloping lip of green till she's a safe distance from the edge, then she springs and sinks across the hay to flop down with her nose against one of the little windows spaced under the eaves. Below her is the gravel area between the round barn, the milkhouse, and the Big House. In the center, leaning on the elm tree with his face buried in the crook of his arm, is Craig. He's six. She can hear his muffled shout: "Niney-eight, niney-nine, *one hunnert,* here I come, ready or not!" He turns, looks all around, then wanders off between the ice-house and the tool house.

Jackie considers running in free, but that's too easy when only two are playing. She rolls over on her back in the new, sweet-smelling hay.

The loft is so full that hay reaches to the very top of the walls. Right over her head, the roof rafters arch up, like the spokes of an umbrella or the brown gills of a mushroom, springing toward the dusty dimness of the center. The fat concrete silo is like the white stem of the mushroom; it rises from the cow barn, from below the cow barn, comes up through the barn floor, and continues through the loft to the roof. Its final few feet before the peak are made of wood, golden brown with age, and topped with a circle of little glassed windows that let light from the barn into the silo. From inside the silo, you can look up and see this odd little floorless room, its ceiling a pointed cap where all the barn beams converge.

In the loft, part way up the beams, is a fretwork of lighter rafters lacing the beams together. Sparrows and pigeons balance their nests on these rafters; the straw sticks out untidily. Jackie listens to the chirping and cooing and the rush of wings. Cobwebs festoon all the rafters, great strands and streamers and ropes of cobwebs, made by generations of spiders. Old webs can't blow away in the round barn. They only grow thicker and heavier with dust.

Above her head, a little way up the slope of the roof, is the metal track for the hay fork. It circles the loft, bolted to each beam. During haying, the track has a thick-rollered trolley hanging from it, and the hay fork is fastened to the trolley. She loves to watch the fork in operation. It swings out over a loaded wagon that's been pulled up onto the barn floor by a team or tractor. It drops, crunching into the hay, and a farmhand helps embed its four great teeth firmly. On command, the horses hitched up outside start to walk, the rope they are pulling strains, the fork lifts. It grips an island of hay in its gigantic two-toothed jaws, a hill torn up by the roots. It carries it to the roof, shedding wisps, swings it sideways with a swish, and, running on the track in a wide curve, carries it to the spot where it's to be dropped. Up in the mow, another farmhand trips the trailing rope, the jaws unclamp, and the island falls with a *schlunk.* The men in the mow attack it with pitchforks and distribute it evenly while the fork rolls back for another bite. At each drop, the dust motes, thickly visible in the sunbeams that stream through the little windows, go crazy.

Jackie wonders what it would be like to climb along that track, like Daddy and Uncle Trever did once when they were little. The barn was new, and so full of hay that they could reach up and grasp the track. They'd pulled themselves onto it and, leaning backward, inched along, reaching from brace to brace, past the safety of the hay beneath them, past the edge of the cliff and out over the barn floor thirty feet below. They'd inched all the way to the start of the track at the barn doors and then sat down and swung their legs. Grama had found them there and screamed. She'd ordered them down instantly, but they couldn't get down in an instant. They had to inch back. Grama couldn't bear to watch. She ordered them to report to the kitchen as soon as they were down. But Daddy and Trever hadn't reported;

Grampa standing before a wall of hay in the round barn loft. A chute is on his right. The construction of the roof is clear.

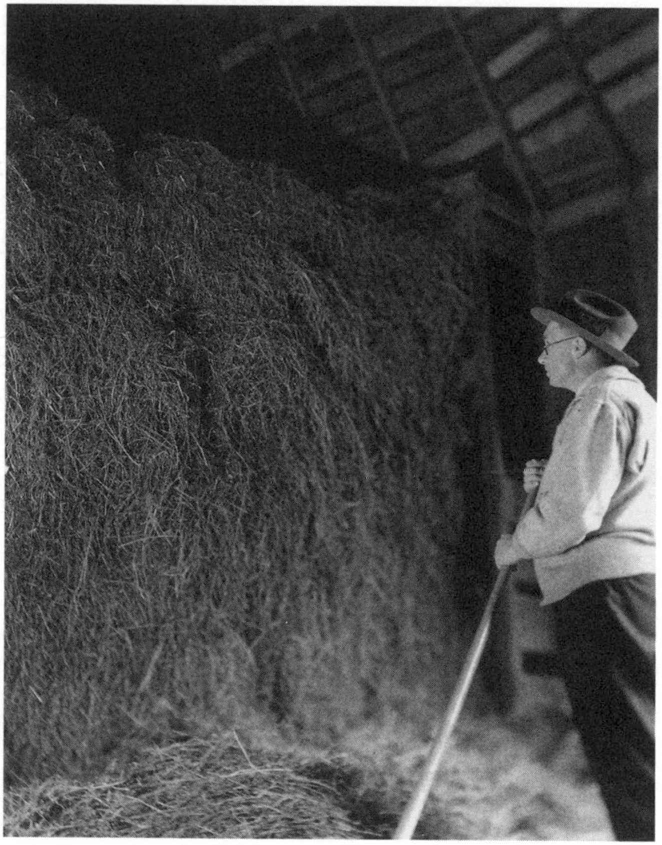

they'd gone behind the horse barn and thrown horse apples at the sparrows till suppertime.

Daddy hadn't been so lucky with the chute. Jackie looks over to where the chute is, alongside the silo, but there's so much hay its top is hidden. She crawls over and finds the hole, a deep black well with a square of light from the cow barn at the bottom. She can see the cement floor. It's like looking through the wrong end of a spyglass. This is the chute Daddy fell down when he was twelve, and even though he landed on a small mound of hay, he broke both his heels. His heels are still strange, with little spurs behind. "Like a bird claw," says Daddy. "I can perch on a twig and clamp from both directions and never fall off."

A pitchfork is stuck upright beside the chute. Jackie runs her fingers along its polished handle, pulls it out, and tries the weight of the hay on its tines. She pitches a pancake of hay into the chute and watches it fall as slowly as Alice down the rabbit hole. It makes the chute dark, until it breaks into the light and lands like a feather on the cow barn floor.

She crawls to the edge of the hay cliff and lies on her stomach, waiting for Craig to come seeking her. On the vast barn floor is where Daddy and Trever had their pulleys. Daddy'd said they'd taken hammers, nails, jackknives, empty spools, and string up onto the barn floor. They'd notched the spools. They'd constructed an ever more elaborate system of pulleys with the string and spools, some strings stretching for long distances. Some went horizontally, some vertically, some diagonally, till the barn floor was a web—from silo to doors to granaries to grain mill.

"We started," Daddy'd said, "with a primary loop fastened to the flywheel of the corn sheller. When we turned on the sheller, it set all the strings and spools rotating. What a grand and satisfying sight! And open to myriad permutations. But after a hired man or two tangled with our strings, we were ordered to dismantle our cats-cradles after every session. And we weren't allowed to take spools or string or nails into the hay, for cows are dumb. They'll swallow anything."

She and Craig have been saving spools from Grama's sewing, ever since Daddy told them about the pulleys.

She's not so eager to try his and Trever's elevator, where they put a rope around a pulley up in the rafters, and on one end tied a gunnysack full of grain, slightly heavier than the weight of one boy. At the other end they made a loop, for sitting in. Then they'd pull the sack up to the top, and as it came down it would pull one of them up. The one at the bottom would let out a little grain, and the boy up top would come down again. "Really educational," Daddy'd said. "A regular Otis elevator!" But Jackie is doubtful—what if the sack fell off or spilled? You'd be one big splat.

She's not so sure about their rope swing, either, where they'd fly from the top of the hay bank right out the barn doors, and then in again.

"If we didn't make it back, it would just oscillate, and we'd eventually make it to the floor," Daddy'd said.

She hears a crunch, too heavy for Craig's bare feet. Grampa comes up beside the feed bin and starts to sort through the pile of old gunnysacks stacked there. He holds them up, one after another. He makes a little crooning noise, like humming to himself and clearing his throat at the same time, like a chicken prowling around the woodpile. He can't hear the little song he makes.

He's standing under the old fashioned printing on the silo, under THE AIMS OF THIS FARM. How could he have signed his name? The letters are big, and high over his head.

"Hello, W. J. Dougan," says Jackie, conversationally. "Hello, Wesson Joseph." She looks around for a way to get Grampa's attention. There's nothing to throw except the pitchfork, and she would never do that. Accidents happen with pitchforks. She doesn't like to think about Daddy accidentally killing the mouse, or the neighbor who threw a pitchfork up into his haymow and it hit a beam and bounced back and killed him.

She feels in a pocket and finds loose corn. It's often there, for she likes to jumble it in her fingers or worry a kernel with her teeth. She's learned these habits from Daddy and Grampa. She throws the corn at Grampa and it peppers his back. He looks up. His face registers huge astonishment. She puts her finger to her lips and points to the barn door. Grampa understands. He laughs silently. Grampa always laughs silently; it's on account of his deafness.

He picks up a gunnysack. He looks up at her, down at the sack. She gets

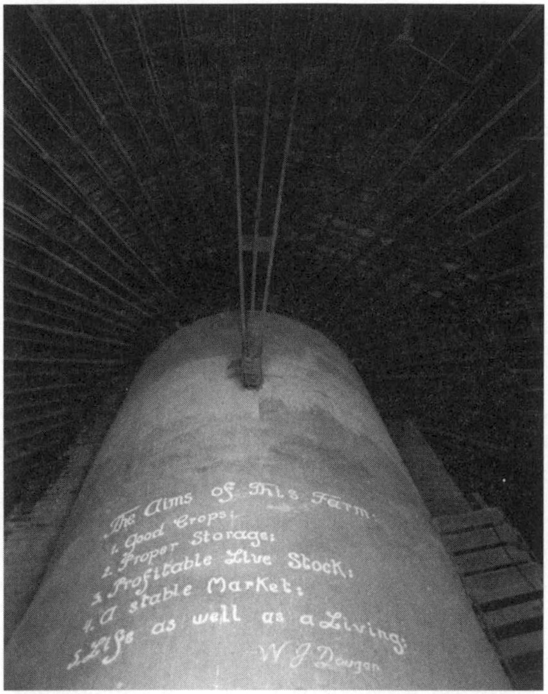

The silo with the AIMS. *The chute Daddy fell down is on the right; the left structure serves as a ventilator to the roof and passageway for climbing up into the silo, as well as the chute for pitching silage to the cow barn below.*

his idea. She motions a question out the door. Grampa looks. "Quick, cubby, he's coming!" he shouts, loudly, because he can't hear himself.

She eases carefully onto the ladder, then scrambles down. Grampa holds open the gunnysack. She dives in, and he closes it with a bit of twine. She can hear his breathing as he ties, and through a hole, she can see the arm of his blue work shirt. Then the arm moves, and she glimpses her brother coming into the barn. He's drinking a half-pint of chocolate milk.

She lies still. The sack smells strongly of grain, and the dust makes her hold her breath to keep from sneezing. She prickles all over from the hay in her clothing and the oat spears stuck in the sack. The loose burlap weave allows a dim light to filter through.

Craig asks out loud, "Grampa, have you seen Jackie?" Through the hole she watches him spell her name on his fingers and look inquiring. She can talk to Grampa with the finger alphabet, too. It was the first thing she learned after learning to read; her sisters taught her. Grampa was greatly pleased when she spelled her first word to him. Before that he'd only pretended to read when she made her hand go. She still can't spell lickety-split like Grama and Daddy. Neither can Craig.

Grampa is playing dumb. He looks puzzled at Craig's spelling.

H-I-D-E A-N-D S-E-E-K, spells Craig.

Grampa's face lights up. He motions toward the loft. "Have you looked in the hay?"

Craig is impatient. He shakes his head. D-I-D Y-O-U S-E-E H-E-R?

Grampa begins to laugh silently. Jackie laughs silently, too. The sack jiggles. Craig grabs at it.

"Hi!" Grampa shouts. "Leave my sack of potatoes alone!"

Jackie rolls and lurches away. Craig's hands beat on her. Chocolate milk spills through the sack.

"You're it!" cries Craig.

The twine parts; the sack bursts open. Jackie stumbles out running and heads for the barn doors.

"I tagged you!" shrills Craig. "You're it!"

"Inside the sack! It doesn't count!" Jackie races down the ramp and reaches the tree. "Home free!"

Craig, looking injured, walks down the incline.

Grampa stands in the doorway, laughing and waving the gunnysack like a semaphore.

18 BIG HOUSE CHRISTMAS

Christmas at the Big House is held on Christmas Eve. Earlier in the week, Grama and Grampa always give a big Christmas supper for all the nonresidential employees and their families, and Christmas bonuses are handed out. There is cold molded chicken salad, and everybody carries home a plate of Grama's special Christmas cookies. But Christmas Eve is the party for the more immediate family—Grampa and Grama and Effie (Grama's maiden niece and helper); Mother and Daddy, Joan, Patsy, Jackie, and Craig over from the Little House; Aunt Lillian, Aunt Ida, and Hazel out from town; and all the hired men who are living at the Big House, unable by distance or work demands to be at their own homes with parents or other family members.

The parlor has the tall tree at the east end. Grama and Grampa's tree, this year as always, has its own familiar ornaments, different from the ones at the Little House, and in the darkened room its many colored lights shed a diffuse glow through the circling mists of angels' hair. Jackie loves to tiptoe into the room and stand, smelling the balsam scent, drinking in the softened colors, feeling the magic of the huge pile of presents under the tree. The quiet heap exhales that magic like perfume emanating from a hay field or warmth rising from a pasture lane. Only a few of the packages will be for her—tonight is more an evening of giving than of getting—but that doesn't lessen the anticipation.

She and the rest of the family brought their gifts over in the afternoon in a wicker laundry basket; she recognizes the wrappings, and these have helped swell the volume of the pile under the branches. On a side table sits a crèche, and its familiar Mary and Joseph and baby Jesus, and all the kings and shepherds and angels and animals, are older, a little chipped, enough different from the crèche set up on the mantle of the Little House to merit yearly reexamination.

Out in the brightly lit dining room there is noise and laughter and much going to and fro from the kitchen. All the hired men are slicked up. Some of them are helping; others are in their sitting room, which opens out from the dining room, basking in watching all the activity. The radio is playing carols. When Jackie isn't making her trips to the sanctuary of the Christmas tree room, she's racing around with her sisters and brother, dodging into the kitchen to snatch snippets of the coming feast, and then being given jobs to keep out of mischief, such as carrying to the table the milk pitchers or bowls of cranberry-orange relish. The waiting for dinner is almost unbearable. It isn't helped any by the huge wooden chopping bowl sitting on its own little table, mounded up with popcorn balls wrapped in wax paper, a treat Grama makes only at Christmas. The smaller bowl of sugared doughnut holes is also a Christmas treat, but sometimes, when Grama is making doughnuts during the year, Jackie is allowed to drop some of the centers into the hot fat, so doughnut holes are not quite so special as popcorn balls. Popcorn balls mean Christmas.

But finally, the meal is ready, the family from town has arrived, and all are seated at the candlelit table with its snowy tablecloth barely visible underneath the best china and silverware, the bowls and plates and pitchers and platters. Grampa lowers his head and gives a long, grateful, and joyous Christmas grace. Then there is so much food that the sideboard is used as a buffet, and everyone has to stand and go past to load up his or her plate with creamed chicken on biscuits and all the fixings. Christmas Eve is always creamed chicken on biscuits. And there are often so many guests that a few card tables have to be set up in the entryway into the living room, and these too have festive cloths and candles.

The grown-ups don't hasten their eating, so there's no point in the children hurrying, either, for they'll have to stay at their seats right through to the mince pie with whipped cream and the coffee for the adults. Jackie, all her life, never does learn to eat quickly—even nonholiday meals on the farm are always a ceremony, deliberate, a time to start, a time to stop, with much conversation and sharing in between. Tonight, there's plenty of time to see who can construct the best mashed-potato pie. Half the hot mashed potato is patted down into a circle, and this is covered with thick shavings of butter all over, for the filling. It is then salted, peppered, and the other half of the potato spread on top for the upper crust. The trick is to get the cold butter on quickly and evenly and then the hot top, so that the butter doesn't melt too soon and mess up the process. The edges must also be rapidly crimped so that the filling doesn't run out onto the plate. It's permissible to prick a little pattern onto the top, like Grama does; and then, of course, once you slice your pie in six and start to eat it, the filling goes all over anyway, as it does in any respectable apple or cherry or rhubarb pie. It's only the pumpkins and minces and custards that don't ooze.

But finally, the dinner is over, and then the dishes have to be cleared and everything tidied before the next phase of the evening. But with so many hands, the cleanup doesn't take long. Jackie's favorite job—if any job at such a time can be a favorite—is to crumb the table, with the crumbing pan made of amber horn, flat with curved sides and with a handle, like a medium-sized dustpan, and then the crumber itself, also horn, shaped like the larger pan in miniature. You have to get the angle just right, to collect the crumbs and guide them into the larger pan. If you go at the job too vigorously, the crumbs behave like tiddledywinks and hop all over the place, even onto the floor. And if you shepherd them all to the edge of the table, then you have to hold the large pan just so under the wide, tableclothed lip, to be sure all the crumbs fall in. It takes care and practice to be a good crumber. At the end of the job, you empty the crumbs into the bucket for the chickens, nest the small pan inside the larger one, and return them to their spot in the buffet drawer. You never wash them.

The presents are not next. The program is. This varies from year to year, but it always begins with Grampa reading aloud the Christmas story from St. Luke: "And it came to pass in those days, that there went out a decree from Caesar Augustus, that all the world should be taxed." Jackie knows it almost by heart.

Other things follow. One year Joan and Patsy sing a duet of all three verses of "Fairest Lord Jesus" while Mother accompanies them on the piano. Joan sings the melody and Patsy sings a high, sweet descant that amazes Jackie: she herself will never be able to sing that high or sweet. One year she and Joan and Patsy are dressed up in crowns and bathrobes, and they each take a solo verse of "We Three Kings," with everyone joining in on the chorus. Joan and Patsy sometimes play their violins. One year, Hazel, who teaches vocal music at Lincoln Junior High School, sings and plays the story of "The Selfish Giant." Grama reads a poem she's written, called "Wrapping Paper."

Another year the hired men put on a shadow pantomime behind a sheet pinned over the door of the office, on the far side of the living room from the tree. The audience sits in the dark room and the lights are bright in the office; there's even a spotlight. A shadow figure climbs on a table before the door and stretches out. A shadow doctor clamps a tit cup over the patient's nose; shadow attendants pin down his flailing limbs until he goes under and flops limp. The attendants hand the doctor his tools for the operation: a large knife, a saw, a hammer, a plumber's wrench, a horse hypodermic, a nose leader. The shadow doctor uses each tool with vigor, and there's much laughter from the audience. Finally, the doctor takes a posthole digger, lowers it into his patient and hauls out a great mass of guts, which the viewers gleefully recognize as spaghetti. The doctor inspects the cavity, reaches in, and brings out and out and out what's apparently been the trouble—a manure fork. The crowd claps and cheers. The doctor replaces the spaghetti and mashes it down well with a hoe. Then using a long gunnysack needle

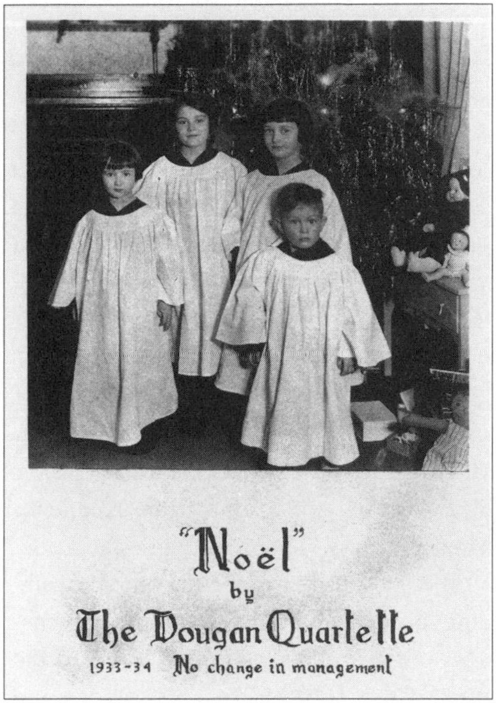

Jackie, Joan, Patsy, and Craig on a family Christmas card by the fireplace and mantle at the Little House.

and twine, one of the attendants elaborately sews the patient back up, the tit cup is removed, the patient sits up and makes the I'VE WON boxing sign, and all the shadows take bows amidst thunderous applause. The hired men, flushed with success, emerge from behind their sheet. And then Mother, or Hazel, plays Christmas carols while everybody sings. Grampa can't hear any of the festivities, but he's the one who enjoys them most of all.

And finally, finally, come the presents! Sometimes Grampa plays Santa Claus, sometimes the children take turns distributing. It's always hard to know what to get the grown-ups, especially Grama and the elderly aunts. Handkerchiefs are such dull gifts, yet everyone can use another handkerchief,

Mother assures. Jackie likes the year Mother suggests little Christmas corsages to pin on coat lapels: these are bright and have bells and ribbon and pine cones and cost only thirty-five cents each at Woolworth's. Grampa is easier. One year Joan gets him a red clay head in a dish; above the head's saucy smile and upturned nose and arched eyebrows his scalp is scored with parallel ridges; you put water in the dish and grass seed in the ridges and the man grows green hair. One year Jackie and Craig get Grampa a present they can't wrap, but have to carry in from where it's been hidden in the office—a goldfish bowl and two goldfish: a gold one with a streamy tail and a black one with bulgy eyes. Grampa laughs so hard at the bulgy-eyed fish that his own eyes disappear.

As for Jackie's presents—there are the mittens Grama knits, connected by a long crocheted string that goes through her coat sleeves, or a pair of blue knee-high knit stockings, beautiful, but which she knows from experience will fall down around her ankles when she runs. There are games and puzzles from the aunts and Hazel and Effie, or something for the whole family. Daddy gets ties and gloves and fishing lures; Mother gets candy and notepaper and scarves. One Christmas when Craig is small, he receives a knitted doll, its clothes part of the knitting—orange top, black pants, orange and black striped socks. It's a long slim boy doll, knit by Aunt Ria in Appleton, and named by Craig, oddly enough, "Jackie-doll." Over many years, Jackie-doll is loved to shreds. One Christmas, Grampa gives Grama a large set of expensive kitchen knives, and Grama is offended. The next year he knows better, and she receives a jeweled brooch. The floor is always littered with bright paper, and Grama tells at least three times every year how when she was a little girl she got only half an orange for Christmas.

The year Jackie remembers most vividly is the one when at the end of the gift exchange Grampa makes them get into their snowsuits and boots and mittens and follow him outside. He won't say for what; he is merry and mysterious. They form a line and Grampa leads them through the snow. Jackie follows behind Patsy. She feels cold and cross. She wants to be back in the Big House, playing with the toys she's received, claiming another popcorn ball. The moon is so bright that they don't need any flashlights. They go this way and that, out into the Big House yard, then behind, past the woodpile and henhouse, then between the barn and Big House, out toward the lane leading to the crick, and then back again to the granary and the corncrib. Jackie gets colder and crosser. Where is Grampa taking them? She finds his suppressed mirth annoying. They round the milkhouse, go past the circle of lilac bushes, and are at the Little House. Grampa leads them into the backyard and stops.

There is a sudden intake of breath from all of them. Glimmering in the moonlight is a playhouse! It's large and white, with dark shutters running the length of both sides. Grampa opens the door, and they crowd through. He strikes a match and lights a candle that is waiting on a small table. The inside flickers to life, throwing their shadows against the white painted walls. Long screened windows are on either side. Two green benches flank the walls.

It's a perfectly wonderful building! Grampa is laughing silently and looking at their faces. Jackie is ashamed that she's been feeling so contrary. She rushes to him and hugs him; Grampa is smothered in a pileup of hugs.

The playhouse is a present from Grampa and Grama, Mother and Daddy. It gets constant use—as a playhouse, a clubhouse, an art gallery, a store, a summer camp, a sleep-out spot, a ticket booth, a museum, a jail. When the family moves up Colley Road to Chez Nous, it stands at the foot of the lane; and on winter days, the four huddle inside for warmth while waiting for the school cab. Then it disappears, and the four think it's stolen; after some years it surfaces on the dairy as a hutch-house for rabbits. Nobody tells them who took it or where it's been. It leads a long and useful life.

But on the night of its arrival, they can only sense its potential. Grampa blows out the candle, and they return to the Big House by the direct route.

There, the grown-ups are waiting to hear how they like it and to tell them how the house had to be secretly delivered and put in place while the Big House party was going on. Daddy had even slipped out to be sure it was really there and to put in the candle, before Grampa started the trek.

And then Christmas Eve, like every Christmas Eve at the Big House, is finally over. Thanks and hugs are exchanged, and the family walks home on the shoveled sidewalk under the bright stars to the Little House, carrying the wicker laundry basket full of the presents they've received, and it's time to hang up stockings, put out the milk and cookies, and go to bed to wait for Santa Claus.

19 THRASHING

Whenever Jackie reads stories about farms, the yearly thrashing is given prominence. That's as it should be. On a farm, thrashing is a major event.

It was an event when Daddy was a little boy. He remembers the harbinger of the thrashing machine, the lumber wagon fuel of soft coal that rumbled into the farm a day or two ahead of time. It was the responsibility of each farmer to provide the coal for his own thrashing. The coal was used to stoke the thrashing machine's steam engine. He remembers better yet that day the thrashing machine arrived for the first time in his life. He was in the upstairs bathroom when he heard the commotion coming up the road from Marstons'. Iron wheels were loud on the gravel; there was the shivering and shaking of metal, the pounding and chuffing and huffing of the steam engine. He ran to the window in his room, and the sight was as awesome as the sound: a metal behemoth lumbering along, filling the whole road. Tubes lying against its sides were like elephant trunks. The men were ants beside it. Ronald rushed downstairs and out to meet it, pitched over a croquet wicket in the front yard, and broke a toe.

He also remembers how it was when the thrashers quit for the day. There'd still be a little steam in the engine. He and Trever would go out and blow the whistle.

Thrashing is always an event for Jackie, too, and her brother and sisters. For days ahead, over in the Big House kitchen, one or another of them sits cross-legged on the flour box, out of traffic, watching Grama and Josie singe and clean chickens, roll out twice as many pies as usual, snip and shape and oil twice as many loaves of bread. Sometimes Jackie helps, snapping beans or stirring a pot. Over in the tiny kitchen of the Little House, Mother, too, and her helper, Geneva, are cooking ahead for the thrashers, long baking pans full of scalloped potatoes and cakes with coconut and brown-sugar frostings. Nearby neighbors, whose farms are part of the thrashing circle, are also preparing. Hattie Blodgett always makes more pies. Mrs. Mackie chops cabbage and celery into pale jellied salad rings that nobody really likes. Lura Marston is responsible for platters of tomatoes and cucumbers. Then the thrashing machine comes, scarcely different from when Daddy was a little boy, except now it's pulled by a tractor and is powered not by steam but by a long belt that stretches from it to a tractor standing nearby. The machine is owned by a group of farmers on Colley Road, and they thrash in turn. Jackie doesn't know where it stays from August to August; it's never wintered on any of the Dougan farms. By not seeing it standing idle through the year, it's always a fresh surprise to her, its size and strength and the mystery of its voluminous innards. She can't see inside it to see how it does what it does, and there's no opportunity during the year to explore.

The thrashing begins. First the thrashing machine pulls in beside the stacked bundles of oats that have already been cut by the binder and brought in behind the barns. These conical stacks are not easy to construct; the bundles have to be placed in such a way that they will drain and still not slide out of the stacks. Daddy says his always bulge or slide. But Albert Marston is the area's master stacker. He starts with the bundles sloping down a little toward the center. When he gets near the top he gradually raises the center until he has a watershed.

Now the spike man, or spike pitcher—another skilled worker—stands on the edge of the stack and organizes the bundles as they're tossed to him from various parts of the stack. He straightens them out and pitches them into the throat of the thrashing machine, always grain heads first. The tractor roars; the belt tautens and spins. The machine gulps the bundles up, shivers, shakes, rattles. The longest tube, now an elephant trunk stretched out, spews the first golden straw onto the green ground, and the straw stack begins building. On the side of the thrashing machine, the oats first trickle, then pour out, into a wagon box.

Children aren't allowed in the field behind the horse barn where the thrashing is taking place. It's too dangerous. But there's a fine view from the horse yard fence or from the lane down to the crick. Jackie and Craig sit on fence posts in the sunshine. Behind them on the dusty lane, the heat rises in shimmering waves.

The elephant trunk rises slowly as the stack grows and grows. The men who are working in the straw are naked to their waists, their chests and faces and hair thick with straw dust. Heaped wagons roll in from the fields, bringing bundles that have just been cut. The work and the noise and the flying straw against the blue sky go on and on. Then everything shivers to a stop. In the sudden stillness, a bird sings. Something has happened to the machine. Usually, it's that someone has lost a pitchfork into it, and the machine breaks down. Then all the men climb off the wagons and stack, drink water from five-gallon milk cans or bottles of orange drink and chocolate, and throw themselves down in the shade while the farm mechanics repair the damage. There is always joking and ribbing that the pitchfork went in on purpose, for thrashing is heavy, dirty, grueling, relentless work.

At noon comes the dinner. Mother is over, to help Grama and Josie, and so is Geneva. Fannie Veihman has come from the Hill Farm. The thrashers wash up and troop into the Big House dining room. They fill the entire extended table. Some years, the dinner is set up on trestles in the front yard of the Big House, and then Jackie and Patsy, Craig and Joan run back and forth replenishing the pitchers of milk, the bowls of meat and gravy and vegetables, the plates of butter. After all the thrashers have eaten, the kitchen crew eats. Then Jackie and the others are employed as dish wipers for the mountains of dirty dishes.

This routine goes on for as many days as it takes to thrash the Dougan grain. As soon as a day's work is over, the four rush to play on the unfinished straw stack. Once the thrashing is finished, they know this will be forbidden.

"Those stacks are carefully built to shed water," Daddy always says when they beg. "Every time you stick a foot in the straw, that makes a pocket to collect water and rot the straw underneath. Sure, it's fun to climb up and slide down. I used to do it, too. But we just can't let you."

And then the machine crawls away, a great prehistoric monster, its rackety din fading down Colley Road. It goes to a neighboring farm where the process is repeated. It leaves behind bin after bin of gleaming grain and two huge and shining stacks of straw.

One summer, 1941, the pattern changes. Grama has been ailing; she's not up to feeding all the thrashers at the Big House. But Grampa and Daddy have an idea. During the past year, Geneva Bown has bought the Subway Cafe down on Third Street near the Beloit Iron Works. Earl Bown still drives a Dougan milk truck, but now if Jackie and the rest want to taste Geneva's chocolate pudding or Lazy Daisy cake, Daddy takes them downtown to sit up at the counter of the Subway.

This year, Grampa and Daddy ask Geneva if she'd be willing to have them bring all the thrashers downtown. Geneva is delighted. She plans to serve the men after the workers from the nearby shops have their noon hour. There is the plate-lunch special for twenty-five cents or the full dinner for thirty-five cents, she says. The full dinner is this: all the bread and crackers the men can eat, along with free coffee and milk. The first course is soup du jour, either bean or vegetable. The entree is roast beef or T-bone steak or two breaded pork chops or fried chicken, with two scoops of mashed potatoes and gravy and side dishes of vegetables. Dessert is chocolate or lemon pudding. A slice of pie is ten cents extra. Daddy and Grampa agree on the thirty-five cent dinner for each thrasher and pie for whoever wants it.

The first day of thrashing, all the thrashers but David Collins wash up, pull on their shirts, and pile into the back of the farm truck. David sits by himself in the shade of a bush, wolfing down the hefty sandwiches his mother has packed for him. He's fifteen years old, a town boy, and is working on the farm for the summer. Every day he pedals out on his bicycle with his sack lunch in his basket and does whatever Grampa tells him to do. Today he's been working in the thrashing. He's a greenhorn. He doesn't realize that thrashing is an event. He only knows that he's much tireder, much dirtier, much pricklier, and much hungrier than he's ever been before.

As the truck leaves the drive, Grampa spots David under the bush. "Stop!" roars Grampa, and the truck stops. "Come along, laddie, get in, get in!" Grampa shouts.

David wipes the crumbs from his mouth and protests. He points to his empty sack, tries to explain he has already eaten, but Grampa is in a hurry and pays no attention.

"Get in, get in!" he insists. "Come along, come get your dinner!"

David shrugs. His job is to do what Daddy Dougan tells him to do. If Daddy Dougan tells him to come eat dinner, then he will eat dinner. He runs to the truck, and the men in the back give him an arm up. The truck rumbles off down Colley Road to the Subway Cafe, where Geneva serves David a second meal.

World War II brings an end to Turtle Township's neighborly exchange in farmwork. As the years go by, there are simply not enough men. No one farm has enough help to be able to take off and spend days thrashing the fields of nearby farms. Mrs. Wehler, when she's ready to thrash, can find in the way of a field hand only one colored man. When two of her neighbors arrive with their teams and wagons to head up the work and see the Negro, they turn around and go home. "We're not going to work with any nigger," they sneer. The anger and animosity this breeds is lasting.

But even with most of the labor force gone, the work must be done. In addition to the country's own needs, Europe, with its food production seriously crippled, places new demands on United States agriculture. Innovations make it possible to produce more food with less labor. The first needs are for silo filling and thrashing. Thus come the forage harvester, the successor to silo filling, and the combine. While the latter is known before the forties, it hasn't been widely used in the Midwest. It goes through a field cutting the standing grain, separates the kernels and funnels them into an accompanying wagon, and spews out the straw, either spreading it on the ground to return to the soil or windrowing it. If windrowed, the straw is baled and carried to the barns in another operation.

In Turtle, in 1944, Ralph Meech and Vern Moore go in together and buy a Gehl Forage Harvester. Phil Holmes, with his own and his father's farm to harvest, looks longingly across the fence at their machine. The next year, he buys one, too. He hires out, and that year, also using his 1943 combine, he fills silo and thrashes for seventeen farms.

By the end of the war, combines have made communal thrashing a thing of the past. The huge thrashing machine disappears; when it occurs to Jackie to wonder what happened to it, nobody seems to know. Perhaps it ends up in Dick Post's barn, dozing to rust with other obsolete machinery. Or perhaps it gets hauled up to Janesville and rattles and chuffs at the yearly Labor Day Thresheree, for the amazement and amusement of droves of city folk. It must also be a wonder to the younger farmers, those who have never lost a pitchfork, accidentally or on purpose, into its insatiable maw.

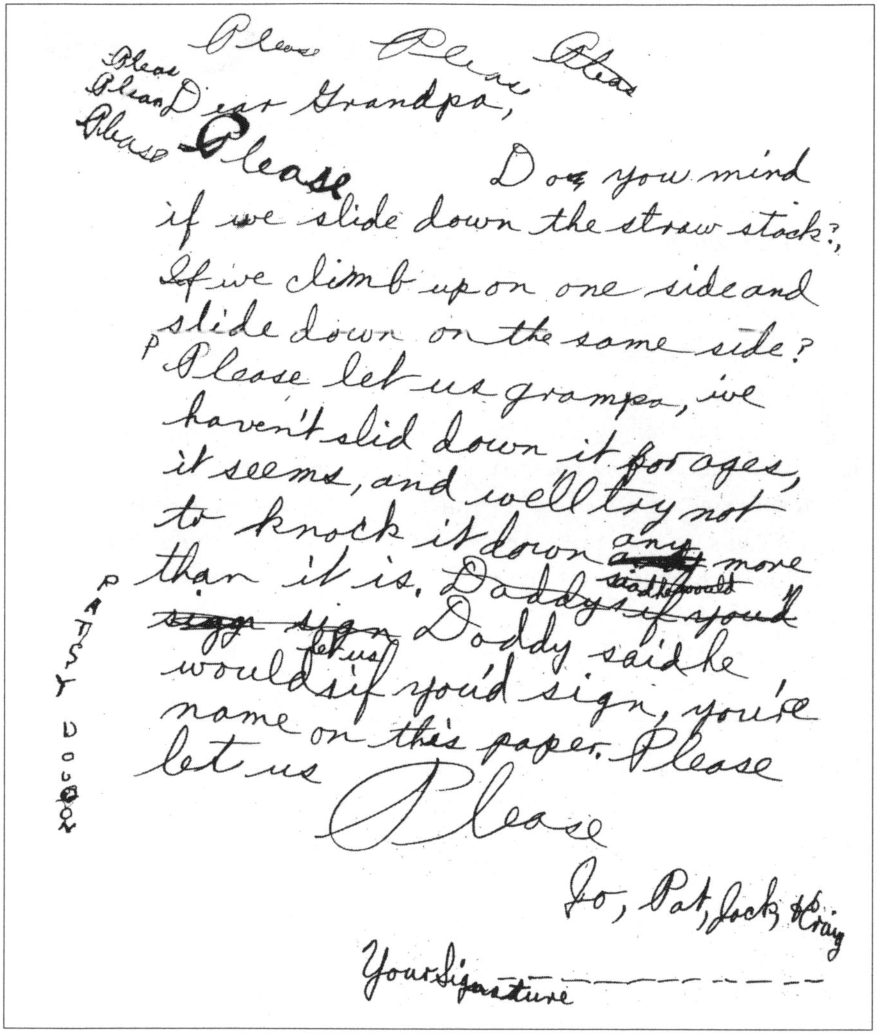

Pleas Pleas Pleas
Pleas
Pleas Dear Grandpa,
Please Please

Do you mind if we slide down the straw stack?, If we climb up on one side and slide down on the same side? Please let us grampa, we haven't slid down it for ages, it seems, and we'll try not to knock it down any more than it is. ~~Daddy if you'd~~ ~~sign sign~~ Daddy said he would let us if you'd sign your name on this paper. Please let us

Please

Jo, Pat, Jack, & Craig

Your Signature ______________

PATSY

This plea (found among farm papers) was probably written by Patsy, though a younger sib seems to have printed Patsy's name along the side. Did Grampa give permission, even though the petition is unsigned?

20 BACK-FENCE WALK

It's a Saturday afternoon in early autumn. Jackie is eight. She and Joan and Patsy and Craig are playing school in the old schoolhouse beside the corncrib. Joan is the teacher. She punishes infractions severely; all her pupils sit facing corners except Jip, who has scratched to be let out for recess.

Grampa flings open the door. "Come along, cubbies!" he shouts. "It's too fine a day to be at lessons indoors. I'll show you some outdoor lessons! Come with me for a back-fence walk."

The four are willing enough to go. They're tired of playing school. So is Jip. He runs ahead when Grampa turns down the lane toward the crick.

"Most people follow roads," Grampa says. "You can see a lot of things on roads, if you keep your eyes open, but there are so many things you miss by not following back fences."

They cross the crick, balancing on the stepping stones, except for Jip who splashes through, pausing midway for a noisy drink. They go through the pasture toward the gravel pit. Jip finds a gopher hole, and Grampa looks around till he finds the gopher's back door. He tells them that little animals that live underground always have a back door for escape if something, like Jip's nose, comes poking in their front door. They know this already. Jackie wonders how Grampa can tell which door is the back one.

The gravel pit is always a good place to play. There's a weathered wooden bridge in it, with a hole as big as a cistern cover in the middle. There's no water under the bridge, just a place to stand a farm cart. The hired men shovel gravel through the hole into the cart below. It's easier to shovel gravel down than up. But when they play, the four of them don't use the hole for its purpose. They jump down through it, in Follow the Leader, or slide down through it with a gunnysack full of stones and sticks over their shoulders, being Santa Claus, or pop up through it as the troll, trying to catch the three Billy Goats Gruff who, one by one, trip-trap over the bridge. This last is the most satisfactory of the games, for there are roles for each of them: Joan as the fierce troll and the other three in ascending order as the billy goat brothers.

On the floor of the gravel pit, Grampa bends and picks up a smooth, round stone. "Do you know how this stone got here?" he asks. "There were great glaciers that covered Wisconsin with ice, and when they melted, they left behind these gravel deposits. Their immense weight grinding over the bedrock crushed it to gravel, and the ice rolled and carried the gravel under and before it, and the streams that flowed out from under the melting glaciers tumbled the stones some more. That's why so many of these stones are smooth and rounded."

They climb the hill on the far side of the gravel pit. At the fence, they turn east. Grampa checks the fence posts and bob wire as they go. He says, "Just as I thought. Some of these posts are rotting out. They'll need replacing. And the wire needs tightening up. We don't want our cows getting into our neighbor's alfalfa." He walks on a bit and adds, "But a three-wire fence never holds a cow if there isn't something in her own field to eat."

There's a kind of broad-bladed grass growing along the fence. Daddy has shown them all how to pluck a blade, place it lengthwise between their thumbs, and blow through the small slit their pressed thumbs leave between them. The blade vibrates and makes a rude noise, rather like a razzberry. They show Grampa their whistles and demonstrate, though he can't hear them.

"You've made whistles," approves Grampa. "I taught your father and uncle to blow on grass blades when they were small. . . . Do you know that all this bromegrass belongs to me?"

They nod.

"The grass knows it too," says Grampa. "Every blade has my initial on it."

He shows them one. In a different shade of green, at about the middle of the blade, an unmistakable *W* stretches from side to side.

"For 'Wesson,'" twinkles Grampa. "Like a cow brand out west. But my brand doesn't hurt them. They grow my initial willingly."

The four pounce on other blades of bromegrass to see whether they all have *W*s. They all do. Joan reaches through the bob wire and plucks a blade. THIS ONE IS ON THE MACKIES' LAND! she writes to Grampa. WHY DOES IT HAVE A *W*, TOO?

"Oh my," says Grampa. "It's just wanting to see if it will grow greener on the other side of the fence!"

They all laugh. They know Grampa is fooling.

Patsy takes a blade, turns it upside down, and points to the marking. She makes a letter *M* in hand language, then spells, *M* F-O-R M-A-C-K-I-E.

"Well, well," says Grampa. "The grass on that side must know they belong to Mr. Mackie."

They reach the end of the field by the Mackies'. Grampa examines the corner post, which has to be in especially good condition because it's so important, supporting fencing from two directions.

"Look at this bob wire," says Grampa. "Notice how it's made, by twisting two wires and regularly inserting the barbs. See how they circle the twist. This wire of mine has only one barb." He walks to the adjoining fence. "This one of Mr. Mackie's has double barbs. And there are other varieties, too. The farm stores have great rolls of different sorts. Bob wire was invented, I think, only fifty miles from here, down at DeKalb. My, you should see the mansions of the families who've made their fortunes on that invention! But have you noticed how some farms have pastures with wooden fences? Those are for horses. Cows won't get tangled up in a bob-wire fence, but horses will. They can rip themselves badly."

C-O-W-S S-M-A-R-T-E-R? spells Joan.

"About fences, certainly," Grampa says.

An early photo of cows crossing the pasture creek. The gravel pit is left, the Mackie farm, right. On the back-fence walk, the pit was larger and there were more Mackie trees.

They follow the fence down to the crick. It's where the stream almost meets the curve in Colley Road. They cross the stream again.

"The school you were just playing in stood right here," Grampa says. "Your daddy went to school here, and so did Trever and Esther and Eloise. Your daddy even taught here for a short while before college. They called it the Dougan School because it was on the corner of my land. Then, when it became cheaper to send you District Twelve children to town than pay for a teacher and supplies and building upkeep, I bought the school for twenty-five dollars and moved it across the field to the farm."

The four nod. Jackie has studied the picture in Grama's album of kids wading in the crick, in front of the schoolhouse. There's a picture, too, of Daddy and all the other boys standing on the roof. And Daddy has told how he and his pupils skated on the crick. At Todd School, there's no wading or skating or climbing on roofs. It would have been a lot more fun if District 12 had decided to keep the old school right here.

Grampa pulls up the bottom strand of bob wire, and one by one, the four lie down on the grass, their arms tight against their sides, and roll under. Then Joan does the same so that Grampa can roll under. Grampa always rolls under bob-wire fences, although the hired men usually step on the bottom strand with their heavy shoes and pull up on the next strand, making a gap to crawl through. Jip always gets through on his own.

Now they are on the Mackies' land. They follow the crick as it winds past the Mackie gravel pit and through a long pasture. A clump of trees is at the far end of it. This is all new territory for Jackie. She hasn't explored beyond the boundaries of the farm. The others haven't, either. Grampa tells them how Spring Brook originates in marshy land beyond Clinton. It flows into Turtle Creek shortly after it goes under Colley Road, close to town. Jackie knows where that is: Spring Brook's spindly red iron bridge and Turtle Creek's flat black bridge are almost double bridges. The two streams meet just beyond the double bridges and just before the railroad bridge, in the flood plain beyond the two bridges.

"Then Turtle Crick joins Rock River in South Beloit, and Rock River joins the Mississippi at Rock Island, and the Mississippi flows into the Gulf of Mexico. We are connected to the sea by our little Spring Brook watershed."

WHERE DOES TURTLE CREEK START? Jackie writes.

"Up near Mukwonago, where Phantom Lake Y camp is. From a shallow lake near it called Mud Lake."

They've reached the end of the pasture; the clump of trees is on the other side of the stream.

"It's a woods!" exclaims Craig. He pulls Grampa's arm and points.

"We'll go over there in a moment," says Grampa. "I want to see something here, first."

Jackie looks down the bank as they walk. Below them the crick has broadened and the water runs still and deep. There are huge ancient willow trees with shaggy bark and slender young shoots springing up beside their thick trunks. The trees lean untidily over the water, dropping their thin yellow leaves. Some leaves are carried sedately downstream by the even current; some, like small curled barques, twirl slowly in dark eddies. Jackie feels delight. Who would have thought there was such an enchanted place so close to home?

Suddenly, their way is blocked by an immense chasm. It's too wide by far to jump across. Its sides drop like cliffs. Its mouth opens into the crick like a waterless river, and the dry riverbed winds back into the land east of them as far as Jackie can see.

Grampa shakes his head. "This is what else I came to check."

They retrace their steps till they find a place they can climb down the bank. They return along the narrow, gravelly stream verge to the gully and stand at the bottom of the great gulch. They walk into it a little way.

Grampa says, "This is a terrible thing. Bad farming practices in the fields above here have caused this erosion. At every storm, rain runs off the land and uses this pathway to get to the crick. The rain carries the topsoil with it, and the force of the water digs this gully wider and deeper. The world depends on its farms for food, you know, and we're letting our precious soil run down into the sea. Have you noticed that after a storm, the crick in our back pasture runs thick brown?"

The four nod vigorously.

"Most of that mud is coming from here." Grampa shakes his head some more. "I should hate to see this spot in a freshet."

Patsy points out the black color of the soil at the top of the gully, and its change to mustard yellow at the bottom.

"Yes," Grampa says. "It's cut through the loam right down to clay and gravel. We have some of the richest and deepest topsoil in the world, right here in Rock County, but every year we're losing inches of it. When we get to clay and gravel, there'll be no more crops."

"Can't it be stopped?" pantomimes Craig.

"Oh, yes. If the hills were left in grass, and not plowed, there'd be scant runoff. The roots would hold the soil. Or if the plowing went around the slopes, instead of up and down, then every furrow would be a little dam. Of course it's not just water that causes erosion. Wind does, too. We're only beginning to recover from the worst erosion this country has ever known, where the Great Plains were plowed, and then came drought, and then wind—and all the topsoil, that's taken tens of thousands of years to build up, has been blown away in dust storms. There's been terrible loss and terrible suffering. You've seen pictures of the dust bowl."

Soberly, the four nod.

"Your father and I are trying to farm so that we increase the soil rather than lose it," Grampa says.

Jackie plucks a snail shell from a band of soil at the level of her hand. She shows Grampa.

"Yes," says Grampa. "That shell's been there a long time. When you're older you'll study geology and learn the workings of the powerful forces that form and fold the rocks"—he flings his arms above his head—"and lift them from the ocean bed to glitter above the clouds!"

N-O M-O-U-N-T-A-I-N-S H-E-R-E, spells Patsy, shaking her head.

"No, but there was once an ocean. This was all a warm shallow sea and that's where the limestone that we have so much of has come from. When sea creatures died, their shells rained down to the bottom; and after eons, the shells built up to such great and heavy thickness that they were pressed into rock. If you study the rocks, you'll find in them the fossils of creatures that once lived."

Jackie tries to imagine such age, such vast numbers of sea creatures. It makes her almost too dizzy to think.

Patsy, Joan, and Jackie, with Craig in front, perhaps a year or two after the back-fence walk. Notice the barbed-wire fence and fence posts.

D-I-N-O-S-A-U-R-S, Craig spells.

"Yes, dinosaurs," Grampa agrees. "Dinosaur bones were recognized for what they are shortly before I was born, and dinosaurs burst into fame when I was a little lad. My, how interested I was in learning everything I could about them! Everyone was filled with wonder that such behemoth creatures once roamed our world."

Grampa hands back the shell and Jackie carefully pockets it. He crumbles a bit of soil from the gully wall and shakes his head some more.

"All this land isn't Grampa's," Joan says, and then spells to her grandfather, W-H-A-T C-A-N Y-O-U D-O? She stabs a finger at him to emphasize the question mark.

"Education," Grampa says. "The university, and the county agents, and the Grange—the federal government, too—are all working to improve farming methods and to let the farmer know about them. I can help there, learning myself and informing my neighbors. What we—your father and I—have been doing, is renting the Snide farm, where this ditch starts, and now your parents are buying it; it's the new farm." He points up the gully, but nobody is tall enough to see over the top. "Now we can fill in the gully up there and then farm so that the erosion slows down and stops. It will be a challenge; that farm is almost as hilly as the Hill Farm."

They walk back down the gully to where it reaches the crick and follow the verge to a shallow place where the water runs quickly over gravel. It makes a cheerful gurgle. Here, the falling willow leaves are swirled and whisked downstream rapidly.

They ford the crick; Jip stops in the middle again for a sloppy drink. On this side, the bank slopes up gently, and behind the willows the woods begin.

Joan is behaving oddly. She looks at the trees, walks a few feet, and looks again. Then, still looking, she walks backward. She tugs Grampa's sleeve. R-O-W-S, she spells, and explains to her sisters and brother, "Look how the trees are all planted in *rows,* and they're all the *same* kind of tree. This is a *planted* woods!"

Jackie walks backward and forward, too. So do Patsy and Craig. It's true. The big trees are in orderly rows. It's strange.

"There's a story to this grove," Grampa says. "Back at the time of the Civil War, men were drafted to serve in the Union Army. But if you had money enough, three hundred dollars I think it was, and could find someone else who was willing to go, you could pay him to go in your place. The man who then owned the Blodgett farm paid a man to go in his stead. That man was killed. Mr. Houston felt terribly guilty. Well, some years later, there came a man along the road with a horse and wagon. He was a Union Army veteran and had lost a leg and was blind in one eye. He was going from farm to farm selling catalpa saplings—catalpa wood makes excellent fence posts. And Mr. Houston felt so guilty that he bought the whole wagon load, to salve his conscience."

"And planted them *here,*" Joan exclaims triumphantly.

"He planted them here," repeats Grampa, not knowing he's repeating. "But he didn't feel so guilty that he used his own strength and sweat to plant them. He had his son-in-law do it. It was a hard, hot job, and the son-in-law thought he'd never get to the end of planting catalpa trees. I know all this because it was the son-in-law—Mr. Hill, who used to live on the Obeck place, who told me the story."

"They must not have used many trees for fence posts," Patsy observes. "There are still a lot here."

"I don't think he ever used these trees for fence posts," Grampa says.

Joan spells to Grampa, Y-O-U N-E-E-D F-E-N-C-E P-O-S-T-S.

"Yes." Grampa laughs. "And we will cut them out of our own woods at the Hill Farm."

The four walk back and forth some more to see the rows shift. Grampa points out the large size of catalpa leaves, and the long seed pods hanging from the branches and littering the ground. They peel back the brown husks and see the hard, fat, shiny seeds lying in a row inside, like beans.

"Some people call catalpas 'bean trees,'" Grampa says. "Locusts are bean trees, too, and some others. Catalpas are late budding out—every other woods will be green before this one. My first spring here, I thought this entire woods was dead."

Jackie adds a bean to the shell in her pocket. She will call this special place "the Catalpa Forest."

They leave the woods and head back to the dairy. As they go through the farm gravel pit again, Jackie picks up a small stone rounded by the glacier and adds it to her treasures. Grampa notices her do it. She spells to him, Y-O-U C-A-N L-E-A-R-N A L-O-T F-R-O-M S-T-O-N-E-S.

"Yes," says Grampa. "God's hand has written history as definitely on the pages of rock beneath our feet as on the pages of Scripture. We just have to learn to read them."

Back at the farm, they thank Grampa for the back-fence walk. He goes off to check on the milking. Jackie sets out the shell, the bean, and the stone on the well lid. She contemplates them. There are many more kinds of reading, she decides, than what Todd School teaches.

21 PARADISE

Joan, Patsy, Jackie, and Craig know what Paradise is. They have dwelt there. It's the room over the milkhouse.

When the milkhouse was first built, that space was a bunkhouse for the hired men. After the Big House had its roof raised and dormitory rooms put in, the bunkhouse became an apartment for a succession of married couples. One of these was Lester and Moo Moo Stam, who moved out in the middle of the night after Moo Moo and Grama had a fight over nobody ever knew what. It has been empty now for quite some time.

There are really several rooms, each commanding a view over a portion of the farm, so that a trip through the apartment lets you see from on high everything that is going on. The floors are broad golden planks, and the walls and ceilings painted white. It's a fresh and sunny place, with built-in cabinets and large drawers forming one whole wall of the largest room. It is this room that turns into Paradise.

It happens this way. The rich relatives who live in Elgin have bought new furniture. They offer to sell Daddy and Mother their old furniture at a very low price. Old Bosworth furniture is much finer than anything Mother and Daddy now have. Besides, they will soon need more furniture, for they are buying the Snide farm up the road, and plan to remodel the large farmhouse.

Mother and Daddy drive a truck down to Elgin to look over the discards and pick out what they want. They return with a bird's-eye maple bedroom suite, a dining room table and eight chairs, several marble-topped bedroom tables, an ornate four-sided pivoting bookcase, and other assorted pieces. Aside from trying out the spin on the bookcase, the four children are not particularly interested in the spoils.

But then Daddy says, "They threw in something for you. Go look in the room over the milkhouse."

The four mount the stairs and enter through the many-paned door. Side by side in the empty front room stand a bear and a barrel. The bear is dark brown, its four legs on wheels, and is big enough to ride. They all make a dash but Craig gets there first and straddles it. He promptly discovers a metal ring in the middle of the bear's shoulders. He pulls it and the bear says, in a low weary voice, "Uuunh." Craig scoots the bear forward. It turns out that one of the wheels is only half a wheel; the bear lists to the side and clunks when it rolls. But that hardly matters. It is a wonderful bear! They take turns riding it and making it go "Uuuunh."

They then turn their attention to the barrel. It is larger than the chocolate powder barrel in the old schoolhouse, larger than the copper sulphate barrel. It's open at the top but covered with tucked-in newspapers. They peel back the papers and make their flabbergasting find. *The barrel is filled with toys!*

After a stunned moment they reach in and start grabbing them out, loudly laying claim, until Joan declares that everything in the barrel has to belong to all of them, just like the bear has to, unless there's something nobody else wants. Patsy, Jackie, and Craig can see the justice of this. They also agree when Joan suggests they remove things one at a time, and examine them together.

Where did all the toys come from? That's easy to figure out. The rich relatives have four daughters, long grown up. The Dougan kids have never known these second cousins, except that Joan once met the youngest, Betsy. Betsy was visiting at the farm and riding a horse, and she told Joan, who was trotting along behind her, breathless with admiration, to go away and quit bothering her—she was too little and might get hurt. Joan was outraged to be ordered off her own fields by a virtual stranger. Forever after, she has resented Betsy Bosworth.

A smaller version of the bear from a Sears catalog. They fail to mention its memorable voice. Perhaps this model had none!

But now, all is forgiven. Somebody put the Bosworth girls' outgrown toys in a barrel and sent the barrel up to the farm, along with the marble-top tables and bird's-eye maple.

The barrel is a cornucopia. Wonder after wonder pours from it. There is a rag doll as tall as Patsy, with a smiling face and yellow yarn braids and a real child's dress and pinafore. Elastic bands are sewed to the bottoms of her feet, so that you can put your feet through the straps and dance with her. There is a metal platter painted with houses and trees and streams and bridges and a train station. When you wind a key on the underside, a little train runs round and round a groove in the edge of the platter. Most of the other windup toys no longer work, but one that still does is an amazement: a little tin woman, with long tin skirts and her hair in a mobcap. She holds a tin carpet sweeper with bristles that really go around, and wound up she darts here and there erratically, pushing the sweeper stiffly before her. She has a no-nonsense expression. Her name is printed on her apron: Bizzy Lizzy.

There are alphabet blocks and anchor blocks. There are books, among them several fat volumes of *Chatterbox,* which turn out to be bound collections of old children's magazines with games and puzzles and continued mystery stories. These come from England, and Jackie immediately adores them. There are toys with missing parts, and parts with missing toys. There are games with no directions jostling for space with games complete in their boxes. There are three ornate cut-glass perfume bottles, elegantly stoppered, fit for a queen's dressing table. The bottles are empty but each retains a trace of faraway fragrance.

These, and some of the toys, come wrapped in funny papers. The four spread the papers out and see comics they recognize, but most are from before their time, such as Little Nemo and Krazy Kat.

When the call for noon dinner comes, they hurry back to the Little House, each carrying a choice item to show Mother and Daddy. Joan brings the beautiful perfume bottles, Patsy clasps Bizzy Lizzy, Jackie and Craig between them lug the bear.

Their parents are happy to share their delight. Mother makes one rule. The barrel toys are to be kept over the milkhouse, for the Little House is cluttered enough, and the long window box is already crammed to the top with toys. That is all right with the four.

Though usually worn and sometimes broken, the new toys are special for several reasons. Fundamentally, they have appeared out of nowhere, totally unsolicited, imagined, longed for, or deserved. It is not Christmas or Easter or anyone's birthday. They are pure manna from heaven. Then, because the Bosworth cousins are so much older, their toys are not the familiar ones in the stores and advertisements. Where could anyone possibly go to buy a Bizzy Lizzy? Her day has come and gone. Add to that the wealth of the Bosworths. The toys they purchased are expensive ones, from unusual catalogs or Chicago department stores like Marshall Field's. They sit on a higher shelf in the economic toyshop than most of the Dougan kids' toys, however plentiful.

But all this is not enough to make the room over the milkhouse Paradise. There is a final factor. At the Little House, play goes on on the living room rug. Extensive villages outlined with blocks and peopled with small ceramic dolls and dogs, elaborate Tinkertoy or Lincoln Log extravaganzas, can last only an afternoon. Sometimes Mother is persuaded to let a particularly absorbing creation stay up till the following day. Then everybody has to be careful to step over it or around it, including the family pets, who are particularly obtuse about such matters.

But over the milkhouse, the spacious room is totally theirs. No grown-up presence taints it. Week after week, the four can play on the sunny floor and never have to pick up anything. *No one ever, ever, ever says: "Time to put your things away."* When they return, everything is as they left it.

But earthly paradises do not last. Patsy arrives at the room one day to find it bare. She is stricken, and so are Joan and Jackie and Craig. They rush to find out what has happened. Their parents don't know. But the answer is soon forthcoming. Grama has decided they've played with the toys long enough. It's time for Trever's children to have a turn. After all, they are Bosworth cousins, too. So, like Moo Moo in the night, the barrel has vanished. It has been loaded up and shipped to Jerry and Karla.

Daddy says it's also history repeating itself in another way; that his Grandmother Delcyetta swiped his toys when he didn't pick them up and hid them in her bottom drawer. They weren't found till she died.

It doesn't make them feel any better. "You at least got them *back*," Patsy wails. She never does get over losing Bizzy Lizzy.

But two things are saved from Armageddon. Jackie happens to have a volume of *Chatterbox* under her pillow at the Little House. And Craig has only recently dragged the bear that says "Uuunh" over to the playhouse, as a guest at a stuffed animal tea party.

22 THE SHOE FACTORY

It's Jackie's ninth birthday. Her present is to go through the Freeman Shoe Factory with the milkman. This is something she's been longing to do ever since she discovered there was such a factory in Beloit.

It's a school day, but Daddy and Mother agree that anyone who requests such an educational present deserves to miss a morning of school. "Tell us what you've learned tonight," says Daddy, "and if there's any trouble, I'll go see your teacher personally."

Now Jackie follows Howard Milner from the loading platform into the factory. He has a wheeled cart that's low to the floor, piled high with milk cases. There are half-pints of white milk, chocolate milk, and orange drink, as well as a few cases of white milk pints.

The first room is big as a barn. It's the cutting room, Howard explains. Jackie marvels. Here are the cowhides that are going to be made into shoes, all piled up like rugs in a furniture store. Howard introduces her to a foreman and he tells her that the hides have already been tanned and dyed, somewhere else.

When the workmen buy milk, they josh about Jackie. "We have a new milkman!" "Better watch out, Howard, she'll take your job away from you!" "That your best girl, Howard?"

Howard grins. "She is for today!" He seems to know all the men. "She wants to know what you do here."

The men show her how the preliminary cutting is done. They give her scraps so that she has pieces of all hues to take home with her—browns, blacks, tans, beiges, even reds.

Then she follows into an even larger room. Noise hits her ears like a blow: clacking, stamping, crunching, clunking. The room is filled with machines in long rows with aisles between them. There are men standing at the machines. Jackie trots behind Howard and the cart, and the workers pause, buy milk, and make remarks.

"What a pretty little milkmaid we have today!"

"What'll you take for her, Howard?"

Jackie doesn't mind the joking. She's fascinated with the machines. She lingers, watching a man stamp out sole after sole, like a giant cookie cutter. The next man is stamping out soles, too, of a different size and color. She wanders slowly down the aisles, staring at first one machine and then the next. Each machine does just one thing, often the next step of the machine before. She tries to follow the progress of a shoe.

At one machine she's startled to see a man from her church. Of course people at church must have jobs during the week, but this has never occurred to her before. Here is redheaded Mr. Harris, in work clothes, running a press! He recognizes her and grins, but there's no opportunity to speak, over the din.

Jackie watches. He puts a flat piece of black leather over a rounded form, clamps it, takes a brush from a pot and smears the leather with liquid, reaches overhead for a lever and hauls down the upper part of the machine. With a crunch it stamps into the leather. He holds it in place several seconds, while steam hisses from the juncture. Then he releases it. The leather beneath has become a permanently rounded shiny toe. He tosses it into a bin beside the machine with other identical toes, takes a fresh piece of leather the same shape as the first, fits it on the form, wets it, and stamps again. Jackie watches him steam the second toe, and a third and fourth, before she trots to catch up with the milkman.

She travels by fits and starts through the factory. They take a large service-type elevator, and as they ride up, Howard tells her that the shoe factory milkman before him, Don Stevens, had a temper. The men would tease him. He'd come back to where he'd left his cart and it would be hidden. Or

Jackie on a milk truck. She was this age when she went through the shoe factory.

they'd have smeared the handles with rubber cement, just to see him get mad. "But I josh around with them all," Howard says as the elevator door opens, "and they don't mess with me!"

They come into a room where it seems a thousand sewing machines are whirring. Jackie watches one woman sew a heel seam, and another heel seam, and another heel seam, over and over and over; the woman next to her takes the work and adds the next seam, over and over and over. The women glance up and smile but their flashing hands never miss a motion. She watches uppers stitched to soles, heels fastened and trimmed, lacing eyelets stamped in place. She sees the progress of a shoe, not always quite in order, but from beginning to end. She's absorbed and fascinated. The only problem is, she wants to stand and watch all day, and Howard keeps moving ahead too quickly with his cart and milk bottles.

When he's finished peddling, he drops Jackie back at Todd School. She thinks about the shoe factory all afternoon. It was as interesting as she thought it would be. But something bothers her about the experience. She tries to figure out what it is.

At supper Mother says, "Well, tell all of us what you've learned."

"I learned how a shoe is made," says Jackie, and spends much of the meal describing with enthusiasm the huge rooms, the hides, the leather pieces moving along and becoming more and more shoelike as they go. Her voice is more tentative when she tells about Mr. Harris stamping out his toe, and the rows of women at their sewing machines, each stitching one seam over and over, over and over, all day long, every day all week, all month, all year.

"That's called mass production," says Joan. "That's the way factories run."

This is how Howard Milner looked when Jackie accompanied him through the shoe factory.

"The cobbler in the fairy tale, the one the elves helped, he'd make a shoe from beginning to end," says Jackie. "It was all his, like when I draw a picture; I don't do one line and let somebody else do the next one."

"But he didn't make very many shoes that way," says Patsy. "That was the trouble."

"We mass produce, too," Joan goes on. "The hired men—there's always the haying; and they milk the cows over and over, every day; and in the milkhouse, the bottling is just like an assembly line; and the milkmen deliver the milk to the same old houses. It's just the same."

Jackie shakes her head vehemently. "It's not the same at all! The cows are fed, and then they're milked, and then they're stripped, and the barn is cleaned—the job's the *same,* but there's so much more *to* it, it keeps it interesting. And in the milkhouse, they bottle the quarts, and then the pints, and then the half-pints, and then the chocolate milk; and they wash the bottles and make butter and cheese—one man doesn't just stand there stamping caps on bottles all day, and that's all he does. And on the route, you're moving around town, and seeing people, and meeting dogs, and . . . and . . . well, going through shoe factories."

"And out in the field," adds Daddy, "the hay is only a little part of it. There's plowing and planting and cultivating, and worrying about the weather . . ."

Jackie nods. "The shoe factory was interesting because I wanted to see how shoes are made, and I went through with the milkman and saw the whole thing. But if I had to stay in one spot all day, indoors, sewing up one little thing, and not being able to talk to anyone on account of how noisy it is—I don't think I could stand it!"

"Unfortunately, a lot of jobs are tedious," says Daddy, "and a lot of people have to work at them whether they like them or not. But I must say I agree with Jackie. I often thank my lucky stars that I'm a farmer."

Jackie takes her last bite of birthday cake. "Me, too," she says.

23 JUDGING COWS

Jackie is nine, Craig seven. They're at the Rock County 4-H Fair with Grampa. Grampa is going to be a cattle judge in the afternoon. They go to the cow barns and look at the animals to be judged. The 4-H members are busy cleaning and currying their calves and cows and steers, readying them for the show ring. Over in the pig barn, they were actually scrubbing the pigs with scrub brushes and soap and buckets of water, and one girl was rubbing mineral oil on her pig to make it gleam. But cow hair is thicker and needs a currycomb.

Jackie envies the kids who have animals at the fair. There are platforms over the pens, for ropes and buckets and feed sacks and bales of hay. There's also space for sleeping bags. Kids live right at the fair, sleeping above their animals. They are part of the fair.

Jackie's only a visitor. But she belongs more than most of the town people, who seldom come into the barns. They come for the rides and game booths and the events in the grandstand. They think the fair is a carnival. She belongs more, too, because Grampa is a judge.

"Would you like a geometry lesson?" Grampa asks.

Jackie frowns. She's not sure what geometry is, but the middle of a cow barn at the fair doesn't seem the place for it. Craig frowns too.

"Cow geometry," says Grampa, twinkling. "It takes cow geometry to judge a cow."

That's different. They both nod vigorously.

To Jackie, cows have never looked all the same, as some people think they do, but she has no idea what makes one cow better than another. She's studied the pictures on the covers of *Hoard's Dairyman* and can't tell. *Hoard's,* every so often, will have a cover divided into four rows, *A, B, C, D,* and the

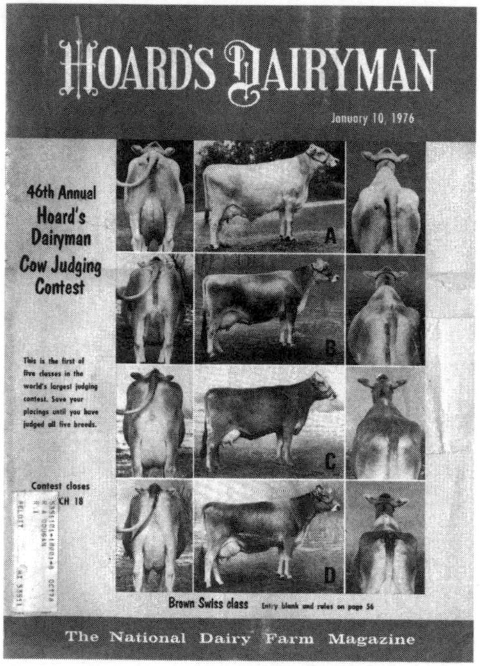

A Hoard's Dairyman *cover, of the sort shown every year for the contest. How would* you *vote? (Thanks to Steve Larson, editor of* Hoard's, *for permission to print this.)*

rows into three pictures. Each row pictures one dairy cow: her hind quarters with her tail held aside to show her udder, then a side view, then a view from a little above her hind quarters showing her back from tail to head.While the cows are not in color, Jackie can add in her imagination the tan and white of the Guernseys, the splotchy red and white of the Ayrshires, the Jerseys all coffee-creamy, and the Brown Swiss, brown. The black and white Holsteins, of course, need no enhancement. The covers look rather like game-boards. It *is* a sort of game, for readers are supposed to judge each breed, and see if they agree with the *Hoard's* judges. There are prizes for the winners, and readers as young as eight years old can enter. Daddy reports a joke cover once—somebody drew it and posted it on a bulletin board at the university. Instead of cows there were four farmers, front, side and back. The cows were to judge the farmers. Daddy says the mean-looking farmer who smoked a cigar while milking and burnt a cow's udder got a rock-bottom score from the cows. But *Hoard's,* so far as Jackie has noticed, has never said anything about cow geometry.

Grampa stops beside a young black Aberdeen Angus tethered outside its pen. Its owner is busy currying.

"If it's a beef animal," Grampa says, "it must be solid and square, like this one. Laddie, may we borrow your steer for a moment?"

The boy flashes a grin and stands back.

"This boy will lead his steer in front of the judging stand," Grampa says, "and try to get it to stand evenly on all four legs." Grampa nudges at the steer's feet with his heavy over-the-ankle farmer's shoe until the steer shifts and is standing as square as a table, one leg down from each corner.

"Then," Grampa continues, "if this lad is as bright as he looks, he'll slip his hand underneath and tickle the steer right in the middle of its stomach," —Grampa does it—"and the steer will arch its back up a little till it's a straight line."

The steer obligingly arches the sway out of its back.

"And there it stands, square as a brick," says Grampa, "and just as solid." He laughs silently; his eyes disappear. Jackie, Craig, and the boy laugh, too.

"Thank you, laddie," Grampa says. "You've raised a handsome steer. It ought to win a blue ribbon."

"Thank you, sir," says the boy as the three start on.

Craig explains over his shoulder, "He can't hear you, or he'd say 'You're welcome.'"

"Now, in a dairy cow," says Grampa, pausing beside another pen, "you don't look for squares. You look for triangles. You look for three important triangles. Take this Guernsey cow. Can you see any triangles?"

Jackie and Craig look hard. They both shake their heads. Grampa takes his tablet of yellow paper, the one he hands to people to write on when they have something to say to him, and his pencil. He makes a funny little sketch of a cow, side view. He draws a triangle over the whole side of the cow. Now they understand.

"It must be heavy in the rear, and straight across the back. And here is the second triangle." Grampa draws another funny picture that doesn't look much like a cow at all:

"This is a top view, from her shoulders back to her flanks. A well-built dairy cow has narrow shoulders and broad flanks. The third triangle," and Grampa draws a funnier picture yet, "is the rear end. Flat and wide across the hips, narrowing down to the knees."

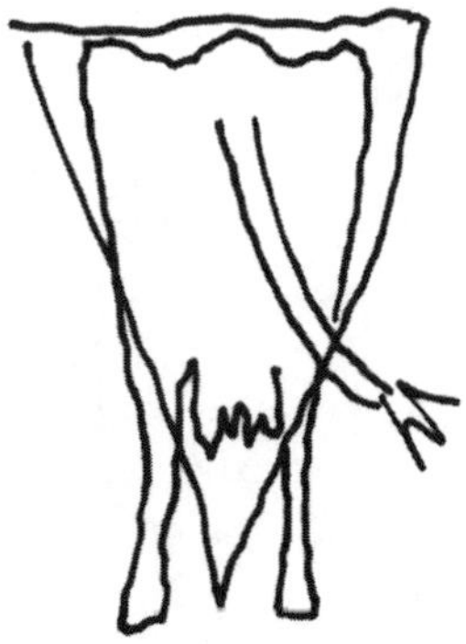

Craig takes Grampa's pad. "Don't all cows have 3 △△△s?" he writes.

"Yes, and that's where the judging comes in: how well does the cow fit the ideal triangles? There are other things to judge, too. She must have good legs and a well-supported udder, not pendulous. There are things a judge can't know without records. But here we judge on looks."

Jackie takes Grampa's pad and draws the face of a cow, the cartoony one she's made up and uses on her papers at school as her trademark. Grampa, laughing, watches her drawing grow. When she's done she draws a triangle over it, from ear to ear to chin. She holds up four fingers.

"Four triangles!" Grampa exclaims, opening his eyes wide. "I see I've been lax! I must be sure to look at their faces, too, when I'm judging."

He takes the paper back. He draws a square with four little circles in it. "Have you ever seen one of these?"

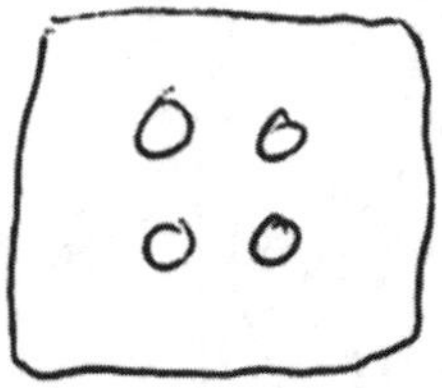

Craig and Jackie shake their heads.

"They're rare nowadays. It's an udder board. Judges used to put a lot of stock in the shape of the udder. A person about to show a cow would put the udder board under her and let the tits hang through the holes. Then, as the bag filled with milk, the udder would settle onto the board and flatten out. Just before she went in the ring he'd take the board off and the udder would hold that square shape with a flat bottom for a while. But it didn't mean a thing."

Grampa tucks his paper and pencil back in his pocket. He looks reflectively along the pens of cattle. "Of course, modern science is now proving that looks don't have much to do with what we value in a cow—how much milk she gives, and butterfat content, and resistance to disease . . . a grade cow may be better in all those than the most beautiful purebred Guernsey. One of our very best milkers in the round barn is the funniest looking."

Jackie nods. She's noticed that cow.

The three walk on through the dairy barn. The geometry lesson is over.

At the judging that afternoon, Jackie sits up in the bleachers beside the show ring. Grampa is in the judging stand with two other men. For a while, she watches the 4-H kids leading their calves and cows around the ring. She tries to figure out the squares and triangles. She gets a little bored. Just as she is about to leave and go do something else, she sees the boy from the morning lead in his black Aberdeen Angus. He stops it in front of the judges' stand. He nudges its hoofs until it's standing absolutely even. Then he bends and tickles it under its stomach, and the steer arches its back. It stands square and solid. The ringmaster motions the boy on.

Jackie waits until the end of the division, and sees the boy go up and get his blue ribbon. She grins. She wonders if he recognizes Grampa in the judges' stand.

24 THE CORNHUSKING CONTEST

It's October 29, 1937. Jackie is nine, there's tremendous activity on Colley Road, and everybody has the measles. Everybody is Joan, Patsy, Jackie, and Craig. They were all exposed at the same time. They are in quarantine.

For almost ten days they've lain in their beds, the shades drawn so that the two bedrooms are enveloped in gloom. They haven't been allowed to read or write or draw, for measles can injure the eyes. Their bodies have been flushed and mottled with red rash. The distinctive sick-sweet-musky-dry smell of the disease has hung in the air and clung to the sheets. Dr. Thayer has stopped out several times. Once they are on the road to recovery, they've been infinitely bored.

But now they are well—well! They're well! They feel fine. The rash is gone; the smell has vanished.

"I'm sorry," Mother says for the twentieth time. "You're not out of quarantine until tomorrow. I can't let you go."

Everyone else has gone, now even Mother. Jackie and Craig have come from their room and joined their older sisters lying across Patsy's bed; it affords a view across the East Twenty. They watch the steady procession of cars streaming up Colley Road, turning at the corner, running along the length of the field till the road dips down for the next turn and heads east again, out of their sight. Not a single car is coming from the other direction. They are all stopping at the next farm, the Blodgett farm, where the very first All-State Cornhusking Contest is being held today.

None of them has ever been to a cornhusking contest. They've seen corn husked, of course, for Daddy and Grampa and the hired men and the agronomy professors from the university husk the Dougan hybrid seed corn yield test plots by hand, so there will be no mix-up on whose corn is whose. But even with most farms now using mechanical pickers, hand husking is practiced. Men wear special husking gloves and carry special husking tools, and they go down the rows picking corn from both sides as fast as they can and slinging the ears against a bangboard that sticks up from the side of a wagon following along. It's an art, an athletic feat, to pick fast. County contests are held every year to see who can pick the fastest. Dick Post has won the Rock County contest for four years. Other states have had state contests, and their winners have gone on to national. Now Wisconsin is having a state contest. Dick Post will probably win it; he may even go on to be national champ. And the marvel is that the state contest is being held on the very next farm!

The Beloit paper has had pictures and articles every day all week. Ten thousand people are expected to come. The Plymouth Farm Bureau band will lead the parade of the sixteen huskers and their horses and wagons to the field. The Turtle Fife and Drum Corps will play. There will be airplane rides just across the road by the Mackies' and seven food tents, including the Turtle Grange's.

Visitors to the sickrooms have kept the four up on all the details. When Grama stopped by yesterday, she reported that Fannie Veihman and Mabel Wallace were running the Grange tent, and all they had were three slow kerosene stoves with three burners each to cook the forty pounds of hamburger they'd ordered. And the Bonnie Bee was going to have more hamburger made up, just in case, and Mabel had ordered one hundred pies from a bakery—think of it! One hundred pies! Grama herself has made five batches of doughnuts, and there will be chocolate and white half-pints of Dougan's milk and orange and grape drink for sale.

Grampa, on his visit, told them that his little bay team, the team he'd bought and broken last spring, was going to pull one of the sixteen wagons, and perhaps win the prize that the Wisconsin State Horse Breeder's Association was offering for the best farm team. The four know that Daddy and Grampa are fixing up a stand to advertise and sell their hybrid seed corn.

There won't be any rides, like at the 4-H Fair, but there might be balloons and those little pink celluloid dolls dressed in feathers on a stick. Most of all there will be crowds—huge crowds, huge excitement.

And now the great day is here, and they are still in quarantine. They lie in a row on the bed, their chins in their hands, watching the cars go by. In every fiber, they crave excitement. The longing to be at the cornhusking contest is unbearable.

"Let's go," Joan says suddenly.

The bed visibly shakes with the shock of the other three—not so much with surprise as that Joan has dared put into words what has been in the minds of them all.

Patsy's voice is cautious. "What if we get caught?"

"With ten thousand people there? Who will notice us?"

"Grama and Mommy will," Craig says with conviction.

"They're in the Grange booth. Mother doesn't intend to come home; she's left lunch for us in the ice box. We just stay away from the booth and watch out for Daddy and Grampa at the hybrid corn booth and anyone else we know. Nobody notices little kids. And we come home before it's over and get back in bed. Who will ever know?"

"What about the measles?" asks Jackie.

"We're well," Joan says. "What's a day?"

What, indeed. The four lie there digesting the unthinkable. The flow of cars begins to slacken. It must be getting on to the time for the contest to start. The unthinkable gradually becomes not only thinkable but quite thinkable, then possible, and finally imperative. Joan rolls off the bed, opens a dresser drawer, and pulls out her underwear. Without a word, the other three also go for their clothing. Even though the house is empty, they are stealthy.

At the front door, Joan turns and says, "No one tells. Promise?"

The other three nod.

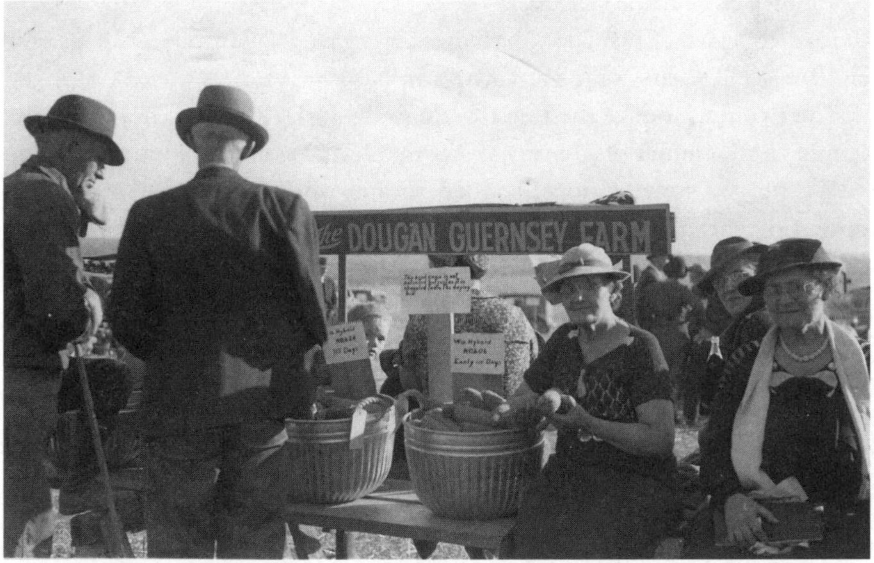

The Dougan seed corn stand at the cornhusking contest. Grama is beside the basket of corn ears. Effie, Grama's niece, peeks from behind. Mr. Griffiths has the skinny neck.

Jip, long deprived of play, is racing and leaping, wild to go, but they close him in. They look both ways as they leave the Little House and keep watching as they cross the yard and climb the fence.

Cutting across the field, they're exposed. "Just walk natural," Joan orders. "Everybody from the farm is there already."

At the Mackie corner, they have to join Colley Road and follow along with the traffic. Parked cars line both sides, making the passageway narrow. The moving cars continue on to a parking field across from the Blodgetts', but the four veer off into the double row of pine trees that surrounds the houses and farm buildings.

"OK, now we split up," Joan instructs. "Patsy and I will go together, and Craig, you go with Jackie. Meet back here in—oh, an hour and a half."

"How can we tell?" Jackie asks.

Joan considers. "Just check back here every once in a while. When we're all here, we'll leave. Come on, Patsy."

The two duck out of the trees. Craig grabs Jackie's hand. They stand listening to the tumult of so many voices that it makes a great hum, punctuated by nearby conversations, sudden shouts, shrill laughter. An airplane drones overhead, dogs bark, a horse whinnies, a wagon creaks. Somewhere a chorus starts to sing. They peer through the branches as their sisters disappear into the shifting mob. They see children dodging and running.

Jackie's feelings are on a seesaw, but a stuck one. Perched on the high side are excitement and anticipation; weighting down the low are guilt and dread. All these, plus the danger, plus the freedom after long confinement, add up almost to delirium. But it's a bottled delirium that mustn't be expressed in her actions. "Let's go," she finally whispers, and she and Craig slide out from behind the tree trunks, too.

The pounding of her heart slows as she and Craig sidle into the crowds, staying in the middle of all the boots and bib-overalled stomachs and bright dresses and jackets. They avoid looking up at faces. They avoid the many food booths, identifiable by their canvas and counters and beckoning, conflicting smells. They do see a booth with balloons and pinwheels and pennants on sticks, and they edge up to it and look at the goods; that's safe enough, for no one from the farm would be at this booth. They don't buy anything. They haven't any money, and besides, how would they explain? They see shiny new farm machinery on exhibit, and corn and grain displays. Jackie spots the Dougan corn stand and Daddy talking to someone there; she clutches Craig's arm and they both melt backward into the throng.

Now they hear a band, and immediately the crowd's aimless meandering changes. Rivulets of people join streams of people, and the streams converge into a river, moving along behind the drums and the trombones, past the biggest barn out toward the cornfield beyond. Jackie and Craig allow themselves to be swept along with the current. Up ahead, they see the horses and wagons positioning themselves. A shot rings out, and the tide surges forward. The cornhusking contest has begun.

They squirm their way to the head of the crowd. Alleyways have been cut out of the field so that there is room for the horses and wagons, room for the people. The cornhuskers move along their corridors in the warm Indian summer sunshine, sweating, picking with a grace and economy of motion. Some huskers are young and brawny; one is older and grizzled, but his wagon is keeping up with all the rest. The golden ears smack the bangboards in an erratic, rapid tattoo. The people follow; each picker has his own cheering section. Jackie wonders which one is Dick Post. He's Rock County's favorite, the one the newspaper thinks has the best chance of winning. Craig spots Grampa's bay team, but the driver and the husker are strangers.

Behind each husker, more slowly, comes a second wagon, with two men walking and stooping beside it, throwing in an occasional ear. A farmer beside Jackie explains to his city companion that those are gleaners; they are picking up what a husker has missed, and this residue will be weighed and then subtracted against his total. Jackie conveys the information to Craig. They both watch to see if the gleaners get much.

The contest is interesting, but after a bit, not that interesting. She and Craig buck the current and squeeze back out of the field to the main grounds. There are still droves of people here. They eye the Turtle Grange booth from a distance until they see that both Mother and Grama are still there. Over by the pigs, they spot their sisters. Joan sees them and gives a little nod. By different routes they arrive back at the trees, go along the road, cut across the field and yard, and into the Little House. Jip greets them reproachfully. They undress, put away their clothes, eat the lunch Mother left, and go back to bed. Jackie sleeps all afternoon.

Husking corn by hand.

It turns out Dick Post does not win the contest. He comes in second, with 29.2 bushels. He had the flu the night before and was not up to snuff, it's later reported around the township by Bob Maxworthy, the driver of his team and wagon. The youngest husker of all, one nobody put any bets on, eighteen-year-old Omer Koopman, from Patch Grove, in Grant County, wins, with 29.3 bushels. In the horse contest, Grampa's bay team takes third prize, though Grampa says had they been judged on performance alone, they'd have been first. He is quite proud of them. He and Daddy are also pleased with the Dougan booth, which chalks up orders for three hundred dollars worth of seed corn, at eight dollars a bushel retail, and six dollars and fifty cents to dealers. The Turtle Grange sells all its hamburgers and pies.

And the children's escapade is not discovered. They none of them tell. It has been a satisfying day.

Many years later, after Jackie is married but before she has children, she's visiting at the farm. Daddy has begun having school tours, first-graders coming out with their teachers to see cows milked, pigs fed, and other farm activities. She's been on these school tours before.

Today, there's a tour but for a different sort of child. An organization of parents is coming. They are bringing their retarded children, perhaps ten mothers, ten children. Daddy asks Jackie to come along.

She accompanies the group, noticing each child and mother, wondering how it must be to bring up a child so far from normal. The mothers chat with one another matter-of-factly, about ordinary things. All the children can walk, but some have strange shambles; some cling so closely to their mothers that walking is difficult for both. Some talk; others are silent and seem oblivious to where they are. Jackie recognizes several gentle children as having what is coming to be called Down's syndrome instead of Mongolian Idiot. And some of the children are hardly children, either in age or size. But they are, in actions—down in the barn when a cow arches her back, lifts her tail, and looses a stream of urine into the gutter, followed by the plop of a hearty cow pie, a husky boy of sixteen or seventeen doubles up with hilarity, pointing and laughing and shouting out "Pee!" like a two-year-old.

Daddy tailors the tour to the group's abilities, showing them how milk comes from a tit, letting calves suck their fingers, letting them hold rabbits. He includes things for the mothers' interest; he recognizes, Jackie realizes, that the outing is as much for the mothers as it is for the children, probably more so. He, too, chats matter-of-factly. Some of the mothers he knows; they are Dougan customers.

Jackie particularly notices a boy of twelve or thirteen who hangs onto his mother's arm with one hand and with the other keeps digging into one eye. Both eye and socket are terribly distorted, swollen, red, and angry looking.

It must hurt, yet the boy's knuckles keep kneading. He's one of the children who, unlike the Down's children or the boy in the barn, seems totally unaware of his surroundings or of any other people except his mother.

Jackie knows that openness is better than pretense in most instances. These parents aren't hiding their children's disabilities. She asks the mother about the boy's eye.

The mother explains. She had rubella when she was pregnant, and her son was born retarded, deaf, and blind. When he works at his eye, he sees flashes of light and color. "It's just about the only entertainment he has," she says.

Jackie has read about rubella. When she was a child, it wasn't known that rubella in pregnancy could cause retardation and other birth defects. There were no vaccines. Ever since she learned this, and that rubella was once called measles, she's had an uneasiness about the cornhusking contest. But she also knows that measles were defined differently then: there were the German measles and the three-day measles, and she and her sisters and Craig had had both varieties. They may also have had a measlelike rash later identified as separate, roseola.

She's asked Mother before, but now that she's actually seen a rubella child, and can imagine all too vividly his life, and the life of the family caring for him, she asks again.

Mother has long since been told about the escapade. She repeats that the measles the four of them had, the day they sneaked over to the cornhusking contest, were the ten-day measles, not rubella. And that no matter what they had, they were surely past the catching stage by their last day of quarantine. Even had they not been, what were the odds of any of them being long enough in the company of a pregnant woman to do any harm?

Jackie is reassured. But once in a very great while she has a nagging edge of doubt. What if there *is* a rubella child, somewhere, digging into his eye, that the four of them by their disobedience are responsible for?

25 THANKSGIVING AT THE BIG HOUSE

It is Thanksgiving dinner at the Big House, and the table is crowded with family and hired men. Jackie perches on a stool at one corner. Grampa has just finished the long Thanksgiving blessing. In the pause after his "Amen," as everyone is looking up from being solemn and thankful, Grampa adds a postscript.

"It gives me great satisfaction to look upon this table," he exclaims. "Do you know that everything for our Thanksgiving dinner has been grown on this farm?"

"Why, that's so, Wesson," says Grama.

Grampa beams, laughing silently, while everyone looks around and begins pointing and enumerating. Jackie looks around, too.

Dominating the table are the Thanksgiving chickens, sharing a huge platter, three of them, golden brown and crackling, with steam escaping from a tender breast where Grama's fork has pierced. Because of Grampa's words, Jackie sees the food and its source at the same time. It's more than a double exposure, however; it's a series of pictures in such quick succession that they seem to be seen all at once, with sounds and smells and feelings rolled in.

She sees the hens as chicks, adorable fluffy balls; as gawky, half-feathered younglings; as grown hens purling and prowling around the woodpile by the Big House kitchen door and racing when she comes with scraps; as laying hens sitting sharp-eyed and sharp-beaked in the box nests in the hen house, herself reaching cautiously under a puffed bosom to ease out an egg. She sees the chopping block and a headless chicken running crazily, like a balloon blown up and let go. She sees Grama plucking and singeing and pulling out all the insides, setting aside the heart and liver for giblet gravy, and with one swift stroke cutting open the gizzard to remove the gravel. She remembers the time she stood in amazement, her eyes scarcely above the marble tabletop, as Grama pulled shell-less, yellow yolks out of a chicken, a whole sequence of them, starting with almost usual size and then gradually smaller and smaller, till there was a final itty-bitty round yolk not as big as a teardrop. And at her request, Grama gathered up those never-to-be-laid eggs, down to the tiniest, and poached them for her breakfast.

And then, all the vegetables! The golden mountain of Hubbard squash, with a peak of snowy mashed potato beside it, both with boulders of butter melting down their sides; the tureen of creamed onions; the sliced carrots swimming in cream and butter; the cucumber pickles; the cabbage slaw; the bowl of stewed tomatoes. She sees, superimposed, the garden in all its seasons: the long row of feathery carrot tops; the tangled masses of squash and cucumber and pumpkin vines, with their gaudy flowers; the rough-leaved potato plants spattered with the yellow-striped potato bugs she loathes to pick off but is sometimes ordered to.

Strawberry jam and ruby-red currant jelly share a divided dish; she sees the strawberry beds with their glimpses of red and, at the edge of the garden, the hedge of bushes laden with sour red currants, each as translucent as the jelly but with faint little stripes from top to bottom, like a beach ball, and with a little pip of something on top, left over from the flower.

The hedge and garden stop at the orchard, and there are rows of gnarled trees, all good for climbing and making separate houses, all bearing different sorts of apples, with different tastes and different consistencies: Snows and Hubbardsons and Northern Spys and Wallingfields and big, fat Northwestern Greenings, for pies, and Daddy's favorite apple, Eastern Maiden's Blush. In the fall, after they are gathered, the potatoes and carrots and turnips and apples and squashes and pumpkins are stored in her most private, most special place on the entire farm, in the part of the basement beneath this table:

26 THE ONE-ARMED MILKMAN

It's a sunny morning in late spring. Jackie and Craig are playing Find-the-Milkman. It's a game they've played all their lives. It goes like this: a milkman is out on his route and Daddy has to get ahold of him for some reason, such as to give him additional milk for a customer or to tell him there's one he's missed. Daddy drives to the area where the milkman is delivering. Any children in the car take opposite windows. "Keep your eyes peeled," says Daddy, and he cruises the streets, going slowly through the intersections while everybody peers up and down, looking for the familiar cream-colored vehicle. Finally someone spots it, yells out, and the game is over. Sometimes the game takes quite a while, for a truck has so many streets it can be on, and houses it can dodge behind, that it can stay hidden for a surprising stretch. And all this without the milkman doing it deliberately—he doesn't realize that he's the object of hide-and-seek. He reacts as though Daddy's running into him on his rounds is a pleasant coincidence.

Today, however, Daddy is perplexed. "Vanished!" he keeps saying. "He's evaporated off the face of the earth!"

"He" is Charlie Heisz, the one-armed milkman. Around eight o'clock calls began coming in from customers on his route that the milkman had missed them. After four or five such calls Daddy'd slung a case of milk in the trunk, taken Craig and Jackie, and headed for town to play Find-the-Milkman.

Following last month's route book, Daddy traces Charlie's route. Charlie, he finds, has delivered the start of it. Then, at a corner, and between one page and the next of the route book, he's disappeared. Everyone before has had milk, those after are the ones telephoning.

Daddy is more and more mystified. At first he'd figured Charlie's truck had broken down, but why then hadn't he called for Erv or Ed, the farm mechanics, to come fix it? And more to the point, where is the broken-down truck? It should be on this very corner.

Daddy goes into a customer's house and calls the police. He returns to the car shaking his head. There have been no accident reports involving a milk truck, but they'll alert all their patrolmen to be on the lookout for a one-armed milkman. The hospital, too, says they haven't recently admitted anyone with only one arm but will call the farm if they do. "Keep your eyes peeled," Daddy repeats to Craig and Jackie, and they all go back to playing Find-the-Milkman around the blocks of Charlie's route.

After ten more minutes Daddy gives up. He speeds back to the dairy, collars Roscoe Ocker, the relief driver who's working in the milkhouse today, and together they load up the farm truck with milk for Charlie's customers. Craig and Jackie perch on the loading platform and drink chocolate milk.

"You kids might as well stay home this time," says Daddy, but the two have no intention of abandoning the search now. They're eager to return to the scene. They climb into the back of the truck with the milk, and bounce and rattle to town.

At the disappearance corner everyone becomes a team. Roscoe drives and calls out orders from the route book. Up behind, Daddy loads carriers and hands them down to Jackie or Craig, who lug the milk and cream up to people's doors as hastily as the weight of the load will permit. Daddy laughs and says, "Never has a route been delivered so fast!" At every corner Jackie still peels her eyes for Charlie's missing truck.

For forty-five minutes they deliver. Then Roscoe rounds another corner, and they are radiator-to-radiator with a Dougan milk truck. The one-armed milkman is just returning to it, his wire carrier swinging jauntily from his single hand.

"Charlie!" shouts Daddy with relief and exasperation.

"Oh, hello," says Charlie, as if he hasn't been the concern of customers, management, police, and hospitals for the past several hours and as if meeting Daddy and Roscoe, Jackie and Craig running his route is an ordinary occurrence.

"Whatever happened to you? Where've you been? We've searched everywhere!" Daddy expostulates. "Your customers have been calling since eight o'clock!"

Charlie looks surprised. He sets down his carrier, scratches his chin, gazes at the sky. Then he grins sheepishly. "Well, today, part way along, I suddenly realized how bored I was, delivering my route the same old way every day. So I just drove to the last house and started going backward. That's all."

Daddy shakes his head wearily. "*Mon Dieu,*" he exclaims. "Tell *me* the next time you get bored, and I'll give you variety!"

But Jackie understands perfectly how Charlie feels. So does Craig.

"Just think," he says as they ride among the milk cases out Colley Road, with Charlie following them in his truck. "Just think how he saved you and me from a boring morning, too."

"And not just us," Jackie replies, considering how very many people were spared a boring morning by their one-armed milkman.

27 COUNTING PHEASANTS

It's fall. Jackie is in fifth grade. Joan is in ninth, Patsy seventh, Craig third. They've just moved up the road from the dairy to the Snide farm, with its newly remodeled house. They now call it "Chez Nous," "Our Home," though the men refer to it as "Ron's place."

Chez Nous sits back from the road on a long lane. Now the school cab stops for them at the end of the lane instead of in front of the dairy. They can't see the cab from the house because of a hill in the way. They have to be at the end of the lane at exactly ten of eight or George is angry. He doesn't like to wait. Now they are no longer the last kids on the route. The Dummer kids are picked up after them. Now the taxi whizzes right past the dairy into town, for kids no longer live there. It seems strange. The Little House has become Daddy's office.

When it isn't a pell-mell run, Jackie loves the walk down the gravelly lane in the morning. It usually is a run, the four of them in straggled order, clutching their lunches, until Patsy gets to the top of the hill and shouts, "He's not there!" Then they can relax and walk. If Patsy shouts, "He's there!" then the pell-mell has to continue, and Jackie climbs into the taxi, gasping for breath with a stitch in her side, and George bawls them out for being late. But in the afternoon, when she can walk back up the lane at leisure, or in the mornings when they're early and know it, Jackie loves the walk.

There's a blue flower, almost a soft lavender, that grows along the lane and down by the road that didn't grow by the dairy, or if it did she never noticed it. It has a yellowish center. It's constructed somewhat like a daisy and grows in little clumps. She learns it's an aster. There are thickets of tangled trees along the east side of the lane and scattered trees along the west. There are other things to see. One sight turns out to be lucrative.

It begins this way, not in the lane at all, not in the school taxi, but in the car, many months before. Daddy is driving. He says something. Jackie, in the backseat, doesn't hear what he says, for she's reading a book. Craig is reading a book. Patsy is reading a book. Joan, in the front seat, is reading a book. Only Mother isn't reading a book and hears him say, "Look! Right on that fence post, there's a red-tailed hawk!" Daddy glances into the backseat and sees the tops of all their heads. They are oblivious to everything but their stories.

"Where are you?" demands Daddy of each of them. Craig, it turns out, is in Oz. Jackie is in a secret garden in Yorkshire. Patsy is trapped in an island cave where a grinning skeleton is guarding gold, in *Pirate's Loot;* and Joan is in Scotland with *Ivanhoe.*

"You are all in Rock County, in Turtle Township," states Daddy. "Life is going on in Turtle Township. Little animals are out scrounging for a bug or two. Red-tailed hawks are sitting on fence posts looking for the little animals who are out scrounging for a bug or two. Life is filled with interest; life is fraught with danger. You missed the hawk; a couple of minutes ago, you missed a woodchuck. Everywhere we go, all you see is print. There's more in the world than books. Now get your noses out of those pages and look around you! I'll give you a dime for every pheasant, a nickel for every partridge, and a penny for every quail! You can read *Ivanhoe* when it's dark."

Jackie's nose jerks rapidly out of her book. Three other noses also come up rapidly. When money speaks, they listen.

Jackie looks out the window the rest of the trip. She's not sure what a partridge or quail looks like. She's probably seen them but not known they were partridge or quail. But she has seen pheasants, once in a while, and there is no mistaking a pheasant. They are as big as chickens, only more streamlined. They are basically brown. The male has a brilliant ring around his neck. They have long tail feathers that are iridescent. They have a way of rising with a great whirr almost straight up out of a ditch or cornfield and then skimming low across the road, into another cornfield. They don't fly high or long.

Jackie will concentrate on the big money. She'll concentrate on pheasants. From now on, when she's in the car, she looks for pheasants. She watches the ditches. She watches the thickets. She begins to recognize the sort of place a pheasant is most likely to be and to watch for it. She gets so she can spot a pheasant half a field away, in spite of its protective coloring. Any motion in a field or pasture catches her eye. She gets so she can spot a pheasant a whole field away, and know for sure it's a pheasant. She can even sometimes spot one two fields away. Her eyes become very sharp for pheasants.

Every week she reports her pheasant count, and Daddy cheerfully pays up the extra twenty, thirty, or forty cents along with her allowance. Joan and Patsy and Craig also report their pheasant counts.

Now it's September. They are living at Chez Nous; they are walking down the lane to the school cab.

"Look!" cries Joan, but it's a soft, compelling, do-nothing-to-startle-it "look."

They stop still. Ahead of them, emerging out of the plum thicket, is a mother pheasant followed by a late brood. In a straggling line they cross the lane and disappear into the tall grass.

"Six, seven, eight!" Patsy finishes counting.

"Eighty cents!" whoops Craig. They all agree on the number. They'll each be considerably richer, come allowance time Saturday.

That afternoon they are walking back up the lane. "Look!" cries Patsy, in the same sort of tone.

The mother pheasant is crossing the lane again, with the seven youngsters behind her. She goes from the tall grass to the plum thicket.

The four argue. Can you collect twice on the same pheasant? How do they know there isn't another mother pheasant in the lane with seven babies? How do they know, when they see a lone pheasant in a field or gliding low across the road, that it isn't the same pheasant they saw yesterday? Daddy never *said* they could collect on one pheasant only once.

Naturally, none of them would be so unscrupulous as to spot a pheasant, blink, then count it again. But these pheasants they'd first seen at eight o'-clock in the morning. It's now four o'clock in the afternoon. That seems a reasonable enough interval.

They all agree it's fair. They count the pheasants.

The next morning they are on the lookout. They see no pheasant family. They get to the plum thicket and peer into it. The mother pheasant is there with her brood. They must live in the plum thicket! Jackie, Patsy, Joan, and Craig count the pheasants again. They are worried that they can see only five chicks. They hope the other two are behind the hen.

That afternoon, the pheasants are again walking across the lane, all eight of them. The four are greatly relieved.

Every day they count the pheasant family. A couple of times, there's not a feather in sight and they're disappointed. Jackie starts to carry a pocketful of corn to leave in the plum thicket, to encourage everybody to stay home.

On Saturday, Jackie pays an early morning visit to the lane. She counts the family in the thicket. On Saturday afternoon, the pheasants are nowhere around. She sits near their usual path and braids long strands of grass. She keeps an eye out. She hears a pheasant call sharply, far away. She realizes that she not only sees but she hears pheasants, that her ears pick out their distinctive "berk-berk" from any other sounds and silences. Sometimes she can even spot the caller. Now she spots Craig. He's coming along, pheasant watching. He joins her in the grass. They talk quietly until the mother pheasant finally shows up and crosses the lane. They count eight pheasants.

Saturday night, Daddy pays up allowances. He pays Joan.

"And six dollars and ninety cents in pheasant money," adds Joan. Patsy claims eight dollars and twenty-one cents; she saw a quail. Craig and Jackie's totals are more than nine dollars. Jackie has the most, nine dollars and ninety cents, for she saw several singleton pheasants in several different fields and two went over the road with a great whirr.

Daddy is incredulous. He demands explanations. The four give them, gleefully interrupting one another. Daddy shakes his head ruefully. He agrees with their reasoning; he pays up. He has even seen the mother and her babies himself but hadn't realized what they were costing him, or he would have relocated them over in the next township.

"However," says Daddy with finality, "our budget can't stand another week of this. I think I don't need to pay you anymore. You've all become seasoned pheasant spotters."

Jackie is regretful. They're all regretful, but they all knew in their heart of hearts that the glorious bonanza would probably kill the goose that laid the golden egg. It's been worth it. The look on Daddy's face was worth it, and they are all considerably wealthier. It's a grand finale to the pheasant spotting, like the last superrocket on the Fourth of July.

Now there are no more ten centses. But Jackie discovers something interesting. She can no longer *not* spot a pheasant. She sees a tag of movement a field away and thinks, *Pheasant.* She sees, *Pheasant.* She hears the familiar berk-berk and her brain automatically registers, *Pheasant.* She rarely reads in the car anymore; it always gave her a headache, anyway. Mainly, she read because she was bored. She's no longer bored in the car, or when she's outside, or when she's anywhere, for there is so much to see. She realizes that by learning to see pheasants she has learned to see everything else as well.

28 ROUTE BOOK

Every milkman has a monthly route book. Each customer has a page in it, in the order of the route. The milkmen are supposed to check off their routes in their route books as they go along, putting down how much milk and other dairy products each customer takes.

Howard Milner is a fast milkman, and prides himself on his memory. He doesn't like to be bothered with constant bookkeeping. He waits to fill in his route book till he's checking out in the office back at the farm. But Daddy is forever after him to fill in his route as he goes, like the other milkmen, for, good memory or not, he sometimes makes mistakes.

"I don't want to see you filling in your route book out here," says Daddy.

"All right, all right," agrees Howard. He changes his ways. But he still doesn't fill in his book after every delivery. At the end of his route, he pulls his truck up under a tree and, holding his route book in his lap, flips the pages and fills in every one.

One morning the phone rings in the office. Ruby answers it. A woman's voice states that she's not a customer, but she simply has to talk to Mr. Dougan. Daddy takes the receiver. The woman gives her address, and Daddy notes that it's near the end of Howard's route. She is clearly agitated.

"Mr. Dougan," she blurts, "I apologize for calling you this way, but I feel I must tell you! It's about your milkman. I'm sure you'd want to know and put a stop to it. Heaven knows *I'd* want to know, if I were running a business, and if I were having that going on, and me not knowing—and right out in public—on the street—he's over there right now, doing it again!"

"Doing what?" Daddy asks. "What is our milkman doing?" He knows that Howard, from time to time, does things that might baffle a customer,

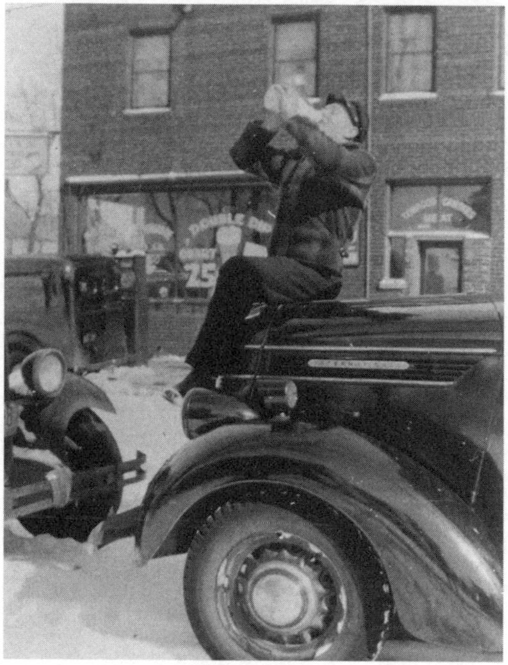

Howard Milner, sitting on the hood of his milk truck and downing a quart of milk.

such as putting snakes on running boards, and he waits to see what tricks Howard is up to now.

"We-ell"—Mrs. Milford takes a deep breath—"your milkman—I really hate to say it—your milkman stops across from my house every day, there by the park entrance, at just about now—and I can see him through his truck window—looking down—and—and—"

"Yes?" encourages Daddy.

"Oh, Mr. Dougan," wails the woman, "I *can't* tell you what he's doing—but it's filthy, and he's been doing it every day at about eleven fifteen or eleven thirty—"

Daddy begins to get the picture but is doubtful. "You say you can see him?"

"Well, I can't exactly see him—I can't see his hands—but he's moving and moving them and, as I said, looking down, and it's perfectly *obvious* what he's doing!"

"I'll certainly see to it that he stops," Daddy vows. "We can't have *that* going on. I do appreciate your calling to tell me, Mrs. Milford."

"I just knew you'd want to know," the woman says, in a relieved-I've-done-my-duty tone, and hangs up.

When Daddy is able to stop laughing, he tells Ruby, and they both double over with mirth. They wait for Howard.

When he returns from his route and climbs up the stairs to the back room of the office over the milkhouse, Daddy accosts him. "Howard, haven't I been telling you to fill in your route book after every couple of deliveries or you'd get yourself in hot water? Well, you're in hot water!"

"I haven't made a mistake in two weeks!" Howard protests.

"Oh, yes, you have. You've made a big mistake to park across from the house of a Mrs. Milford while you leaf through your route book. She's convinced you're a naughty boy." He tells him about the phone call, and all the milkmen in the office whoop. This time, Ruby laughs till the tears roll down her cheeks.

The episode doesn't cure Howard. He still doesn't fill in his route book after every delivery. He does, however, change his parking spot to an alley where no one can see him.

29 THE BEST DRINK IN TOWN

It's a hot summer day in 1940. Craig is ten. He and his friends, John Eldred, Ed Grutzner, and Delmar DeLong, are riding home from Mukwonago. They have just spent a glorious week at the Phantom Lake YMCA camp, and now Grampa has fetched them, in the blue Dodge.

As they drive through the Wisconsin countryside, the day gets hotter and hotter. The boys are thirsty. They talk among themselves of pop and root beer. Craig indicates to Grampa that they are all parched—he makes a strangling motion with his hands around his neck, takes a long swig from an imaginary bottle, heaves an exaggerated sigh of satisfaction, and then looks expectantly at Grampa. Grampa glances over at the pantomime while driving. At the end of it he nods.

"You boys are thirsty."

Craig beams and nods vigorously. The three in the backseat nod and beam, too.

"When we get to Delavan," Grampa says, "I'll see that you boys get the best drink in town."

The boys are rapturous. They discuss what the drink can be. Ordinary bottled pop, obtainable anywhere, doesn't seem to fit the definition. Grampa must know of an ice cream parlor in Delavan that sells superior ice cream sodas, malteds, and black cows. They jiggle on the seats and wait impatiently for the miles to roll by. They talk and talk about what can be the best drink in town. No dehydrated castaways bobbing on a raft in the tropical seas could have covered the topic more thoroughly.

At last they arrive in Delavan. Grampa slows down for the residential section, and Craig again throttles himself to remind Grampa of his promise.

Grampa hasn't forgotten. "The best drink in town," he repeats.

At the business district they hang out the windows, trying to spot where Grampa is planning to treat them.

"There's a drug store!" cries John.

"Ice cream shop! Ice cream shop!" yips Delmar.

Grampa slows and turns off the main street. He drives to the end of the block and pulls the car to the curb. The boys jump out, looking for the store.

Grampa clambers out, too. "Here it is, laddies!" he announces. "The best drink in town!"

The boys whirl. They hadn't even noticed it, but Grampa is bending and drinking from an ornamental porcelain bubbler at the edge of the sidewalk. It has a basin circling the bottom, filled with overflow, so that even dogs may drink.

"Help yourselves," Grampa says, straightening and wiping his mouth. "Drink all you want!" His face is alight with pleasure; he hasn't the slightest idea that he has disappointed anybody. "This water is from an artesian well. The rains that formed it fell north of Baraboo thousands of years ago, where the St. Peter's sandstone outcrops. It's been percolating down here ever since."

The boys look at each other. They've all had a long enough acquaintance with Grampa Dougan to know better than to argue or try to explain their expectations.

"Baraboozle," mutters Ed.

Crestfallen, they take turns drinking from the best drink in town.

30 THE ROMAN CATHOLIC COW

Father O'Reilly is the Roman Catholic priest at St. Thomas Church near downtown Beloit. One year he calls up Daddy.

"Ron," he says, "every year we have a big bazaar down here, a big carnival, in our church basement, to raise money. It lasts for three days, from ten in the morning till ten at night, and a couple thousand people come. This year we're selling space to local merchants, to set up their displays and advertise their wares. Can I reserve you a space?"

"Father," responds Daddy, "the only way I can use your space is if I bring you a cow."

Father O'Reilly doesn't even hesitate. "Ah, Ron, that's a splendid idea," he says, "but it'll cost you two spaces. Tell you what, I'll give you a discount on the second one."

Daddy argues. He tells Father O'Reilly the dimensions of a stall. He says he'll bring down his smallest cow, who he is sure can be fitted into one space unless she's allotted only a tabletop. He points out that he's running a real risk, exposing a naive Methodist cow who has never left home to the Whore of Babylon. Father O'Reilly laughs and signs Daddy up for one space.

Fair time arrives, and Daddy and a hired man transport a gentle Guernsey cow down to the church. She's sleek and handsome and named T-12, but Daddy paints a sign to go on her pen, calling her Bathsheba. They fix her up with sawdust bedding, and a salt block, and hay and water and a sack of grain from which she will get her daily scoops. Daddy hires a boy to stay near her and shovel up her cow pies when she makes them, and carry away the wet sawdust when she pees. The boy also sells half-pints of Dougan's chocolate milk to the fairgoers.

All during the carnival Bathsheba looks out at the crowds with soft brown eyes. Sometimes she eats hay; sometimes she lies down and chews her cud. Every morning early, Russ Ullius, the herdsman, drives downtown to milk her, and Father O'Reilly unlocks the church basement and lets him in. Bathsheba moos a quiet welcome from among the still displays. Afternoons, Daddy does the milkings. He wears a white cap and apron, and black boots, and makes the milk zing into the pail as the crowds press round the pen. He squirts milk into children's mouths with fine accuracy. After Bathsheba is finished, Jackie and Craig pour her warm milk into paper cups. Whoever wishes to can have a drink.

When they aren't busy at the pen, Jackie and Craig wander among the many booths and exhibits and eat doughnuts and cotton candy. They feel strange to be in a Roman Catholic church, even if it is the basement. It doesn't seem very different from the Methodist church basement, although Craig points out a calendar where Jesus' heart is outside his body, with rays coming out from it.

The final day, Daddy rounds up a lot of children under twelve to enter a milking contest. They sit awkwardly on the three-legged stool and hold the tits as if they are hot. Daddy instructs them. But one girl needs no instruction. She settles onto the stool, presses her head into Bathsheba's belly, and milks like a pro. Daddy recognizes her; she's the daughter of the one Roman Catholic family in Turtle Township. He gives her a prize of a book of milk tickets that she can exchange for chocolate milk.

Throughout the carnival, Bathsheba is the center of attraction. She's a model guest, placid and well behaved. The *Beloit Daily News* comes and takes her picture during the milking contest, and it makes the front page. The headline reads HOLY COW! Daddy and Father O'Reilly and everybody are well pleased. Bathsheba is invited back for next year.

In only one way does she cause any problem. Though the carnival is in progress, upstairs in the church the services continue on schedule. Father

O'Reilly celebrates daily masses. These are quiet affairs, and Bathsheba is not aware of them, nor are the worshippers aware of a cow's presence below. But on the last day of the carnival, there is a wedding. The organ booms out with the wedding march. Bathsheba stretches her neck, raises her voice, and bellows along. When the organ plays "Ave Maria," Bathsheba's voice is louder than the soloist's. And when the organ starts the recessional, Bathsheba fairly trumpets down the house. It's not a wedding that anyone will soon forget.

Back home, Bathsheba settles into the round barn routine as if she'd never been away. Fame and bright lights haven't turned her head. She's the same sweet and unspoiled bovine that she was before she became a celebrity.

When Daddy shows any visitors through the round barn he points her out. "All of our cows are Methodist," he says, "except for that one apostate. That is Bathsheba, our Roman Catholic cow."

Bathsheba (or one of her sisters) singing in the cow yard.

31 BLOAT

There have probably been a number of incidents of bloat on the farm. Jackie knows the stories of two. The first happened well before she was born, the second well after she'd moved away, so she's never seen a bloated animal dead or dying. But it takes little imagination to know it's a painful death.

She hears the first bloat story when she's thirteen. Dr. Knilans, the vet, leaving the farm office as she is coming in, mentions to Daddy in parting that a farmer in Lima township has just lost several cows to bloat.

"What's bloat?" Jackie asks, and Daddy tells her. His explanation goes like this.

It happens in cattle, and other cud-chewing animals, when methane gas builds up in their first stomach, the rumen. The gas is produced by fermentation, through the bacterial action that breaks down the cellulose of the plants they eat. Ordinarily, gas escapes when the animal burps up its cud. But if the buildup is faster than the animal can belch, it bloats.

"Or if a cow, or goat, or yak—any ruminant—were to fall upside down in a ditch and not be able to get out again, it would bloat and die, for the food in the rumen would be blocking the natural outlet."

Jackie does not find this at all a pretty picture.

Bloat in cattle, Daddy goes on, is usually caused by a too-rich mix of protein, which speeds up fermentation, and the regurgitation of the cud can't handle it fast enough. Rapidly growing spring grass has a strong growth protein, which causes this faster fermentation. The cows bloat, and if they're not helped, they die from the pressure of the rumen on their lungs and heart.

"Some farmers keep their cattle off wet grass in the spring," Daddy says, "but it isn't the wetness that's the problem; it's that the wetness causes the grass to grow fast, producing lots of protein. What they should do is feed their cows on fresh growth sparingly, then move them to an older pasture, or augment the fresh growth with hay. At any time, you should move cows to a fresh pasture with care, for their stomachs are used to the rate of fermentation of the pasture they're on. A new, richer pasture can give them too much protein and cause trouble."

"So what can cure them?" Jackie asks. "They just swell up and die and that's that?"

"You puncture them."

"What?" cries Jackie. "How?"

"Well, if there's time, there's a less drastic way. But a bloated cow has to have the pressure relieved. She can be tubed—that's when you work a length of hose down her throat into the rumen. The gas comes up the hose. But if a cow is too far gone for tubing, or a tube isn't handy, you puncture the rumen with anything sharp, and the gas rushes out like air from a pricked balloon. You can hear it whoosh."

Daddy rummages far into his desk drawer and brings out a small instrument. "This is standard equipment in most barns. A vet always carries a supply. It's a trocar."

He hands it to Jackie. She's fiddled with something like it before; there's one on a shelf beside the silo in the lower barn, where the daily records are kept, but she never bothered to ask what it was for.

"It has two parts," Daddy says. "That sharp triangular middle part is the *stylet*—it does the puncturing; and the tube that fits around it, the cannula, is left behind in the wound for a while to keep it open."

"How do you know where to puncture the cow? What if you hit her heart or something?"

Daddy laughs ruefully. "There's no question. The rumen is bulging so grotesquely, you just strike at the height of her distention. The left side, below her final rib."

"And then she's OK?"

"Once the pressure's relieved she usually recovers in short order. The wound never seems to present a problem—it may bleed or ooze a little, but it closes up and the cow gets on with her business."

Jackie pushes the stylet in and out a few times and then returns the instrument. "Why do you keep one here in the office?"

"I don't know. It's been in the drawer a long time. Maybe to remind myself of when I lost a bunch of Grampa's cows, myself, when I was seventeen."

Jackie waits expectantly, and Daddy tells her. He was working on the farm the year between high school and college. That spring, his parents had to be away for three days, and they left him in charge. One night it frosted, and the next morning he turned the cows into a fresh pasture of Sudan grass. When he went to fetch them for milking, he could hear them a long way off, groaning, trying to belch, but they couldn't. He ran and found most of them down, bloated.

"I was frantic. There wasn't time for tubing even if I'd had a tube. But I had a jackknife. I rushed from cow to cow, puncturing rumens. I saved a lot, but six didn't make it."

"How awful," breathes Jackie, hearing and picturing the scene of carnage.

"I was heartsick, of course, and dreaded Grampa's return. He felt terrible, too, for the suffering of the animals, and the economic hardship of their loss, but he didn't blame me. He blamed himself. I didn't know, and he hadn't warned me. He said only an old, experienced cowman would have known. And it turned out, we learned later, that the cows that died really died of prussic acid poisoning; the poison made them bloat."

"Poison!" Jackie cries. "Where did they get prussic acid?"

"It was in the grass. It poisoned them, they went down, and bloated. I found out that young Sudan grass contains a high level of prussic acid, especially after a frost."

He goes to an office file cabinet and finds a booklet titled *Forage Crop Varieties and Seeding Mixtures,* published by the university's College of Agriculture. Jackie looks over his shoulder as he leafs through it. It deals with legumes, then grasses. Under "Sudans and Sorghum-Sudan Hybrids" Daddy points to a paragraph titled "For Pasture."

He reads aloud, "'Sudan grass and hybrid Sudan grass are suggested because of low prussic acid, few grazing management problems, and high yields. They should not be grazed before they are at least 18 to 20 inches tall since prussic acid content is always highest in the shorter growth and younger plant parts.'"

Daddy points farther. Jackie reads for herself. "Piper" Sudan grass gets top billing under "Most Promising Varieties" for it is "low in glucoside which is converted to prussic acid and therefore much less poisonous to livestock." And under "Less Promising Varieties" is "Sweet Sudan," a Texas strain high in poisonous properties, only fair in yield when grown in Wisconsin, and moderately susceptible to diseases. It has, however, "sweet stalks and is palatable to cattle." "Common" Sudan grass is described as an old-type commercial Sudan grass, "moderately high in poisonous properties," and under "For Green Chopping," "The danger of prussic acid poisoning is generally greater with hybrids than with Sudan grass."

Jackie is highly dubious. Why should Sudan grass be grown at all, however palatable? If it kills what feeds on it, can it be profitable? She pokes through the booklet a bit more. She's impressed with all she doesn't know about pastures and forage crops, and the kind of land they thrive on. To her, a pasture has always been just a pasture—a place where grass comes up and cows eat it, whatever grass they don't ruin by making a cow pie on it.

She tosses the booklet down. "But why didn't they all die? Didn't they all eat the Sudan grass?"

Daddy shrugs. "Some maybe ate more than others. Maybe some were hardier cows. Not everybody in Europe died of the bubonic plague."

Jackie hears about the second bloat episode when she's more than twice thirteen. Dick Knilans, who's a little older than Jackie and has been in partnership with his father for a number of years, is treating a cow in the Chez Nous barn. Jackie, home for a visit, sees his van and goes down. He's clad in coveralls and boots and has his equipment in a large bucket, in contrast to his father's formal barn wear and Boston bag.

"What's up, Doc?" she asks.

Dick grins. "Mind you never call old Doc that," he says. "When my wife was first helping out at the clinic she answered the phone one day and repeated the message just as the farmer said it—'Tell Doc my cow has cast her withers and he should come right away.' My dad said to Marie, 'It is not "cast her withers," it's "the cow has an inverted uterus," and I am not a "doc," I am a Doctor of Veterinary Medicine. A "doc" is a horse trader.'"

"What did Marie say?" Jackie asks, grinning too. She's glad in all her years of knowing the senior vet she's never presumed to call him "Doc."

"He wasn't bawling her out," Dick assures. "He was teaching her, and she knew it. She smiled at him and said, oh so sweetly, 'Doctor Knilans, a farmer wants you to come see about a cow who has an inverted uterus.'"

They both laugh. Dick explains that once in a while in a difficult birth, a cow will expel the calf with such force that the uterus comes out, too, and inside out. Then it has to be turned right side out and replaced. Jackie, who has birthed two daughters, grimaces.

Dick is treating a sore hoof. He goes on to entertain Jackie by giving her an account of the farm's recent mysterious bout with bloat. The cows on her dad's place—as she knows—are the young ones, not milking yet, and the dry ones. And one day several of them are found dead or dying in the barnyard, bloated. The rest, wandering around, seem OK. Dick rushes down. By the time he gets there a few more are affected.

"Those that were dead, were dead," Dick says. "I didn't have any idea what was causing it, because they'd not been on pasture, and they'd all had the same

Dick Knilans, the vet, notching a pig's ear for identification.

feed, but I treated those that were down with dextrose, a detoxifier, and whatever it was, that saved 'em. Then we began an investigation, trying to find out what had happened. We asked questions of the help, and it took us a couple of hours to figure it out. You know the feed mill up in the round barn?"

Jackie knows it well. All her life, oats and barley and corn have been ground in the feed mill and the ground grain transferred to the bin with the double sloping bottom alongside the silo, ready to go down the chute to the feed cart below.

The Chez Nous barnyard, with the manger where the fatal bag of feed was poured. Only the cows who ate from the poisoned section became bloated.

"Well," says Dick, "they've been using urea—a nitrate product—to add protein to the system. It helps with their rumination. You can get it in a lick, too, big cakes on a little wheel, and the cows lick it and get a small amount that way. But up in the round barn, they have it in bags, powdered. At the feed mill, they'll pour in a couple of bags of urea and so much corn and oats, and anything else they're using as a supplement, and grind it all up and mix it thoroughly with a rake and take it to the grain bin, where it'll be ready to go down to the barn below. But first, they fill three bags for the cows up here at Ron's and set them by the barn door. Then, the next morning, somebody loads those three bags on a truck and brings them up here and pours them into that long wooden manger that's over there alongside the barn."

Jackie nods, following the story.

"Well, that morning they'd finished the milking, and one of the Vanderkooi brothers went up to grind the grain. He threw the urea in the mill, and some corn, and then something happened and he was called away. Meanwhile, Bob George—Ron's farm manager—decided that because more heifers had been brought up here they'd better give 'em more feed, so he told the one in charge of bringing the three bags to bring one more. The guy loaded the bags that were waiting, and then went to the mill and drew off a fourth, and this one had a terrific concentration of urea because whichever Vanderkooi it was hadn't finished mixing. So, the cows that got that bag were the ones poisoned. When you do have concentrations of feed that are toxic, you have to be awfully careful—the Vanderkoois hadn't realized that somebody might come back and take feed. Often you never *do* discover what causes something."

Jackie tells Dick Daddy's story of the Sudan grass and prussic acid, which he hadn't heard before. Then he tells her that all bloat isn't simply gas that can be expelled by tubing or using a trocar.

"Sometimes it's a foam—we call it 'frothy bloat'—and that's a more complicated problem. We tube what we can, and give medication to slow the fermentation, and get a surface tension agent into the rumen so that the bubbles can't form, like you throw oil on water. Our standard treatment is detergent."

"Detergent!" Jackie exclaims.

"Yes, well, soap works, too; you could sprinkle soap over your cow's feed every day if you wanted to, and she'd never bloat, and some farmers used to do that as a preventative, but then, after the war, when detergent had been developed, they started using that every day instead, and that was effective, too. Until they noticed that the fat content of their milk began to drop. The detergent circles the fat, or whatever it does, and the fat doesn't go into the milk. They found out they were getting about a 1 percent fat content. The deposition of fat in the udder changed. And on beef cattle, they wouldn't get a good deposition of fat all over. It cut down the marbling. So they quit. But we still use it if a cow has frothy bloat."

Dick has long since finished treating the cow's hoof. He gives the animal a slap on the flank and picks up the bucket he carries his medicines in.

"Horses can bloat, too," he says. "A cow has all her gas up front; she belches all the time. But in a horse, the fermentation takes place in the cecum, the blind gut. Horses fart a lot. When a horse gets bloated, he has to be relieved mechanically, by a vet. He's like a rodent. . . . Did you know horses and rats can't vomit? If they do, their stomachs rupture. That's why you can kill rats with products that cause them to vomit, like Warfarin. . . . Do you know I have a horse that can talk?"

"Sure," says Jackie. "You ask him if he wants some oats and he says, 'A feeeeeeew.'"

"I guess we grew up on the same raunchy jokes," says Dick.

Jackie walks with him to his van. "Where next, Doc?"

Dick grins. "Gotta go over on the Shopiere Road. There's a cow there that's cast her withers."

32 SCRAP DRIVE

World War II is on. Jackie is in eighth grade at Roosevelt Junior High School. The school is having a scrap metal drive, to assist the war effort. Every homeroom has a goal of so many pounds, and the homeroom that has the most will be honored. Also, the individual student who brings in the most weight will receive a prize, a twenty-five dollar war bond.

Competition runs strong. All the students are combing their neighborhoods. Jackie combs the dairy, and Chez Nous, and the Hill Farm. Grampa's policy, and Daddy's, too, of not letting junk accumulate, of keeping things tidy, works against her, until she discovers that the farm dump has a fair amount of metal in it. And she does find an occasional roll of rusted fencing, in some distant field, and manages to wrestle it out of the weeds that have grown into and around it. She argues over broken shovels that have not yet been given new shafts, bent milk cases, pails with holes, and all the metal odds and ends in the toolhouse that are there because they might be just what is needed for a future repair job. To aid the war effort, Grampa is willing to give some of these up.

Mother and Daddy go to a monthly bridge club that rotates at the homes of the members. After an elegant potluck, they all play cards. One session comes at the height of the scrap drive. Over dinner, Mrs. Wootton talks to Mother about the competition. "Joanne is just going over the neighborhood inch by inch," she says, "and you wouldn't believe how much she's found and brought home. We keep having all these junior mountains pile up in the driveway, and then she takes it all in and has it weighed. She's far ahead in her homeroom. I told her she was sure to win the war bond, but she says no, that on the last day Jackie Dougan will show up driving a tractor."

Mother laughs sympathetically, but doesn't say, "Oh, no." For all she knows, Jackie just might find a tractor.

Jackie works hard. Craig helps her. They press the neighbors. No contribution is too small: a coffee can of rusty nails, the metal hinges off an old door. And then they make their big find—a side-delivery hay rake along the back fence of a neighbor's field. It's long been unused; they get permission to take it for the scrap drive. It isn't a very big find, as farm machinery goes, for a side delivery is a relatively light conveyance, dealing with a relatively light product—it turns drying hay in the field and rolls it into a windrow for the hay loader to pick up. Still, it has wheels and a tractor seat and a metal frame.

The side delivery can't travel on its own, so on the last day of the drive, a farmhand carries it to the school on the back of a wagon, along with the final scrap that Jackie and Craig have managed to amass.

Joanne Wootton, dragging an ornate wrought-iron gate, sees it come, and her heart sinks.

But Jackie Dougan does not win the war bond. A triumphant Fritzi Veihman, who used to live on the Hill Farm and now lives between the dairy and town, next to where the Perrigo clay excavation was abandoned, clanks up to school at the very last minute, riding on an old steam scoop shovel.

33 HORSES

In all the books of that sort that Jackie has ever read, there's always a special bond between a girl and her horse. Between a boy and his, too, of course, but most of the horse books seem to be about girls.

Jackie, too, has a special bond with her horse. On the horse's side, it's hatred. On her side, it's a determination to force the animal to her will. She gets Paint when she's fourteen, when she goes with Daddy to a farm auction. One of the sale items is a small brown and white horse; the white is in large splashes. Jackie hangs on the fence, admiring him.

"You want a horse?" Daddy asks.

"Sure," says Jackie, surprised.

Daddy enters the bidding and gets him and his tack for a hundred dollars. They saddle up the horse—Paint, Jackie immediately names him—and well pleased, she leaves the barnyard and starts on the fifteen-mile ride home. The horse walks along a bit reluctantly. Jackie doesn't blame him. He's leaving home, and they have to get used to each other. She talks out loud to him in a friendly fashion.

The first hint of trouble comes a half mile or so along the country road, where on either side low concrete walls flank a culvert. Paint slows down and stops. He turns and takes sideways steps. Jackie reins him forward and urges him on, but it's apparent that he doesn't want to walk between the little walls. He seems frightened. She digs him with her heels and he circles. Finally, he leaps between the walls at a gallop and won't slow down for another half mile.

"Well, what was that all about?" Jackie pants. It soon becomes evident. They approach another culvert, and the episode is repeated. Then there is a tatter of white cloth caught in a bob-wire fence, fluttering. The horse shies.

He's finally persuaded to mince past, on the far side of the road, and once clear again gallops till the danger is far past. The trip progresses by fits and starts, much stopping, backing and filling, strange footwork. The horse is afraid of anything remotely unusual. He rolls angry eyes over his shoulder at Jackie, with the whites showing. Finally, he slows down and stops, for no apparent reason, and nothing she can do will get him moving again. She gets off and tries to lead him. He won't budge. They have come perhaps one-third of the way. It is here Daddy overtakes her. She's fighting back tears.

Daddy speeds on ahead to the farm, picks up a hired man, and returns. Jackie is not much farther along. The hired man takes the wheel, and she climbs into the cab beside him. Daddy swings up onto the horse; as the truck drives away, Jackie watches out the cab's rear window.

"You have to show him who's boss," Daddy says when he arrives home some time later. Jackie has meanwhile fixed up a stall in the Chez Nous barn, put in hay, and located a brush and currycomb in the feed room. She rubs down her horse and curries him. Paint rolls his eyes at her.

Over the next months she tries to win the horse's goodwill through apples, carrots, ears of corn. Paint accepts her gifts but not her. She does all the feeding and grooming and tending. Paint flattens his ears and nips whenever he gets a chance. She finally accepts that they will never be friends. She doesn't like him, either. But she insists on riding him every day.

He loathes every minute of it. Going any direction away from the barn, he drags his hoofs; as soon as he's allowed to turn back, he burns up the turf. Jackie has to duck her head as they careen through the barn door and come to a halt that nearly pitches her over his head.

Every ride is a battle of wills. Jackie matches stubbornness with stubbornness and wins, though not always gracefully. Out on the road, the culverts continue to cause first a refusal, then a mad gallop. Paint also doesn't like cars to pass him. Most afternoons there's a race with the mailman—the horse hogs the center of the road and gallops; Jackie bobs on top in her red cap and

Santa Claus bringing the pony to Joan, Patsy, and Jackie, in the yard of the Little House. Grama's rat terrier Bounce looks on. The Big House is across the way.

tries vainly to get him to slow down and pull over. The contest never ends until the mailman, with a cheerful wave, is able to turn off on a side road.

In the wintertime, Jackie rides Paint over the fields to the Catalpa Forest. She tethers him to a tree, laces up her skates and skates on the black transparent ice of the crick. Sometimes June Dummer rides over the fields from Blodgetts' on a workhorse; sometimes Judy Livingston rides over from the Freeman farm on her horse, and they all skate. The forest is about equidistant from the three farms. But Paint hates the cold weather, and he hates the other horses.

Most of all he hates being ridden at night. He travels grudgingly over the fields until the glad moment comes when he can turn and dash back to the barn. Jackie has strong twinges of longing for her moonlit rides with Jeff.

Jeff was the horse before Paint. Even before Jeff, there was the pony. But she hardly counts. She was shaggy and brown, and Santa Claus brought her in person, Jackie's second Christmas. A photograph shows Joan, Patsy, and Jackie on the pony's back, though Jackie has no memory of this occasion. Standing in the snow and holding the bridle is a rather thin and glum-looking Santa. Joan names the pony Star because she has a white star in the middle of her forehead, but the hired men call her Mona.

During the Little House years, none of the children see much of Star. She's used to fetch the cows, and is always out in some back pasture. Because she's inaccessible, they forget about her. And no one on the busy farm thinks to catch her and bridle her up for them. Perhaps it crosses Mother's mind, but she's a city girl, not used to fetching ponies in pastures, and she is overworked with taking care of four little children.

The pony does get trotted out now and again for a birthday party, then forgotten once more. When Jackie is old enough to ask about her, nobody seems to know where she is. It's an idle question on Jackie's part, anyway, more to confirm that in spite of the Santa Claus photos, the pony isn't a dream. Much later, she learns that because his grandchildren weren't interested, Grampa took Mona over to the Hill Farm for Fritzi Veihman to take care of and ride. Star is a loss of Jackie's childhood; Mona, a gain of Fritzi's.

But Jeff is another matter. He is a handsome chestnut and arrives when Jackie is nine. His owner has ridden him in Beloit parades and in various lodge functions for years but has to part with him for reasons Jackie never learns. The old horse needs a place to live, and Grampa offers him haven. Jackie and her sisters and Craig are by now very ready to have a horse. They all suggest names, and Joan writes them out in a long list. They pore over these and settle on "Lord Jeffrey," shortened to "Lord Jeff" and, eventually, "Jeff."

On Jeff's first day at the farm, Daddy demonstrates how to mount. The horse stands bareback in the drive before the Big House. "Always mount from the left," Daddy says. He grasps the reins and a fistful of mane in his left hand, clucks to get the horse moving, runs a few steps alongside while pressing on the horse's back with his other hand, and then pulls hard on the mane and makes a tremendous leap, aided by the momentum of the horse. Instead of landing on the horse, he sails right over and onto the ground. He's a bit sheepish when he picks himself up. The next attempt, he calculates better and lands on Jeff's back.

Jackie tries, but she's not tall enough to mount this way. While the horse stands still, she uses Daddy's hand for a step that heaves her up. Once she's on and has the reins, Daddy does something thoughtless. He gives Jeff a slap on his flank to start him going. The horse leaps forward at a dead gallop and streaks across the lawn of the Big House. Jackie gasps and hangs on. An instant later a clothesline catches her across the throat; she's swept over the rear of the horse and flung to the grass. It's the shortest horseback ride she ever will have, and luckily, it is bareback. The red line across her neck takes two weeks to fade.

She learns to fetch Jeff from the pasture. The first time is scary—the walk down the lane carrying the halter and looped lead in one hand, an ear of corn in the other. The apprehensive approach, speaking in a gentle conversational voice, holding the corn at arm's length. The horse notices and ambles over; while he fumbles at the cob, trying for a bite, she slips on the halter and snaps the lead. It's easy! She glows as he follows her up the lane to the horse barn.

She learns to put the bit in Jeff's mouth and work the bridle over his forehead and ears. She learns to smooth the quilted saddle blanket onto his back and sling the saddle up, positioning it close behind his shoulder bones. The saddle is neither a western nor an English but an army saddle—it has a lengthwise split down the middle and a raised rim, front and back, but no pommel. There's a trick to tightening the girth. Daddy tells her a horse will hold its breath to keep the saddle loose, and it's true. You tighten the girth as far as you can; then, holding it at that point, wait several moments,

Jackie riding a neighbor's horse.

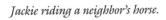

whistling nonchalantly, till the horse thinks he's outsmarted you and relaxes. Then you give a final pull and fasten the worn leather strap around the ring in a special hitch, so that it lies flat and can't backslide. Jackie also learns to adjust the stirrups if anybody has changed them and to mount using a stump from the woodpile or the low concrete wall at the bottom of the ramp to the round barn.

Jeff has a stall in the horse barn and is fed and cared for with the workhorses. After a ride, Jackie unsaddles him and hangs the saddle and blanket on a peg; then she rubs him down and curries him. She allows him a long drink in the horse trough after he's cooled off. She likes to watch him push out his lips and suck water up. She likes to rub his velvety nose, and stroke his chin, which is velvet with bristles. She likes to give him an apple; he wrinkles and wrinkles his upper lip as he opens his yellow teeth to take it.

She learns, more or less, to ride. Occasionally, she ventures onto Colley Road but mostly takes leisurely walks down the lane, across the crick, and around the pastures and cornfields beyond. After her clothesline experience, she's alert to keep the horse firmly reined. Jeff wants to gallop, but she's afraid to let him go beyond a trot. And she doesn't let him do that often, for his trot jars her teeth out of their sockets and kills her rump, even when she manages a kind of post. It's like riding a bicycle over a rutty field. One day, however, she lets down her guard. Jeff, trotting, senses this. He breaks into a gallop, and after a second of panic, Jackie realizes that she's riding in an armchair on a cloud. She finds she's posting rhythmically without any effort, standing in the stirrups, then sitting easily in the saddle. She hardly has to use the reins. The wind streams through her hair, the ground disappears beneath her, and she shouts with delight. She's on Pegasus! After that she makes Jeff spring from a walk to a gallop with only a moment's transition of trotting. She rues the months she was afraid.

Joan and Patsy and Craig ride some but not as much as she does. When the family moves up the road to Chez Nous, Jeff stays behind in the horse barn; the men use him to go after the cows mornings and afternoons, and he's ridden in detasseling. But Jackie sometimes gets off the school cab at the dairy and rides, or she comes back later, having changed into her jeans.

One afternoon, she and Jeff are riding on Colley Road, near where the railroad tracks cross beyond Marstons'. Behind them, a monstrous noise blasts out. The horse is so startled he leaps almost straight up, lands at a gallop, and streaks for home. Jackie's response matches his. It's the first time either has ever heard a diesel whistle. It's not many years before the familiar steam whistle is a thing of the past. She doesn't realize how much she misses that friendly sound until it is gone.

There is another train episode. Occasionally, she stays overnight at the Big House, and before bed, she saddles Jeff and they go for a ride in the moonlight. She loves the feel of the lane and pasture in the dark; she loves splashing through the iridescent crick. She loves the feel of the quiet horse moving under her. Jeff seems to enjoy these night rambles, too.

On one of these rides, she is near the railroad tracks when she hears a humming that rapidly increases; a train appears in the distance and almost as suddenly is upon them, a dark cylinder punctuated its entire length with tiny

The back pasture with a train going past.

yellow windows and people's silhouettes in each window. It whooshes past and is gone, the thunder and rumble and hum receding. Then all is quiet and starlit and alone again. It is a luminous moment that is never repeated, never forgotten.

Jeff is a comfortable horse who takes life in stride. Jackie grieves when he dies. She's horseless then until she goes to the farm auction, gets Paint, and begins the battles of wills.

Their relationship remains a stalemate for more than three years. Then Paint, out in the pasture, puts his leg through a bob-wire fence and badly rips the flesh. He's moved down to the horse barn at the dairy, where he can be tended more easily.

The leg takes months to heal. Jackie stops by now and then to contemplate the angry wounds, the proud flesh. It's an ugly sight.

Uncle Trever makes a visit to the farm, and they look at the injured horse together. Paint looks back, angry. Trever tells Jackie about his own experience. The rich relatives who had a summer place on the banks of Lake

Geneva wanted to get rid of a black Shetland pony. They gave it to him, and he was thrilled to death. He was supposed to ride the pony all the way to Beloit; he was maybe nine.

"She was stubborn as a jackass," Trever says, "and we'd go two or three blocks, and she'd slow up and slow up and finally stop. Just like this one. So, at last I took off my red sweater and wrapped it around that pony's eyes, and swung her around about a dozen times, and then she'd go on for a while before I had to do it again. It was a long, long ride! I never wanted to see the damn pony again!"

Jackie well knows the feeling.

When Paint's wound finally heals, the long-unridden horse is so wild that nobody dares mount him. He's sold—maybe for dog food. Like Uncle Trever, Jackie isn't sorry to see him go.

34 THE Y CABIN

When Ron returns from France in 1924, newly married, he and Vera live downtown at Aunt Ida's while Ron takes his senior year at Beloit College. He stays in close touch with the farm, however, with the neighbors, with Turtle Township.

He hears that one of the Turtle boys, Murel Holmbeck, wrote to the Boy Scouts and asked how a country boy could get into scouting. They sent him information and a booklet for a correspondence program. He has been working away on his own, a Lone Scout.

In Château Thierry, one of Ron's duties was to lead a Boy Scout troop. Now he sees a need in his own township. He sends out word that he's ready to lead a boys' group. He invites any boys interested to meet at the Big House.

On the appointed date, a dozen boys show up. Murel Holmbeck, along with two brothers and a cousin; Bub Wehler; Jimmy Anderson; Ralph and Vernon Howland; John Holmes; Bob Maxworthy; a few others. Not all who come are old enough to be scouts, but they come with their big brothers. They talk about their organization; they play games; they have refreshments. Each boy drinks a quart of chocolate milk. The troop is launched.

The boys meet weekly, rotating houses. They conduct Boy Scout business, progress on merit badges, have a program, and finish with games and refreshments.

The favorite game is called Hot Hand. One boy leans his head into a pillow against a wall, exposing his elevated rump. The group figures out the longest run in the room, a run where speed can be built up. Then one of the boys runs at the leaning boy and whacks him with as much force as he can muster. "It" has to guess who hit him. If he doesn't guess correctly, he buries his head again for another boy to deliver a blow. Some of the blows are delivered with such force that "It" is practically lifted off his feet. Some of the blows really hurt. Phil Holmes is one of the little brothers; he's too small to play. If he sees his brother, John, having a hard time of it, he will dart in and give him just a little tap. Then John will turn around and guess that it is Phil. The other boys cry out, "No fair!" But Phil is too softhearted to let John's punishment, or anyone else's, go on and on.

Sometimes Vera makes waffles for the group when they meet at the Little House. Sometimes it's doughnuts at Sally Holmes's, or cookies at Maxworthys', or other treats at other members' houses.

The program is usually a speaker on some interesting topic, not necessarily connected with scouting. Sometimes the group has a day activity: Ronald once leads the group on a hike from Zilley School to Bergen, seven miles

Most of the first troop. Back: Erling and Cliff Holmbeck, Ron Dougan, Vern Howland, and Murel and Andrew Holmbeck. Front: Jim Anderson, John Holmes, Lee Holmbeck, Bob Maxworthy, and Bub Wehler.

away, where they visit a phone company and a creamery. Or the program is a night activity: a rope hike in the dark or a snipe hunt for an unsuspecting new member. One night they spear suckers in the crick behind Gundersons'. It's an activity they've done before. When Ron hears of it, he wants to learn how. The boys have sticks with fish spears on the ends. They light flares on the banks by a shallow rapids. When the foot-long suckers swim up the rapids, they make easy prey. Ron joins in the melee. After a bit he abandons his spear and gets right in the water. He catches suckers with his bare hands.

Ron is the leader of the scout troop for several years. But his work presses him, and he is getting his own children faster than a dog gets fleas. He suggests to a new employee that he take over. At the same time, Chet Welch of the County Y suggests that the scout troop become a rural YMCA group.

The metamorphosis is made. Ron hands over the leadership to Roy Veihman and his wife, Fannie, and the organization becomes the Turtle Y. The older scouts have gone on to other things; the group is now mostly younger Turtle boys, perhaps thirty of them. Their meetings now start with the reading of a story from a Bible stories book. After this bow to religion, they go on with their business, programs, and fun. They, too, meet at one another's houses, but the group is too large. They need a clubhouse. They ask Daddy Dougan if they can build a cabin in his woods at the Hill Farm, where Roy Veihman lives. W. J. gives his consent.

One Sunday afternoon, five or six of the boys meet at the Hill Farm with W. J. and the Veihmans. In at least a foot of snow, they mush through the thickest part of the woods, back past the clearing, till they find a spot that is fairly open. There they mark off the dimensions of the cabin, with W. J. giving permission to cut down certain trees. They stake it off. Somehow, a mistake is made or else the boys don't realize how serious Daddy Dougan is about his trees. When the snow melts and ground clearing begins, he shows up to discover the cabin's dimensions have shifted, and the boys are in the process of felling a large unauthorized tree.

W. J. is upset. He gives the boys a long sermon. He orders all work to cease while he considers whether he'll change his mind about his offer. He's not sure he wants to allow a lot of people back in the woods. He wonders if the boys really need a clubhouse and, if they do, whether they might not be better off in another location.

Roy and Fannie rally to the emergency. They talk persuasively to W. J. The boys are contrite. Plans are gone over carefully. Daddy Dougan again gives his consent but with stern caveats. He supervises every tree cut down. He watches on every workday until the structure is far enough along that there will be no surprises.

The group hasn't money to build a cabin. Each boy agrees to bring eight poles from his farm, for framing the building, and as many logs as he can manage. The assembled logs range from six to ten inches in diameter and are of every variety—elm, wild cherry, willow. They are too short to lay horizontally, so the boys position them upright. And because they don't fit snugly together, the gaps are plugged with cement the boys mix themselves. In one wall they build a fireplace out of fieldstone. For the mantle, Daddy Dougan gives them a reconciliation present, a long oak plank, two inches thick and seven inches wide. Someone has some small windows in a storage space on his farm and donates them. These are set in place. The floor is left dirt. A stove is made by cutting out one end of a metal barrel, inserting a stove door, and adding four metal legs and a stovepipe. The boys raise some money to buy corrugated metal for the roof. It's a cabin to be proud of, even though when the first spring comes along and the ground gets soaked, the willow logs start to grow. There are sprouts outside and inside the cabin. The boys just peel them off; it is no problem. They also discover that they've placed their structure on a thistle bed. There is enough light from the windows for the thistles to keep coming up through the dirt floor, even though the ground has been tightly packed.

Getting ready for the dedication. The many folding chairs for the large audience are yet to be put in place, but the little organ is already there.

When it's finished, there's a gala dedication of the cabin, with County Y officials and all of Turtle Township there, and a potluck. It's Sunday; W. J. Dougan preaches the sermon. He is as proud of the cabin as the boys and the Veihmans are. There's a problem, though, for this first big gathering. One of the earliest constructions on the grounds has been a little outhouse, back in the woods behind the cabin. Just before the big celebration, it occurs to someone that women will be coming—mothers and grandmothers and sisters and Y officials' wives. They have to have another outhouse! But how to manage this? There isn't time to build one. There isn't money to buy one. There isn't time to dig a hole and transport a neighbor's outhouse in on a wagon or truck, even if they could find one that was movable. They solve the problem by making two signs. One has an arrow and says GIRLS

Grampa, preaching at the dedication of the cabin.

TOILET. The other has an arrow and says BOYS TOILET. Each points to a path, and the paths go off in different directions. But very shortly, they snake around, and both meet at the one facility.

After a few years, the boys rebuild the cabin. They solicit groups in town. Through Mr. Zimmerman, in charge at Wisconsin Power and Light, the utility company donates old telephone poles, runs electricity into the site, and digs a well. Carpenters and a stonemason donate their services. The boys tear the old cabin down, all except the fireplace, and make a bigger structure around it, this time laying the logs horizontally. W. J. does not object to the few trees that must come down to accommodate the larger building.

The boys pour a cement floor. The old metal barrel is still the stove and heater. They build a heavy wooden box hockey set, which results in many sore knuckles and sorer feelings—tempers sometimes run so high during this game that the players forget about the puck and clobber one another with their hockey sticks.

The cabin becomes not only the Y clubhouse but a hub of the township. An ecumenical church service, dubbed "The Church in Wildwood," with its all-township potluck dinner and ball game, is held there twice a year. Sometimes more than one hundred people come. Turtle residents borrow the cabin for parties and fish fries and other gatherings. Someone makes a gift of ducks. The ensuing duck dinner is so enjoyed that it's held a second year and tickets are sold. By the third year, the crowds are so great that the popular event has no fourth year. And because the cabin is in the Dougan woods, the Dougan kids are free to use it for birthday parties, the destination of hayrides, church youth group meetings, and camp outs with their friends. They use it often.

The boys are appreciative. Ten years after the building of the cabin, they give Grampa a beautiful oak speaker's stand, made by one of their members, and the Chief Ranger of the Turtle Pioneers, Russell Gunderson, says in his formal speech of presentation to "Daddy": "Today it's my most welcome privilege to represent a 'Y' association of approximately fifty members with facilities in advance of most rural 'Y' clubs today. An association that has flourished and won the praise and recognition of local as well as distant 'Y' directors and has built an excellent and envious record of success; but most important of all, an association that has given the boys and girls an opportunity to work and fellowship together in something worthwhile; to broaden their lives and grow by learning and doing and following the 'Y' ideals for perfect triangular development—Spiritually, Mentally and Physically.

"To have had a substantial responsibility in the origin of such work must be a source of personal satisfaction to you and is most assuredly a source of great appreciation by us. We hope that this gift may be a useful and lasting reminder to you of that appreciation."

Roy and Fannie Veihman use the cabin for a Christmas card. The cabin, rebuilt, has horizontal logs, but the mantle is still the broad plank Grampa donated.

Grampa makes his thank-you speech standing at that stand.

When the Veihmans retire as leaders, the Clinton Y takes over. At some point the Y administration changes, and the group is under the jurisdiction of the Tri-County Y; both Grampa and Daddy are on the board. This occasions little change at the local level. When the boys grow older yet, and are dating and marrying, they change their name to YPCA—Young People's Christian Association—and then all the Turtle young women are welcomed as members. A number are already wives or girlfriends. Then a YPCA meeting might end in a shower or shivaree.

She leaps from bed and pulls on her jeans. She doesn't ask the emergency. She knows from experience that if you wait for details, you might be left behind. With Daddy talking that way, whatever it is will be important. Were it merely the bottle washer again, or a problem with the well, he'd have said, "I'll be down as soon as I have my coffee," and she'd have rolled over and gone back to sleep till six o'clock and detasseling time.

She hops into the passenger seat just as Daddy slides into the driver's. He shakes his head and explains as they roar down the lane and onto Colley Road.

"The silo's splitting. Libby's silage is wet, wetter than anything we've ever put in before. It must weigh tons more than the silo's designed to withstand in lateral thrust. Harlan just discovered a crack—down in the cow barn. He slipped on some ooze in the center by the grain bins and nearly broke his skull."

A chill grips Jackie. A herdsman's skull is bad enough, but what about the silo? What if it splits right in two? What will happen to the barn?

"Those trucks were leaking like an old man's nose," Daddy says, "even after coming all the way from Janesville. I should have thought about it." He careens into the drive, pulls right up to the cow barn door and slams on the brakes.

Jackie jumps out on her side. She can hear the milking motor in the upstairs barn pulsing calmly, as if nothing were the matter. Inside the cow barn, she can hear it too, only more muffled. She follows Daddy around the sidewalk and up a walk between the cows to the inner circle of the barn. The cows are rolling their eyes and snorting at the activity before them. Grampa and four or five hired men are standing between the cows and the silo, looking at the concrete.

"Ron's here," somebody says. They stand back as Daddy comes up.

Harlan, the herdsman, points. "There it is."

Jackie looks. There it is, all right—a narrow wavering vertical fissure, whitish against the grayer concrete, starting almost at the floor and disappearing into the ceiling.

"I'll be a son of a bitch," Daddy repeats. The men glance at Grampa, for when they were hired, they had to promise not to smoke, drink, or use improper language on the place. But Ron is Ron, and Grampa can't hear him.

Juice is oozing from the bottom of the crack and making a pool on the concrete. "That's how I discovered it," says Harlan. "I slipped on the puddle."

A gunnysack is lying in the juice, but it's caked with grain dust. Even if it weren't, it wouldn't be effective as a sponge. Wet trickles from under it into a cow's manger. The cow whose trough it is licks it up as fast as it runs in. Her neighbors on either side stretch their long necks and tongues in vain. Jackie understands their desire; she's sucked on many a corn stalk and knows how sweet the juice is.

Her attention returns to the crack. She's sick with foreboding. What can possibly be done? She listens to Daddy, Grampa, the men. They all talk about the problem. Daddy spells to Grampa; Grampa considers. They all consider. Will the reinforcing iron rods in the concrete hold, or will the pressure snap them? To take the silage out of the silo would be a difficult and dangerous job, more so because it would have to be done quickly. And there's no technique for emptying a silo quickly; silos are emptied fork by fork. But can they repair the silo with the silage left in? Might the water somehow be siphoned off, to relieve the pressure? How long do they have before the silo splits more?

"Yes," says Daddy to Harlan, "finish the milking, but get the cows out as quickly as you can."

The dread in Jackie's heart increases.

Daddy remembers where there's an old dismantled stave silo west of town. Jackie knows stave silos. They are wooden, made up of many vertical slats belted at intervals by steel bands. Daddy spells to Grampa: might they belt up the splitting concrete silo with stave silo bands? Grampa nods thoughtfully and follows Daddy toward the office telephone. The barn hands get on with the milking. Everyone else waits, watching, conjecturing, running a finger along the crack, as if to feel it makes it more believable.

Jackie looks at the fissure where it disappears into the cow barn ceiling. She goes into the passageway between the round barn and side barn and climbs the narrow stairs to the upper barn. She wants to find where the crack ends. As she comes out onto the barn floor, the milking motor throbs suddenly loud, and THE AIMS OF THIS FARM high on the silo's side seem to throb, too. She averts her eyes and scrambles up onto the hay. She springs around to the far side of the silo, for she calculates the crack must come up behind the grain storage bins. She climbs the chute and studies the concrete but can find no sign of a break. That's a relief.

She returns to the loft floor and studies the silo. She pictures it splitting, taking the barn, fragile as an eggshell in comparison with that gigantic core, right with it. She sees the barn's curved, white-painted sides smashed like kindling, spilling out grain, spilling out hay, the silo pinning the barn down like a tree struck by lightning. She sees the AIMS cracked and exposed to the sky.

She addresses the silo out loud. "You've gotta hang on! Help is coming!"

Inaction is more than she can bear. She opens the narrow door into the dark silo shaft and swings onto the rungs, scaling them fast as a monkey. She pictures herself part of the kindling, but she wants to see. She can hear voices coming up the shaft from the cow barn. She climbs toward the light to where the last shutter ends and peers over its lip. The silo interior is dim, but she can make out the silage level three or four feet below her. The well of the great cylinder is more than half full. The chopped cornstalks lie there, looking and smelling green and fresh, unfermented. As soon as they smell like silage, the cow whose manger gets the trickle will be perpetually drunk. She gives a snort of laughter.

She looks for the crack, where it should be, but can't see it up here, either. Maybe it doesn't extend very far. She climbs back down and onto the loft floor. Through the open doors she sees Daddy and Grampa hurrying from the office. She swings into the shaft again and climbs to the lower level. No one sees her emerge; they are all attending the crack.

Daddy reports that the farmer will sell the silo. He and Grampa will take two men to go after the bands, and Erv will head into town for bolts as soon as the hardware store is open. Farm stores open early, Jackie knows, often before seven. Grampa squares his shoulders resolutely and cries in ringing tones, "We'll fetch it!" which is what he always says when things get rough. It seems particularly appropriate for this occasion: the situation is very rough, and there is actual fetching to be done. Grampa's phrase cheers Jackie.

A milkhouse hand, just arrived, wanders onto the scene and peers through the crowd. "Hey, that silo's got a crack in it!" he exclaims. "Shouldn't somebody be doing something about it?"

"You're the very man I need, Sparky," says Daddy. "Come here."

Sparky does.

"Put your thumb there where it widens out a little," Daddy instructs.

Sparky puts his thumb in the crack. "Now what?"

"Now," says Daddy, "stay right there until we get back, and holler like anything if the dike breaks!"

Everybody laughs except Sparky, who turns a little red and pulls back his hand.

Jackie decides she'll show up late for detasseling and follow the action. She climbs into the back of the truck with the men. As they bump up the lane to the farm west of town, she spots the remains of the stave silo near the barnyard. The staves are in neat fat rolls, like giant snow fencing. The steel bands are in much smaller, narrower rolls. The men jump down and hoist the bands onto the truck while Grampa and Daddy talk to the farmer. Jackie listens again to the details of the possible catastrophe. A collie appears and

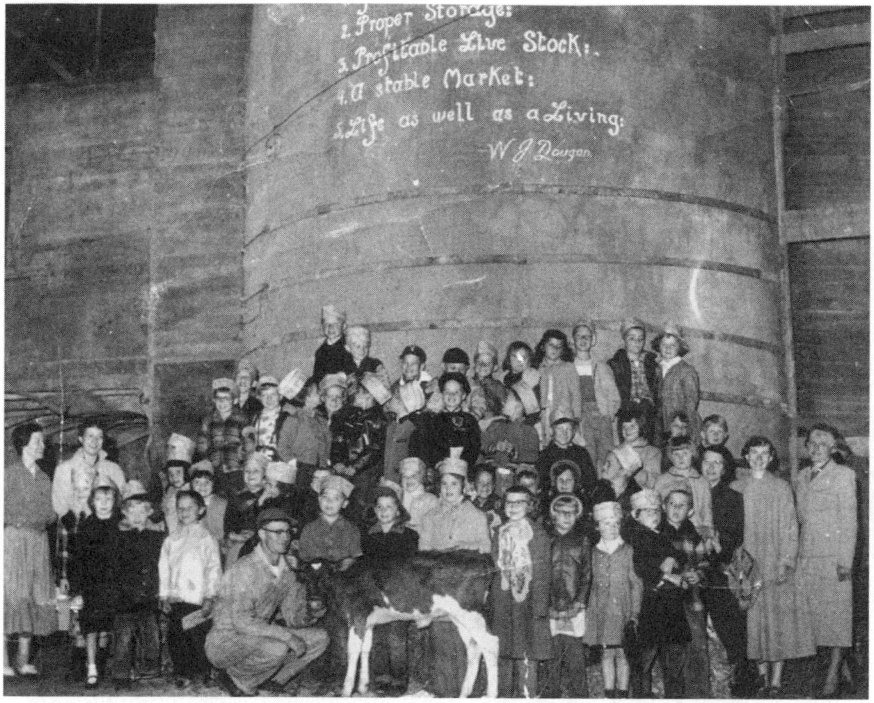

Cunningham School first grade, barn hand, and calf. Note the steel bands that keep the silo from splitting further, and, on the left, how the bands can be tightened.

rubs against her, and three gray kittens come running, their little tails straight up like spikes, and their fur, when she pats them, is soft as thistledown.

When the price is agreed on and the bands loaded—Daddy says they'll return for the staves another time—she climbs back in the truck and settles herself amid the coils. The sun caresses her face; the wind tousles her hair. The men laugh and joke as they speed back toward the dairy. Jackie sends a mental message to the silo. "Keep hanging on! We're fetching it!"

In the now empty cow barn, Erv is ready with his arc welder. The barn hands leave off the cleanup to help. The men thread a steel band around the silo, just under the ceiling. It goes behind the chute and the ventilator, over the crack, and behind the grain bin. As it comes around to the start, Jackie's heart gives a lurch. There's a two-foot gap between the ends! But Erv bends the ends out, burns a hole in each with his acetylene torch, and inserts a long double-threaded steel rod. He screws nuts on the ends and twists. The more he twists, the more the two ends of the belt are pulled together.

She watches as they put another band below the first one and tighten it. The crack isn't closing, but it can't widen anymore, either, unless it breaks the steel. And with enough steel bands, it won't be able to. Grampa tells them that when the silo is empty and the crack has dried out, they'll caulk it. Till that can happen, some time in the winter, corn juices will leak out. They'll have to keep cloths down, on account of the slipperiness of the concrete floor. On account of the tipsy cow, too, thinks Jackie.

Erv and his team decide they can fit three more bands in the cow barn and eight in the upper barn, stopping just under the AIMS. It's going to work! Daddy is cheerful. Grampa is cheerful. Jackie is cheerful, too, and gives the concrete a pat. "We fetched it," she tells the silo.

She's suddenly hungry. She goes to the milkhouse. Chocolate milk is rippling down the cooling coils above the bottling machine. She darts her hand in and plucks a just-filled half-pint off the assembly line, leaving the capping machine to stamp down on emptiness. She goes out in the sunshine to drink.

She looks up the ramp, through the open barn doors, to the "Aims." She thinks about the second one, "Proper Storage." The silo has stored faithfully and properly, ever since it was built. It just never had to cope with Libby's soaking-wet silage before. Soon, with thirteen belts, it will store properly again.

She finishes her milk and strolls toward the office, to find out what field the detasslers are in. The excitement is over. She guesses it's time to get to work. She looks forward to telling Craig all about it.

36 GOATS

Butter is the first goat to arrive at the farm, when Jackie is in third grade. The vet brings her; she's a baby kid, white, with tiny wattles at her throat and a half-pear tail with no hair on the underside, only warm pink skin. She's motherless. She doesn't know how to drink from a bottle. She kneels on her front legs, in the nursing position, and tries and tries, while the family take turns holding the bottle. But she only chews frantically on the nipple. She doesn't get much milk that way. When, after a day and a half of futile feedings, she suddenly gets the hang of sucking, it's like a miracle. She empties the bottle as fast as pouring sand down a rat hole. Her tail wags madly. Her slurps and gulps are music to everyone's ears.

The kid drinks vast quantities and grows rapidly. Even though she has a pen in the backyard of the Little House, she's soon big enough to jump the fence. She chooses to make her bed in the window box outside the living room. From there she keeps tabs on everything that's going on inside the house. When the front door opens, she rushes in and either runs to the end of the living room and leaps on top of the baby grand piano or clatters up the stairs like a mountain goat and gallops through Jackie and Craig's bedroom to Mother and Daddy's room on the sleeping porch. That's as far as she can go; she jumps on the bed and faces her pursuers, skipping sideways and doing a little you-can't-catch-me dance on the bedspread.

She follows the children all over the farm. She nibbles grass. She nibbles bushes. She nibbles Grama's petunias and nasturtiums. The four try her out on every sort of leaf. There are few she doesn't like, but her passion is elm leaves, either fresh off a branch or dried and curled on the ground. On her own, when the children are at school, she discovers the oat bin that occupies part of the toolshed, and she gorges herself. She discovers the garden across the road and eats a whole row of young lettuce down to the nubs.

Grampa is grave. "That goat must be contained," he says.

A hired man extends the fence of Butter's pen upward. Butter wanders dolefully around her yard, blatting all the time.

"I can't stand listening to that unhappy animal all day," Mother says. The four take her for walks after school, but two have to hold the rope she's on; a child alone will promptly get dragged to the oat bin.

She learns to jump the second tier of fencing and is on the loose again. She loves to climb. She jumps onto the running board of a car; then, its fender, its hood, and its top; then, she slides down the sloping back, leaving long scratches. Dr. Thayer, when he comes out for any sick call at the farm, learns to park his torpedo-back Buick one-third of a mile down the road. She'll leap onto the flat roof of the milkhouse overhang and skip up its peaked roof. She'll caper on the rooftree and look down like an Alpine climber. She'll daintily nibble the elm leaves now within reach, bobbing her white head, swinging her wattles like bell clappers.

Lester Stam, one of the milkmen, drives an ancient automobile. It has a tan cloth roof. He drives it out from town and parks it near the milkhouse while he loads his truck, goes on his route, and returns. One day, climbing into his front seat, he's brushed in the face by a shred of tattered canvas. He looks up and finds his roof has rips in it, almost from front to back, as though something large and messy has fallen through. He does detective work. There is no big branch on top of his car, nor any large rocks inside. He does find white hairs on the upholstery. Between thumb and forefinger he carries the evidence to Daddy in the office. Daddy goes with him to look at the car. He notes that the windows are down so that something could have fallen through and jumped out. He notes that the car is parked in the shade beneath a tree with leafy, low-hanging branches—an elm. Butter stands indicted. Daddy begins the search for a replacement roof for Lester's car. Such

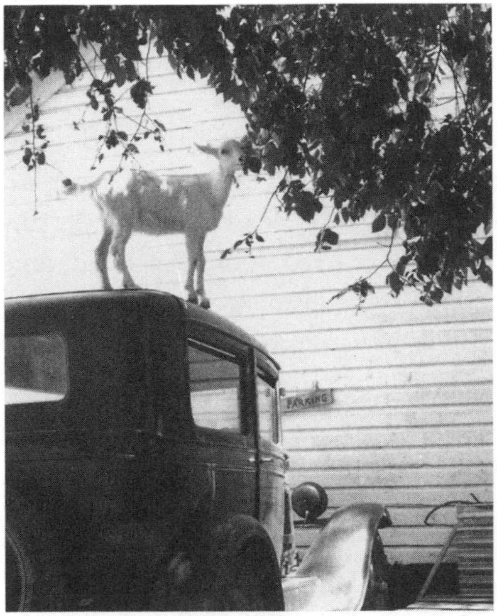

Butter enjoying elm leaves from the top of a car parked near the milkhouse.

roofs, even as the cars they fit, scarcely exist anymore. It takes him time and ingenuity to find one. And it costs more than it should.

Daddy and Grampa decide that Butter is impossible to pen and too destructive to keep. Grama wants her gone, too—the goat has totally destroyed a little willow tree and rosebushes where she was trying to create a beauty area around the new well behind the Big House. Mother tries to mollify the children by pointing out that Butter needs other goats. All this is true. Butter goes to a farm that has goats and in due time is the mother of triplets.

Jackie grieves the most at Butter's departure. The goat had become mainly hers. She gets another a few years later, when the family has moved up the road to Chez Nous, away from oat bins and milkhouse roofs and elm trees. This time the artificial inseminator is the one to bring her, driving rapidly into the yard, slamming on his brakes, flinging open his door as the half-grown kid bursts forth. "I've never been so glad to get rid of anything in my life," Amos shouts, and he drives away before anyone can catch the animal and shove her back in.

Sugarpuss, like Butter, is a white goat. She roams the farm by day; by night she sleeps in a box stall in the barn. She shows affection in goatlike ways: she will be grazing on the lawn, with Jackie nearby. Jackie will slip behind a tree. After a bit, Sugar will raise her head, look all around, and start running erratically, blatting short bleats of distress. The moment she sees Jackie behind the tree, she drops her head and begins cropping grass again.

One summer evening, Mother and Daddy are away; Craig is with them. Jo and Pat have been home for some hours from a trip to Madison for their

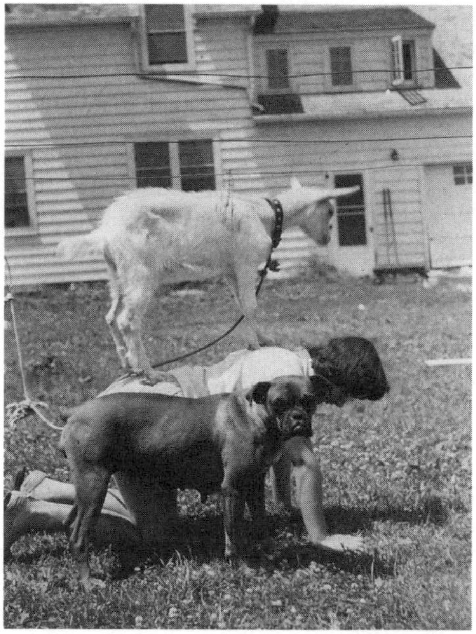

Jackie with Sugarpuss and boxer Boxie at Chez Nous. Craig, when eleven, wrote on the back of this snapshot, "Jackie is the one with the intelligent expression."

weekly violin lessons. Joan now has a driver's license. Outside, Sugarpuss wanders around in the dark, blatting mournfully.

"Jackie!" Jo shouts. "Go put your goat to bed!"

Then she and Pat look at each other. Where is Jackie? They remember. She went along for a cello lesson, something she hasn't been doing in the summer. They drove the fifty miles home without her!

They call frantically all over Madison and no one knows where Jackie is. The last anyone saw she was sitting on the porch rail of the Wisconsin School of Music, swinging her legs. Finally, they locate her at the home of one of Joan's fiddler friends. Jackie repays her sisters by having a splendid time, staying three days, and finally coming home on a Greyhound bus. While she's gone, they have to feed Sugarpuss and put her to bed.

Jackie's high-school goat, Firecracker, likes to eat cigarettes and clarinet reeds. Her end is not like her predecessors, going on to motherhood at another farm. Jackie is busy with many activities and pays only sporadic attention to her pet. She lets her run with the young heifers, and a hired man feeds her along with the other stock. Cracker thinks she's a cow. At some point, when Jackie is away at music clinic in Madison and then at camp, the goat gets shipped to market with a group of bull calves.

Jackie is upset; Grampa is contrite. "She seemed a useless animal that nobody wanted," he confesses. It's not for another year that insult is added to injury, when Jackie learns that Cracker fetched only eighty-seven cents at the stockyards.

The final goat is Skyrocket, arriving, as did Firecracker, around the Fourth of July. Jackie has finished her freshman year at college and has a job for August as a counselor at Phantom Lake Y Camp girls' session. She asks the director if she can bring her goat. Rocky is young and winsome, and she thinks the little girls—especially the city girls—will enjoy her. Max Clowers reluctantly agrees, provided Jackie takes full responsibility for the animal. If it becomes a nuisance in any way, it will have to go back to the farm.

Rocky rides into camp with her head out the farm truck window. Her rectangle-pupiled yellow eyes are alive with interest, her cylinder ears alert. She wanders around in the circle of tents, nibbling and exploring, while Jackie unloads a gunnysack of ground meal and an empty barrel. The barrel is for Rocky's bed, against the side of the tent platform.

When her campers come, Jackie explains that the goat will stay as long as she doesn't get into trouble. Only constant vigilance keeps a goat out of trouble. Would her tent like to form the Rocky Club? All it takes to be a member is to help take care of Rocky, a large share of which is preventing trouble.

All her campers eagerly join. They gather dry grass from the hillside to make the barrel soft. They fill the feed pan and water pan. They sweep up Rocky's marbles that bounce and scatter on the tent floor when the goat comes in to investigate. They shove her off the bunks and pull her head out of their suitcases. Rocky flattens her tail against her back and springs outside to visit another tent. Before long, most of the girls in camp are members of the Rocky Club.

Rocky is a constant presence at Phantom Lake. She goes on hikes and gets underfoot in the stables. She dodges into the crafts tent and before being routed eats a length of red raffia from an unfinished lanyard and samples willow wands softening in a water bucket. On Stunt Night, she stars in three different skits. During the all-camp hide-and-seek, where the counselors hide and the campers have an hour to locate them, Rocky helps the campers win by calling attention to the last counselor, hidden behind the big chimney on the Rec Hall roof.

At the waterfront, she comes dancing out on the long dock; in dodging those trying to catch her, she skids on the wet planks and falls in. She swims to shore, and that night at the Council Circle, she's awarded both a certificate for passing her fish test and a demerit for running on the dock. She eats them both.

Jackie with her last goat, Skyrocket, and family dog Haaken, named after the king of Norway.

All along, Max keeps a stern eye on her. "She's skating on thin ice," he warns Jackie after every escapade.

There is one place that's absolutely forbidden to the goat—the mess hall. This makes a problem. During meals, Rocky wanders the veranda, bleating lonesomely and looking in the screen doors. When a meal is over, Jackie and her campers need to beat everyone out, for Rocky always litters the boards with a copious supply of droppings. They have to sweep up the marbles before Max sees them: they keep a broom and dustpan in a discreet corner of the porch.

Sunday is Visiting Day. One Sunday noon, Jackie hurries out of mess to discover someone has beaten her to it. An elderly woman is stooped over, sweeping marbles into the dustpan. Jackie rushes to relieve her of her task, but too late—the camp director is coming out the door. The woman turns to him and thrusts the dustpan under his nose. He stares down at goat droppings. This is it, Jackie thinks. Outsiders are involved. Fast talking can't save Rocky's hide this time.

"Oh, Mr. Clowers!" exclaims the woman. "Do you know where I can get any more of these? They're exactly what I need for my African violets!"

Rocky finishes camp in triumph. She's awarded a cherished Phantom Lake patch at the final ceremony. She rides back to Chez Nous in the farm truck, and a year later goes on to another farm and matrimony.

She is the last of Jackie's goats. But all her life, Jackie has a soft spot in her heart for the genus *Capra*.

37 DAN GOLDSMITH

Almost always when Jackie goes into the round barn and anyone is there, music is playing. The men listen to the radio while they milk or clean. The radio is on a little shelf up against the central silo, the shelf that holds the day-to-day barn records and the cows' nose-lead. And always the radio station they have tuned in to is WLS, the Prairie Farmer Station.

Jackie is familiar with this station. It's the same one the men listen to in their sitting room over at the Big House when they're waiting for dinner. In the early mornings, on nights when she's slept over at the Big House, she herself listens to Jolly Joe advertising Cocowheats and conducting dressing races that sometimes the boys win and sometimes the girls. Jackie and Craig are scornful—he must make it up, for how can he *see?* WLS has Lulubelle and Scotty, with their guitars, and the Hoosier Hot Shots, Craig's favorites; and people sing twangy songs like "Yippee Ti-Yi-Yo, Git Along, Little Dogies" or "Don't Fence Me In!" There are also whiney ones, "I'm Gonna Buy a Paper Doll," and a singer called the Betsy Ross Girl who belts out "Yankee Doodle Dandy."

Down in the barn, the cows listen to "Yippee Ti-Yi-Yo" while they munch their hay and while the milking machines tug rhythmically at their tits.

"Do the cows really *like* music?" Jackie asks Billy Beadle once.

"They love it," Billy responds. "It soothes 'em and calms 'em, and they let down their milk and give lots of it." He whistles along with "Yippee Ti-Yi-Yo" while he changes a milking machine. Jackie thinks privately that if she were a cow, her milk would come out all curdled if she were listening to one rhythm while her milking machine was pumping away on a different beat.

One year Daddy puts an ad in *Hoard's Dairyman* for a herdsman. He gets an answer from a man named Dan Goldsmith, in White River Junction,

Vermont. Daddy likes the sound of Dan's letter, writes him, and offers him the job. Six months later, Dan shows up on the farm. He's been slow coming, he explains, because the letter went to White River Junction, New Hampshire. It only just reached him.

Dan is a tall man, thin, loose jointed, and bald. He has a prominent nose, and the tragedy of all Jewish history is in the depths of his deep brown eyes. Daddy makes room for him in the barn and the Big House.

Jackie is now busy at Beloit College. She's not around the barn much these days, and with Grama and Grampa retired and living on the edge of town, she doesn't go often into the Big House, either. She doesn't know anything about Dan Goldsmith until Daddy remarks one night at supper, "We have an unusual man in the barn."

"Oh?" says Mother. "What's unusual about him?"

"Have you noticed any difference in the milk? He's got the cows listening to Mozart symphonies," Daddy says.

Jackie and Pat—who is also going to Beloit College and living at home—prick up their ears.

"He tunes in WHA instead of WLS," Daddy goes on. "He listens to "Chapter-a-Day" and is following Professor Easum's history lectures on the Middle Ages. We had quite a chat about Alcuin."

WHA is "the Oldest Station in the Nation," broadcast out of the University of Wisconsin at Madison. It's totally educational. The family is even more intrigued.

Daddy says, "I heard him whistling a Bach cantata today, and I said, 'You must have a love of good music, Dan.' He told me he has a degree in string bass from Julliard."

Julliard! At this point Jackie and Pat are electrified; the account has become distinctly practical. Julliard is one of the finest music conservatories in the country. A Julliard graduate milking cows in the round barn! It's unbelievable. They leave the table, leap in the car, and speed down to the Big House.

They meet Dan. Yes, he's a Julliard graduate. No, he doesn't have his bass with him, though he owns a fine one of native bird's-eye maple, made early last century by the New Hampshire contrabass maker, Abraham Prescott. Yes, he misses playing. If they can find him a decent instrument, he'd be delighted to join the Madison String Sinfonia that Pat and Jackie play in on Saturday afternoons.

Thereafter, at noon every Saturday, Jackie sprints out of her class at Morse-Ingersoll Hall. Pat doesn't have a Saturday class. She and Dan are waiting with a farm truck. Jackie's cello, Pat's violin, and Dan's borrowed bass are in the back. They gun the fifteen miles up to Janesville where Betty, Corky, and Suzie, carrying two more cellos and a string bass, vault into the back of the truck. They then all speed to Madison, thirty-five miles farther. At one-thirty, Marie Endres starts rehearsal, and the Beloit-Janesville contingent, still breathless, have their strings tuned and bows tightened in time for the first downbeat. Dan folds his long frame over his string bass, and watching the conductor with his deep, sad eyes, he draws deep, sad tones from the guts of his instrument. He's a first-rate player. Everyone is enthusiastic about the Dougan herdsman.

Sinfonia isn't the only orchestra Dan joins. Pat's fiancé, Lewie Dalvit, has a dance band in which Pat plays jazz fiddle and Craig plays saxophone. Now Dan goes along, too, on Friday and Saturday nights, and plunks out the rhythms. Sometimes he arrives home barely in time to fetch the cows from the pasture for early milking.

One night the band plays for a dance at the Turtle Grange. A husky farmer who has recently inherited a ramshackle farm and woodlot over on the State Line Road watches the players. At a break he speaks to Dan. His name is Marshall Miller, he says, and diffidently adds that he himself plays the string bass. Dan presses him to take a turn on the next set. Marshall plays

Herdsman Dan Goldsmith playing bass in Lew Dalvit's dance band. Pat Dougan Dalvit played jazz fiddle in the band, and Craig Dougan, sax. Craig took photos of the band, including this one, for a Beloit College photography class project.

a mean bass. It turns out that he's a graduate of Curtiss, another stellar music school. From then on there's another passenger and another bass fiddle in the truck on Saturdays.

Daddy tells the story to a group of Mother's Federation of Music Clubs friends who visit the round barn and are surprised that the cows are milking to Mendelssohn.

"Lift up a burdock leaf anywhere in Turtle Township," he brags, "and chances are you'll find a conservatory-trained, string-bass-playing farmer!"

38 THE SEA OF GALILEE

Grampa is not a singer. That's understandable, on account of his deafness. But Daddy isn't a singer, either. Once in a while he sings "The Spanish Cavalier" or "The World Owes Me a Living," and when he has his many grandchildren visiting at the Pleasant Lake cottage, he leads them single file over the hill to the little local tavern for root beers, with all of them beating on pans and singing, "We're Marching to Zion."

Daddy says he thinks he doesn't sing for a couple of reasons. "When I was twelve I rode my bicycle down to a tent meeting—those bicycles were called 'ice wagons' because you got so cold riding them—and I was singing in the choir. And when I got home I said to my mother, 'Why does Mr. Putney do such funny things with his voice? He goes way down and way up and he doesn't follow the tune. What's the matter with him?' 'Why, he's singing bass,' my mother said. I was confused, because I was sitting in the bass section and singing just as low as I could. I figured I'd been making a fool of myself."

And then there was Grama's singing. It was always embarrassing to stand next to her in church. She sang out on the hymns in such a loud and piercing alto that he always wanted to crawl under the pew.

"I did join the Glee Club in college," Daddy says, "because everybody in our fraternity had to, but after the tryout I never sang, only looked like I was."

Daddy often has vivid dreams. He has one once about singing. He tells it to everyone at the breakfast table.

"I'd been asked to sing in a quartet," he says. "We were going to sing on the steps of the Congregational church that overlooks the park, and the park was just full of a big crowd of people. The other members were Bill Shauffer and Hobart Weirick and Percy Herman, and it seemed a long way off so I said yes. Then, like it does in dreams, time flew, and here we were, dressed in tuxedos, standing back in the church ready to go on, and we'd never done any practicing. I was scared to death. I said to Bill Shauffer, 'What are we going to sing? Don't we need to practice or something?' 'Oh, we don't need to practice,' Bill said. 'We'll do "Spanish Cavalier" or "Down by the Old Mill Stream" or something like that.'

"Just then, through the open door of the church, I saw one of my milk trucks go by. I leapt out of that church as fast as I could go; I stopped the truck and said, 'Langklotz, will you do something for me for fifty dollars?' Langklotz said, 'Ron, I'd do anything for you for fifty dollars!' 'Then get in that church and sing in a quartet,' I said, and I headed off down the street in the milk truck to deliver milk, still in my tuxedo, and Langklotz, in his route clothes, went into the church."

Everybody's favorites of Daddy's dreams, though, are the Spring Brook ones.

Ronald is grown up. He's married, has children. But in his dream he's little again, maybe eight years old. He's down at the crick in the back pasture, dangling his feet over the bank. Fishing. It's the part of the crick that he and Trever have dammed up with rocks and clods of sod to make a swimming hole.

He looks up and sees a luminous figure gliding toward him across the water. The figure has a beard, a long, flowing robe, and a benign expression on his face. He looks like the Sunday School pictures of Jesus. Ronald knows that he is Jesus.

"Little boy," says Jesus, "is this the Sea of Galilee?"

"No, sir," says Ronald. "This is Spring Brook."

A puzzled expression crosses Jesus' face. "Then what in the world am I doing here?" he asks, and the dream is over.

The second Spring Brook dream comes a number of years later. Again he's down by the crick, but this time he seems to be his own age. Across the little stream, on the hillside, three figures are sitting on a bench. They are hooded and completely concealed. They are Green Bay Packers. But Ronald knows they are also the Trinity.

God says, "I started this world going."

The hoods of Jesus and the Holy Ghost nod agreement.

"And then I got busy with other things and forgot all about it," says God.

The hoods nod.

"And now that I've remembered and stopped by, I see that things are a mess."

The other two nod again.

"I see three things I could do," God says. "I could just destroy everything and let it go as a bad job."

The two nod.

"Or I could roll everything back to the primordial ooze and let everything start evolving all over again."

The two nod.

"Or"—God gives a weary sigh—"I could just watch it a while longer, see what develops."

All three hoods sit silent, brooding.

Finally one hood turns toward Ronald.

"Ronald," says Jesus, "what do you suggest?"

39 GAEA

Jackie lives at home while she attends Beloit College. She graduates in 1950, marries, and goes to the University of Michigan in the fall to earn a master's in Latin. Her husband is getting his degree in English. They live twelve miles away in Willow Run Village, a community of paper shanties hastily built at the start of the war to house workers at the airplane plant near Ypsilanti. Now the war is over, and the Village is one of married students; most of the men are veterans on the GI Bill. Rent for a one-bedroom apartment is twenty-three dollars a month; all three of their rooms would fit in the living room of Chez Nous. Morning and evening, university buses run back and forth between Willow Run and Ann Arbor.

The Village is drab. The identical one-story units, strung end to end, are gray, the roadways are gravel. The Village borders on country, but the land doesn't seem to be farmed. Jackie finds fields of yellow grass and weeds, with no grazing animals and only an occasional sagging fence. There are no farm buildings anywhere. This is all right; she likes deserted lands where she can wander and no one will stop her. She finds a scruffy woods with old trees, hardly an acre. In the fall she sometimes climbs a certain oak with a long horizontal branch, and does her reading there.

But with painting the walls of the shanty, fixing up furniture and bookcases, commuting, studying, learning to cook for two, and learning to be married, Jackie hasn't time for hiking the fields. She's taking a full load of classes and playing cello in the university orchestra. Her favorite academic class is "Ancient Near Eastern History," and she comes to love the Sumerians and old Egyptian boys. But her main, most important class is a weekly tutorial with a fine writing teacher, the Hopwood director Roy Cowden. He's in his last year before retirement and has white hair and sharp eyes with a glint of humor. He is quiet; he is gentle; he is wise. "Write another *Alice,*" he tells Jackie at one of their sessions.

It's the first time Jackie has been away from home for any length of time, and this is a permanent move. This is now home; that's what marriage is. Jo married and moved to Madison, fifty miles from home. Pat married, and she and Lewie are living at Chez Nous while building a house on the edge of the dairy; they are building it all, even pouring the cement into molds to make the cement blocks, and gathering fieldstone for the massive chimney. Craig is still at Beloit College, living at home. Jackie is the farthest away.

She doesn't admit it to herself, because it's not a feeling she recognizes as having, but somewhere below thoughts and words she's homesick. She's lonesome not so much for specific persons but for the everything-going-on-all-the-time-ness of home. She's lonesome for being able to go outside and climb on the bullwalk of ordinary activities, lonesome for being a part of the busy, productive life of many people doing fundamental things.

She subscribes to the *Beloit Daily News* to keep in touch with what's happening in and around Beloit. One day in midwinter she comes from the bus, collects the mail, enters the empty apartment, unrolls the paper, and still standing peruses the news. The front page is unusual—instead of printing, it's almost all a large map, which she immediately recognizes. It's the east side of Beloit, just the edge, the Turtle Creek Valley with Colley Road bisecting the center, heading east with all its familiar turns, and the State Line Road roughly parallel south of it, and the highway, Milwaukee Road, angling northeast above it. But there are unfamiliar lines running parallel, north–south. She perceives this in an instant, and only a fraction of a second later, she sees the headline: PROPOSED ROUTE OF NEW HIGHWAY. She sits down quite suddenly on the couch. She is not sure she's breathing.

After a moment she spreads the paper carefully on the floor and gets down onto her hands and knees to study it. The superhighway, Interstate 90, will run from Chicago northwest toward Minneapolis. She positions one finger on the dairy, one on Chez Nous. What the sick feeling in her stomach forebode is true: the proposed route runs right through part of the dairy's land, right over the house Pat and Lewie are still building, through Blodgetts' and Mackies' fields, right alongside the Catalpa Forest. There will be a half cloverleaf at the State Line Road one mile south of Colley Road. There will be a full cloverleaf at Milwaukee Road, a mile and a half north. The highway will continue to another cloverleaf at the Shopiere Road and then head straight north to bypass Janesville on that town's east side. Chez Nous will not be touched, but it will be on the other side of the four-lane highway. Colley Road will have to go over or under it.

Interstate 90 before opening, showing its proximity to the farm and the truncation of fields. Colley Road previously made a right angle beyond the highway.

Pat and Lewie building their house. It turned out to be directly in the path of Interstate 90.

Jackie sits back on her heels. A superhighway. It will change things. It will change things a lot. For the first time she feels in her own body what has before been but a phrase in poorly written books. She now knows it isn't just hyperbole. She hears the death knell. Her blood runs cold.

When the rates are low, she telephones the farm. Daddy says the paper is the first any of them had heard of it. That the highway really ought to go west of town, where the land isn't as good. That some farmers were thinking of getting a lawyer, but there probably wasn't much anyone could do. That the land would be taken by eminent domain, and they'd all be paid, but probably not the full value. That some farms, the cloverleaf ones, would be hit harder than theirs. That it wouldn't happen right away. And, who knows? Things might change.

It is not a comforting conversation.

The winter progresses. Her studies go well; her writing goes well. She and her husband make friends with other graduate students. At noon, in an empty classroom near the English department where they all eat their sack lunches, they play literary guessing games and compose together scurrilous, literary limericks.

When spring comes, there's a moment she'll never forget. Winter has made the Village even drabber than in the summer and fall. It's the first warm, windy day, and spring is palpably in the air, quickening everything. She's restless, she takes a study break and goes outdoors. She walks between two gray units and sees something she thought existed only in pictures, in stories, in e. e. cummings's poem, "far and wee." It's a genuine balloon man! He has gas-filled balloons, red, green, orange, blue, straining at their strings, a massive clump of brilliant globed colors! The old man himself is drab, but not the children running from every direction in their striped sweaters, yellow caps, blue cords. She watches as the man separates strings and frees balloons, and the children go dancing off, the balloons punctuating the gray buildings and shouting their colors into the pale washed sky. The sight gives her a surge of joy so intense it almost brings tears. She's afraid to move, to go closer, afraid the whole scene will dissolve.

The end of the semester approaches, the pause in the academic clock. Jackie has always lived by that familiar clock, ever since kindergarten. Every year has been a school year; academia ticks deep within her veins.

Midspring she goes out again to the fields. She wanders to the little waste woods, she climbs the gnarled oak and leans against its trunk, and then climbs down again. She scuffs through the brittle winter weeds, green flushing again around their roots. Somewhere in her meanderings a sentence begins to form in her mind. But a paragraph goes before that sentence, and the paragraph is this.

There has been another clock within her. She didn't set it nor place it there. It's been geared not to hours but to cycles: the daily precession of milking and bottling, feeding and cleaning, the yearly precession of planting, cultivating, harvesting. It's been set to sun, moon, heat, cold, wet, dry. But now if there's a heavy spring freeze, she puts on a coat without sensing the loss of crops that might result from too-late planting. If the sky lowers black, she takes an umbrella without feeling the sway of the hay wagon racing to reach the barn before the cloudburst. Her dailiness is now this class, that lecture, the next trip to the stacks. This was true before, too, but the steady throb of the milking machine was the heartbeat of the dailiness, the Greenwich underneath, that all the other clocks were timed to. It was the ground she'd stood on, the air she'd breathed.

She has no special moment, no epiphany to explain the realization of loss that comes over her. She only knows that something elemental is gone and has been gone for some time. That it's probably irretrievable, unless she changes the path she's treading. Child of Gaea, she has become an Antaeus, held too long from the earth.

Jackie stands very still amid the oaks and tawny grass. She says out loud to no one, "The clock has gone out of my feet."

40 THE RESCUE

It's a blustery afternoon in early March; it's 1955. The sky is the thin blue of an oft-washed work shirt; the sun is almost white. It's chilly. The ice has recently gone out on Turtle Creek in great heaving floes. The flood waters have risen up and over Colley Road, down toward where Spring Brook and Turtle Creek come within a splash of each other, and have now receded a little, leaving great slabs of ice helter-skelter on the banks of Spring Brook and on the floodplain between the two streams.

Spring Brook, known to town kids as "Dead Bed" because of its usual state, is still swollen and flowing across the road. This is because there's no longer an old red iron bridge over it; it's been replaced by two galvanized corrugated culverts, side by side, each over three feet in diameter. In flood time, the volume of water is more than the culverts' capacities. When the water is too deep, the milk trucks and all other traffic have to go around by the State Line Road.

Ron Dougan is heading toward town. As he slows and stops at the edge of the water to assess the depth of the ford, his attention is caught by a woman in a fur coat, off to the other side of the crick. She's jumping erratically up and down. Suddenly she runs along the bank, darts into the water of the ford, throws herself into Spring Brook, and disappears.

Daddy is aghast. He drives into the middle of the ford, stops, and leaps out of the car. He stands there with the flood swirling past his knees, looking north at the spot where the woman vanished. There's no sign of her, only two wide whirlpools being sucked into the invisible culverts below. The woman must have been sucked into one of them, too. He looks south to where the water foams out. Nothing. His mind races. Should he go in after

41 "BRAHMS' LULLABY"

It's a May morning in 1958. The air is tender; the leaves are tender; the narrow green blades of grass are tender. A kindergarten class from Todd School is visiting the farm. This is Mrs. Wildermuth's fourth farm outing, so she knows what to expect—not every detail, for each tour brings surprises, but there are certain popular features that she knows will be repeated.

The children are tender, too, but as they burst from the cars, all elbows and knees and noise, they seem hardy little plants indeed. They, too, know what to expect, for they've heard about the farm visits from classmates and siblings in upper grades. And they have a secret. They and their teacher have been preparing it. It has to do with something Mr. Dougan said to Mrs. Wildermuth when last year's kindergarten sang the chicken to sleep. "Why is it that the only lullaby kids know is 'Rockabye Baby'?" he'd asked. "Gertrude is always glad to hear the children sing, of course, but she wonders why it's always the same song."

The class whispers together. Mr. Dougan is going to be surprised this year! And Gertrude, too!

Mr. Dougan meets them in front of the milkhouse. He greets Mrs. Wildermuth and the two mother-helpers. He repeats each child's name: Alison, Freddy, Billy, Charlene, Kenneth. . . . There is nudging and giggling and warning shakes of heads as they think of the surprise. Ron Dougan doesn't notice anything unusual; in his experience, all five- and six-year-olds nudge and giggle.

The first stop is the cow barn. The cows are still in the pasture, but Ronald explains about the round barn and its advantages. The children all crowd to the center section and take turns peering down the silo shaft into the depths

Ron Dougan and pigs with Brownie troop from Strong School, Beloit, on June 28, 1954.

of the near-empty cylinder and then looking up its vast height to the wooden fretwork and tiny windows at the top.

"The cows eat silage all winter long, when they can't go out to pasture," says Mr. Dougan. He picks up a handful of silage from the trolley and offers it around, himself nibbling a disk of corn. A few accept, taste tentatively, and screw up their faces.

"The sourness is from fermentation, which keeps the corn from spoiling," Mr. Dougan says. "Then the cows' bodies turn the silage, along with their hay and grain, into milk. They think silage is as good as candy."

Those who tasted the silage look disbelieving.

"Can we milk a cow? My sister milked a cow last year!" cries Raymond.

"Later," promises their host. He shows them the cows' drinking cups, positioned low between every other stanchion. "All summer we use a large tank on wheels to take water to the cows in the pasture; when they're in the barnyard, they drink from the big concrete cow tank. But in the winter, or when they get thirsty here in the barn, they'll use these drinking cups. Cows have broad round noses, you'll see, and when they press their noses against this curved grill in the cup, it releases a valve that lets the water in. They have to share, two to a cup. Do you ever have to share?"

Everyone agrees they do. Ronald lets the children clean out the straw bits, then press the grills and fill the cups with water. Next he organizes races on the circular walk behind the gutter. He tells how he and his brother used to race their wagons around this same track, and so did his own children. Now his grandchildren race when they come to visit.

The class goes down the passageway into the side barn, and Ronald pokes two fingers into a calf stall. A calf with wobbly legs and rolling eyes grabs and sucks noisily. A few brave students poke their fingers in, too, and calves seize them eagerly. The children squeal and jerk their hands out again, tingling and slobber covered.

Then all troop down the back lane, pause to swing on a metal gate wide enough for a hay wagon, and go through to a pasture. "Watch out for cow pies," warns Mr. Dougan, pointing out an impressive green-brown splat on the grass. "You wouldn't want to step in one, would you?" Each child shows respectful interest in the cow pie while giving it wide berth. They look around to mark any other spots of danger.

At the crick, Mr. Dougan says, "This is Spring Brook Crick, it runs into Turtle Crick down closer to town. If your teacher tells you you should say 'creek,' you tell her that all good Turtle Township farm kids say 'crick.' Tell her that's colloquial English."

Ralphie asks, "Are there any frogs in the crick?"

"Look close; you might see tadpoles."

The group crouches on the bank and studies the shallows.

"What's that? It's moving!" cries Charlene.

"Aha, what sharp eyes you have! It's a hair snake."

Charlene blushes with pleasure as Mr. Dougan gently extricates a smooth black string coiled around a reed and holds it writhing on his palm. "It's harmless. When I was a kid, I used to put hairs from horses' tails in the crick, hoping they'd turn into hair snakes, but they never did. Never could figure out why." He sits back on his heels. "Listen to the birds, singing and marking out their territories. I know where a killdeer's nest is; you can see it if you're very careful. The mother will pretend she has a broken wing; she'll try to lure us away from her eggs. You'll have to cross the crick on the stepping stones."

Girl Scouts with a calf, in front of the round barn.

He leads the group farther into the pasture, and, sure enough, a brown bird rises from the grass and hops and flutters ahead of them. But they aren't fooled and approach close enough to see the speckled eggs lying in a hollow on the ground. Then they back carefully away.

"She'll return as soon as we're gone," says Ron Dougan. "Look. The cows in the next field are coming to see us. Did you notice that they were in that far corner when we first arrived? Now they're almost here. Cows don't look it, but they're very curious. If you run and yell they'll bolt, but if you stand quietly by the fence, they'll come right up to you. That single strand is an electric fence—it gives the cows a small shock, enough to keep them in the pasture. Don't you try touching it!"

While the cows graze their way toward them, Ronald relates the story of when he was ten and given a dime to tend cows but let them wander into Mr. Blodgett's corn because he was so absorbed reading a book. By the end of the story, the cows are in a row before the still children. Two of the boldest cows stretch their necks over the fence and chuff their grassy breath into the children's faces. There is a long, quiet pause of child-cow communication. Suddenly there's a screech. The cows rear back, the children jump back, and then there's another, wilder screech.

When the moment is untangled, the cows have hightailed away, Billy is blubbering with his fingers in his mouth, and Charlene, bawling, is struggling up from the ground. She's smeared with manure from shoes to hair ribbons. The class is aghast, the teacher and mothers frozen.

Mr. Dougan strides to the little girl and pulls her up by one slippery arm. He pats Billy on the back. "Now we've all learned that electric fences work," he says cheerfully. "Billy's a true scientist, experiment and see. Stop crying, Charlene, any kid that can spot a hair snake can handle a little cow dung. We'll go to the Big House and you'll be right in no time."

At the crick, he and Charlene scrub their hands, and Ronald wets his

Schoolkids hang over the horse yard fence, watching farm animals. The girl on the right is Jackie's third daughter, Gillian.

handkerchief to wipe the worst from her face. Then, with a sniffling Charlene holding one of his hands and a chastened Billy holding the other, he leads the way back up the lane. He tells them all, "It's a matter of how you're raised. A country kid can run through a pasture and never step on anything, while a town kid picks his way and steps on everything." Charlene manages a wan smile.

He tells them Mrs. Anderson lives at the Big House and cooks and cleans for the hired men. She's the sort of woman, he says, who is a match for any emergency.

At the back door he introduces Charlene. "We have a little job for you here, Pat." With clucks of sympathy, Mrs. Anderson is already pulling Charlene into the house.

Ronald takes the others into an empty circular metal grain bin and closes the door. "This is the hollering house," he tells them in the dark. "Let's hear you holler." The deafening reverberations that roll off the metal are highly satisfactory to all the hollerers.

They go to the milkhouse and Ronald sets first Mike and then Betsy on a huge scales. "Just as I thought," he says. "A kindergartener still weighs about half as much as a full milk can." He shows them the bottling process and passes out white milk-room caps for everyone, with an extra to the teacher for Charlene. As they leave, they meet a child dashing out the back door of the Big House. She's dressed in shirt and blue jeans, the sleeves and cuffs rolled up and the waist well belted in. It's Charlene, dressed in the clothes of Mrs. Anderson's youngest son. She's had a shower, shampoo, and her clothes are in the washing machine.

The children troop up into the haymow of the round barn. At this time of year the hay is practically gone, and the dark rafters are far overhead. Mr. Dougan reads them "The Aims of This Farm," printed on the silo. A photographer shows up and takes their picture throwing ears of corn into the feed-grinding machine. They wince at its rattle and bang, and then poke their fingers into the stream of bran and corn meal pouring from the spout. Ronald munches, but they decline to taste it. Then they go again to the lower barn.

The cows are there, now, lined up in their stanchions. The barn hands are washing udders before milking. Ronald shows how to hold the tits. Billy is the first one on the milking stool; he manages to squeeze out a few drops. After everyone who wants a turn has had one, Ronald takes over and squirts milk into the mouths of the daring while all the rest squeal. He never misses. "I could hit a sparrow at ten feet when I was your age," he brags. "Well, maybe not five or six years old. But by the time I was eight, I was milking two cows a day. I knew every freckle on Daisy's udder." The kindergarten faces show respect and envy.

Someone remembers the secret. "When do we sing Gertrude to sleep?"

"Let's get her now," says Ronald. They go to the henhouse and crowd in to see the eggs. The laying hens look at the intruders with sharp-eyed distrust.

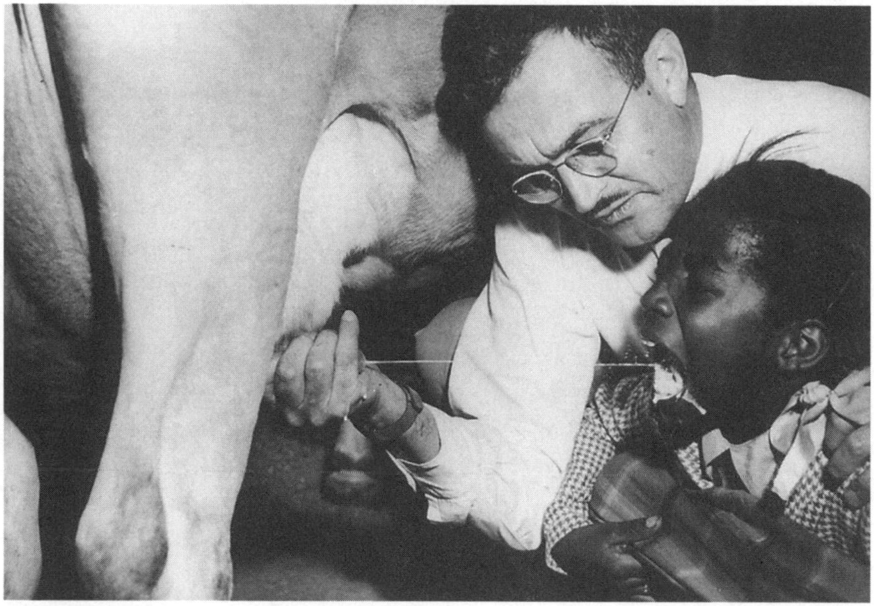

Ron Dougan has an unerring aim when it comes to squirting milk into schoolkids' mouths.

"Where are you, Gertrude?" Ronald croons. "Ah, there you are. Here's a fine bunch of children waiting to sing to you." The children whisper and nudge as he captures a white hen and tucks her under his arm. They go to the lawn in front of the milkhouse and sit in a circle. Ronald flexes Gertrude's foot for them, showing how she and other birds can go to sleep on a perch and not fall off, since their weight settling down on their legs causes the claws to tighten, rather than relax, and grip the branch firmly.

"Now what does a bird do with her head when she's ready for sleep?"

"She puts it under her wing!" cries Alison.

Ronald tucks Gertrude's head under her wing and holds her in front of him like a neat package. "Now, if you'll sing a lullaby while I rock her, I

Not all the children's names are in the records, but the little girl in the scarf is Kathy Martingilio of Gaston School.

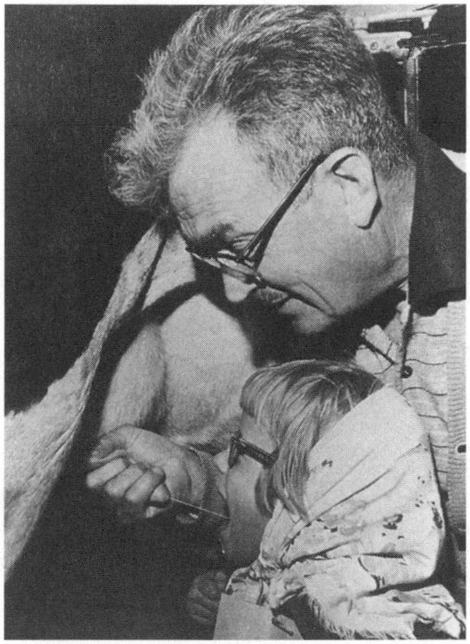

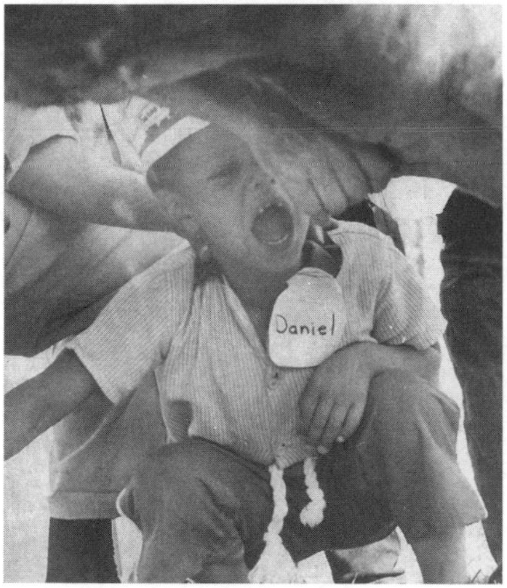

The black-clad ankle is unmistakably Ron Dougan's.

think we can put her to sleep. But you must sing very sweetly and soothingly. Can you do that?"

All heads bob vigorously, eyes dart at one another, giggles are smothered.

"Ready, boys and girls?" says Mrs. Wildermuth, and hums a note. Then their voices ring out, "Lullaby, and good night, wi-ith roses bedi-ight . . ."

Ronald, swinging the chicken back and forth, opens his eyes and mouth wide. He grins all the way through the lullaby, and the children's eyes dance while they sing. At the last note he sets the chicken carefully on the grass. She lies there, motionless. Everyone is quiet and breathless, watching her.

"Your singing has put her into an enchanted sleep," Ronald whispers. "It's the first time she's ever heard 'Brahms' Lullaby.' Before, it's always been 'Rockabye Baby.' Maybe she'll sleep a hundred years. How can we wake her?"

"With a kiss! My brother told me!" bursts out Ralphie.

"Do you want to be the prince who kisses her awake?"

Ralphie recoils. "I wouldn't kiss a chicken!"

But Charlene will. She creeps forward on hands and knees and kisses Gertrude's feathers. The chicken leaps up with a flap and squawk, and Charlene falls backward for the second time that day. Everyone cheers. Ronald catches Gertrude and gives her to a hired man who has just come up with a case of chocolate milk.

"Are you ready for a treat?"

"Yes!" cries the class and whirls to look not at Ron Dougan and the milk but at one of the mothers, who is coming with a broad, flat box. She sets it on the grass beside the milk case, and the class squirms into a tight knot around their host. "Open it! Open it!"

"Something will jump out and bite me," objects Ronald.

"No, no! Open it!"

As Ronald lifts the lid, Mrs. Wildermuth gives a note again, and the class bawls out, "Happy birthday to you, happy birthday to you . . ."

"A cake!" Ronald cries. "How did anyone know it's my birthday today?"

"It was listed in the church bulletin," Mrs. Wildermuth says.

"And we made you cards!" says Freddy. The other mother produces a sheaf of brightly colored manila folders.

Ronald cuts the cake, after admiring the frosting: chocolate, with a white chicken, white egg, white bottle of milk, and white writing saying HAPPY BIRTHDAY RON DOUGAN. Then everyone eats cake and drinks chocolate milk. Ronald exclaims over each card and identifies the artist. Charlene snuggles close as a burr until Mrs. Anderson calls from the Big House. Then she scampers off, to return in a few minutes in her own clothes. They have been washed, dried, and her hair ribbons ironed.

She holds Ronald's hand as they walk to the cars. "Can I write about your accident in a Dougan's milk ad?" he asks. "Put it in the newspaper?"

"Oh, no!" cries Charlene, mortified.

He shakes his head regretfully. He'd like to use the line about town kids and country kids. Maybe on the next visit someone will only step in a cow pie. And there's plenty else to write about from this visit. The hair snake. The killdeer nest. Billy touching the electric fence. The birthday surprise. The different song.

"Thank you for the party," he says to the children. "And thank you for 'Brahms' Lullaby.' Will you tell your little brothers and sisters that that's the lullaby Gertrude wants when Mrs. Wildermuth comes again with next year's kindergarten?"

"Yes! Yes!" they all cry.

"It's such a long time away," says Ronald. "How about an encore right now?"

Mrs. Wildermuth gives the note and there's a final sweet chorus before the class climbs into the cars and is driven away. Ronald watches them out of sight, then turns toward the office. Time to squeeze in some of the more humdrum aspects of running a business; two more classes of schoolchildren will show up tomorrow, morning and afternoon. It's great advertising to have every kid in the city visit Dougan's. But that's not the only reason he does it. He hums the tune of "Brahms' Lullaby" as he goes inside.

42 AUNT LILLIAN'S BURIAL REQUESTS

Though five years older, Aunt Lillian outlives her brother, Wesson, by about fourteen months. Nobody finds her two letters about her burial, written in black ink in her firm wide handwriting, until years after she's buried. They are among Grampa's private papers. The first is written August 18, 1934, when Lillian is seventy and the Great Depression is severe; the envelope is labeled IMPORTANT.

> To my brother W. J. Dougan (or to Ronald Dougan):
>
> Wesson dear should you outlive me I request this of you. First, it is from *preference.* Second, I wish to set a *precedence* that a poor man may be able and *dare* to die without pauperizing his family for years, by having to pay for padded boxes and silver mountings and still be called a sane man. This is my wish—to be buried in an oak box made by Mark Kellor, if convenient, wood from the Hill Farm, with iron handles. No padding inside and out, a bed of alfalfa and pillow of same covered with a white sheet. I wish to be wrapped in a white sheet, if summer, and wool blanket, if winter. I prefer no *aid* from undertaker or beauty parlor man or hearse. I am very sincere in this as have seen so many put under heavy expense for all the foolishness. One family in Stevens Point who in trying to pay, died in turn—were poor people but proud—living in a rented house keeping boarders. In about four years, three beautiful girls died. Why such foolishness. It's just got to come down. My box will be strong and pure with iron handles and no tapestry inside or out. My hearse a farm truck and the lads from farm to carry me. It does not matter where I am put to rest; but I love the farm. Next to Mother would be near the farm, where you could give me a thought as you pass by.
>
> I know you will do it for my sake and others.
>
> Sister Lillian

The second letter is on another sheet and was written in 1936 or 1937. She has changed her mind about where she wants to be buried:

> Dear Family—
>
> Should anything happen to me I prefer my last home to be in Grove Prairie Cemetery beside Father. Now this does not make anything happen just sensible precaution—and I doubt if much if any extra expense as there is no place here in Beloit and I prefer the old cemetery—when the time comes. It's about three miles from Reeseville where I worked four years.
>
> Love, Lillian
>
> I'm so happy Ronalds are going to have a farm house.

This last sentence refers to Ronald and Vera's recent purchase of the Snide farm up the road from the dairy, and their preparing to remodel the house.

In 1942, with Gladys Moore, who works in the office, as the witness, Lillian writes on the envelope that contains the documents of her loans to her nephew and her brother, "To anyone who is concerned: in case anything happens to me, my note of three thousand dollars against Ron Dougan is canceled—also note against W. J. Dougan of one thousand, four hundred and fifty dollars also canceled *after funeral expenses.* Lillian Dougan."

Aunt Lillian dies July 7, 1950. She is buried in a two-hundred-eighty-dollar commercial casket with a white quilted lining. It's doubtful the fittings are silver. She wears a Sunday dress and is shrouded in neither sheet nor blanket. A hearse carries her to the family plot in the cemetery at the start of Colley Road, where there is space for her beside her mother and near her sister Ida, with whom she continually quarreled. (Grampa writes to their sister Della in 1935, "Ida is better than she was last year. Lillian's health is not good and their relations do not improve any." However, when Della makes a rare visit to her two sisters, the bickering in the house on Bushnell Street is nonstop and three way; Grampa is lucky not to be able to hear it.) Aunt Lillian's interment

-loved brother Wesson. Her total funeral expenses are
-nty dollars, reduced to three hundred and forty-six dol-
-ount is settled in less than ten days.

idea of a farm wagon and homemade box. She especially
-f spending eternity on a bed of alfalfa, like an oyster Rocke-
-ant her pillow covered with a Dougan Hybrid Seed Corn sack,
-ten, when she passes by the corner of the cemetery where the
graves can be seen, she remembers Aunt Lillian's wish for a thought
gives her one, and a kindly one at that—even though Aunt Lillian did al-
-ways favor Craig, because he was the boy, and gave him the most dessert.

43 STEALING MELONS

Ron's grandchildren, Peter, Jerry, and Katie, ages seven, six, and five, are visiting from Madison. They're Joan's kids; it's summer, 1956. They've done most of the things the Beloit schoolchildren do when they visit the farm, such as putting a chicken to sleep, and some things the schoolchildren don't, such as picking sweet corn in the garden and eating it fifteen minutes later boiled and dripping with butter.

"What are we going to do today?" Peter asks, his elbows on his grandfather's desk at the dairy office, his chin in his hands, his bottom waggling from side to side.

Ron pauses over his ledger. He considers. His eyes brighten. "My neighbor has a melon patch that I've been keeping a watch on. I think they're at the peak of perfection right now. What say we steal melons?"

"Steal melons!" gasp all three.

"Stealing's *wrong,* " declares Katie.

Ronald rolls his eyes heavenward. "Well, yes, but I think the Lord would forgive us for one or two little melons. And Albert Marston has such a lot, he'll never miss a few. Why, he might have so many he'll have to feed them to the pigs."

The three look dubious.

"Tell you what," their grandfather says. "I'll do the stealing. Because you are underage, the law probably won't consider you accessories. And when you good little Catholics go to confession, just tell the priest your pagan Grampa led you into sin. He'll give you a few Hail Marys. A small price to pay for a delicious stolen melon. They'll be prayers of thanksgiving rather than penance. Come on!"

"He's just fooling," Peter advises his sister and brother.

They follow their grandfather to the Big House. He borrows a sharp knife, four spoons, and a salt shaker.

"Don't get caught," warns Pat Anderson. "People who have their melons stolen can turn ugly."

"I know," says Ron. "We'll be hidden by the cornfield, except for that one open space where we'll have to keep low."

He gives them each a spoon to carry. The grandchildren's eyes are wide. Grandpa isn't kidding after all! They scamper alongside him down Colley Road.

"Keep a lookout. If anyone comes along, hide your spoons and act like we're just taking a walk. Now quick! Here's where we dodge into the corn."

Ronald crouches down and scuttles across the ditch and under the fence. The three follow. Once in the field, they straighten up.

"Now tiptoe behind me," their grandfather instructs. "Don't talk above a whisper."

In single file, they sneak well into the field, following a corn row.

"We're about level with the melon patch behind the barn now," breathes Ron. "If we turn here we'll be going straight toward it. Keep looking down the rows we pass, and tell me if you see anyone on the road."

Every few steps there's a new corn aisle to peer down furtively, but they can't see the road; too many corn leaves get in the way. The excitement of the escapade begins to tell on the three. They giggle.

"Quiet!" warns their grandfather. There is instant silence.

Just before the corn ends, when they can see open land through the stalks and leaves ahead, they all hunker down.

"There's the melon patch," Ron whispers, pointing across a cleared space to a low tangle of green leaves with buff-colored globes scattered among them. "Muskmelons! My mouth is watering already."

"How do we get across?" whispers Jerry.

"First we reconnoiter—look all around. Is anyone coming? Now we crawl. Keep down; here's where they can see us!"

On hands and knees, the three creep over the rough grass behind their grandfather.

"Run!" he instructs, and hunched over, they all race for the patch, throwing themselves on their stomachs beside it.

"We're safe," pants Ron. "Hidden behind the barn! Now—there's an art to eating melons. You've heard of Japanese tea ceremonies? Well, this is the Turtle Township muskmelon ceremony. In it we must use all our senses and not omit any. First, we listen. We have to thump a melon to be sure it's ripe." He rises to his knees and thumps the nearest melon, cocking his head. "No—too green." He thumps another one. "Ah! That's more like it. Hear the difference?" He snaps it from the stem.

"Now we look and feel and smell." He caresses the melon, takes a long sniff, and then holds it where the three can study it. "See what a beautiful round shape!"

"It's got a pattern all over of little raised ridges, like rivers," observes Peter.

"Sort of yellow ridges," says Jerry.

"And green skin just underneath," adds Katie.

They take turns holding the melon, rubbing their hands over it, putting their noses close, and taking deep breaths of its fragrance.

"There's no perfume on this earth sweeter than a ripe, sun-warmed melon," their grandfather says. "And finally, we taste!" He takes the knife and cuts a wedge, like carving the eye of a jack-o'-lantern. The wedge comes out orange and juicy, a pale seed clinging to the end.

"That's called 'plugging a melon.' Here, tell me if we've made a good choice."

He flicks off the seed and holds the wedge while each takes a nibble. They all chew thoughtfully and nod. He then bites off the remainder, close to the rind.

"You're right, an excellent one," says Ron, swallowing. He cuts the melon in half and with his spoon guts the wet pulp and seeds onto the ground. He gives the halves to Katie and Jerry, along with the salt shaker. "Just a tap of salt," he instructs, "to bring out the flavor!"

He and Peter each pick their own melons, thumping and rejecting several first. They all sit cross-legged beside the melon patch and spoon in the orange meat.

"For this part of the ceremony, it's good manners to gobble and slurp," says their grandfather. "Dribble! Get juice up to your ears!"

They gobble and slurp all the melon they can eat. There is melon over everybody; melon mess litters the grass.

"What a feast!" sighs Ron. "I'm replete! Now we have to sneak away as cautiously as we came, so Mr. Marston will never know!"

"But what about the rinds?" worries Katie. "He can tell somebody's been here!"

"The rinds," their grandfather considers. "I'm forgetting the end of the ceremony. Here's what we do with the rinds." He picks one up, rips it across, tears it with his teeth, and flings it into the patch. "Now he'll think raccoons have done it!"

The three rip and fling their rinds with energy. Then they creep and dash across the open ground to the protection of the cornfield, peek behind to be sure they've not been seen, and follow corn aisles east and north till they regain Colley Road.

"I'm relieved you're back safely," says Pat Anderson when they return the spoons and knife and salt. "Melon stealing can be dangerous."

"Every kid should have the experience of stealing a melon," Ron says with satisfaction. "We have here a gang that Fagin would be proud of."

The three beam and nod vigorously. They are sticky from ear to ear, from head to toe.

"Let's go wash in the cow tank," their grandfather says. "Then I've got to get back to the office."

Jerry's eyes dance as they leave the kitchen. "What are we going to steal tomorrow, Grandpa?" he asks.

44 ESTHER, THE REST OF THE STORY

On December 27, 1923, when Ronald is halfway through his year in France, he receives family photos sent to him for Christmas. He comments with warmth and enthusiasm on the portraits of his parents and brother, and then he writes:

> But Esther! What has the girl been doing with herself? She has always been attractive, but in this picture she is doubly delightful. I want to get home so I can take her and show her off. For a minute I thought Trever was sending me a picture of a beauty prize winner at Madison.

But not long after that, he responds to an agitated letter from his mother about a hired hand who's made advances to Esther:

> Your letter about O. J. made me wish I were proficient in profanity. I've just written to Trev airing my feelings and imagine I'll still be angry enough when I get home to give O. J. a hot half hour. I'm big enough to rather disfigure him. Will write to Esther. I'm all for the kid. She is as surely my sister as if she got her pug nose from Dad.

His letter to Trever is even more vehement:

> Of all the low-down hounds I've ever heard of! The longer I live the less confidence I have in the average human. That's not quite true, because I have known more of the decent sort than the rotters. Just the same, from time to time I've run across some pant-wearing sons of bitches that would turn the stomach of a worm. . . . But about O. J. That bastard makes me want to air every profanity I've ever heard. Don't know what you have done, but if I should hear you had met him somewhere, and battered in his face I'd be all for you. I imagine I'll stay sore enough so that when I see him I'll give him a nasty half hour. Look out for the police, but at that there are worse things than a night in jail. Use your head

> if anything comes up. Hit him for me if you can. Whatever may be said to the contrary there is a lot of satisfaction in fists.

Trever is now starting his second semester at the university. On February 23 he writes, in a letter to his parents,

> I'm beginning to agree with you, Dad, that Esther is fairly wise for her age. I was talking to Ernest and he said, "It surely is queer the way Esther can hoodwink her parents." I said that she wasn't getting by with much that you and mother didn't know about. Then I asked him where he got all his information. He said that he wasn't on the place a day before he heard that she was "fast" and that she knew how to "spoof" her folks. She seemed to be the subject of conversation around the place. He said that she let Walley "pet" her and that she didn't go to choir practice sometimes when she was supposed to be there. Mother, please don't say anything to her about the source of this information. You probably know as much as I've told you already, but she will bear watching a little closer I think. As you say, if we can only get her through this critical period safely she will grow to be an extraordinary woman. See how impressions of her are acquired, though. I've often wondered if she thinks of Ron and me as brothers. I wondered more than ever when she kissed me good bye. It didn't seem at all like a little sister's peck ought to be—as I've often said, she would be lots better off in a good girls' school. From all the girls I've met, I think the girls that go away to school are the best behaved, best appearing, and most reserved. I think that your opinion of the boarding-school type is not characteristic of the majority of them, judging from those that I've met. At any rate she would be better off than where she is: in a school where she has no decent companions, dirty little evil minded boys and silly, boy crazy girls, and at home where she is eyed by a bunch of evil minded no-accounts.

Wesson takes some note of Trever's warning, and when he can find a sufficient work-related reason, he lets Walley—Walter Lake—go. He and Eunice do not alter Esther's schooling, however. He writes to Trever, a month or two later, in the spring:

> We realize that our perplexing kids are emerging into the most dependable and beautiful strong manhood and will take their places in the

> world's work, help lift its burdens and share its joys. You have me approaching old age too fast. I am not nearly sixty. I am only fifty six and I do not expect to be any more aged in four years. Not with my boys and girl to help with the lift. Yes, the girl. Esther is a very sweet happy little girl these days. Much better since "W" left. We do hope to tide her over these critical years and save her for usefulness and her happiness.

Ronald has become engaged to an American girl in France and then, to everyone's astonishment and some consternation, married. His and Vera's letters of their wedding precede them home. Esther rushes to relate the event to Eloise, who is slowly recovering from a winter of pneumonia and scarlet fever: "And a dog and a cat slept on Vera's wedding gown, where it was laid out on a bed the night before, and a soiled patch had to be cut out, but from a place it didn't really show; and Vera wrote, 'There'll be no dogs and cats underfoot in our house for a while!' That's what she said!"

The newlyweds arrive in Beloit in late summer, and Vera meets the whole family. Esther shows Vera her room, and Vera notices the doll sitting on a small chair beside the dresser. "What is her name?" Vera asks, and Esther tells her the doll's name is Agnes.

During Esther's sophomore and junior years, Vera pays attention to her young sister-in-law. She gives her piano lessons. She teaches her singing and accompanies her as Esther sings in a clear, sweet soprano. She gives her parties with her friends, a birthday party and a treasure hunt. They put on little entertainments in the parlor of the Big House where Esther sings and recites. Esther helps with baby Joan. Vera convinces her mother-in-law to buy Esther a white chiffon dress, on sale, just her size. Esther is thrilled. She sings in it at one of the programs and it gets smudged. When Eunice washes it, it shrinks. Vera finds Esther in her bedroom, holding the ruined frock and crying. It's the first really attractive dress she's ever had.

Esther has several high-school boyfriends and connections with college men. Eunice mentions to Trever, in his sophomore year at the university,

Esther at sixteen.

"Esther has just gone out with Harold Risley; I guess you know him; he was in school with you. I don't know him, but the Burnetts say he is a nice boy. So many boys wanting to take her out—I don't know what I am to do as she grows older."

After a snowstorm, several college men come to take her to a school event but can't get past the railroad tracks at Marstons' because of drifts. They leave the car on the far side of the tracks and mush to the farm, fetch Esther, wade back on the tracks they've made, and thence to town. Later Eunice says to Lura, in Eloise's hearing, "Well, you can certainly say one thing for Esther, and that's that she's popular with the boys. It's too bad Eloise isn't." Lura is furious. But Eloise knows that Esther has something to sell.

It's at this point that Esther's thievery finally becomes apparent to the family. Ronald has kept a coin collection since boyhood. When the money came in from the routes, he would go through the change and trade common pennies for the rare 1909 Lincoln penny with *VDB* on the bottom, which had been discontinued shortly after its minting. He had fifty or sixty such pennies. He also had liberty head nickels and a number of coins, both foreign and domestic, given him by people knowing his interest. At some point, he goes to add some unusual French coins to his collection. He finds that it's been stripped of everything that will pass for money. And Vera's lovely French underthings, bought in Paris from her own small salary for her trousseau, gradually vanish from her dresser drawers.

When Esther is asked about these losses she knows nothing. But Wesson moves the cashbox from his desk to the apartment of Lester and Mildred Stam, over the milkhouse, and the routemen must now go up there to check in their money.

The family isn't aware of high-school whispers, but Eloise is. In Esther's sophomore year, Eloise reports again to Esther the rumors that she is pregnant. Esther laughs, tosses her head, and retorts, "I don't care what anyone says!"

By that spring, matters have so escalated that Wesson feels constrained to write to Esther's caseworker at the orphanage:

> Mrs. Grube
> Sparta, Wisconsin
>
> Dear Madam,
>
> I am writing you in regard to Esther. There is no need for immediate attention to this, but I feel you should be kept in close knowledge of her attitude and movements. We are very anxious that she should develop to be the beautiful and useful woman that she is capable of being, if we only can direct her aright.
>
> The great trouble with her is her subtle deceitfulness, lying, and secretiveness. She tells us nothing except as we face her with the facts and she must confess. Then she goes no farther than she has to. She justifies herself in this because she is afraid to tell us. This is all nonsense, as we have

never punished her, and are entirely in sympathy with the young. When she is caught in stealing and lying, we do not condone it and tell her it is all right, as she seems to have an idea other parents do. We try to show her the wrong of it and try to fix some penalty which will enforce the lesson. For example, last December Mrs. Dougan and I had to go away on a lecturing trip. We were gone three days. We placed Esther on her honor. Mrs. Dougan told her not to have any company, and not to go out, but to help in the home, study, and attend to her schoolwork. Esther was wanting a new coat. Mrs. Dougan told her if she lived right while we were away, she could have one, if not, she must wear the old one all winter. When we came home she told us she had gone to a movie with one of the boys from town. We withheld the coat. It is in this way we have tried to control her and teach her.

It seems to me she is growing worse in her deceit than when she was younger. She is now justifying herself in it. The recent developments alarm us. Esther is bright enough and forward enough to carry her plans to serious consequences. She has taken to forging Mrs. Dougan's name to excuses for absences and requests for excuses from school. She has gone to a store and purchased for herself and had the bill charged to Mrs. Dougan. (This is the incident Mrs. Dougan told you of. I do not know of others yet, but do not know when they will turn up.) If Esther can carry this through now, what will she do when she goes into college and wants fur coats and diamonds?

This shoe dealer remarked, "The trouble is, your daughter makes a wonderful impression, and could get trusted anywhere."

Yesterday morning the school secretary telephoned to Mrs. Dougan to find out if she knew Esther had been out of school all day the day before. Of course it was a surprise to us. We started to investigate, both myself and Mrs. Dougan giving our entire day and evening trying to unravel the facts. After three hours of questioning of Esther, I had gathered only partial accounts of her absences and forged excuses, and where she went, and with whom. In the afternoon we went to the principal of the high school, and found that Esther had not told of one-half of her absences. She had repeatedly lied to the Secretary, putting in a forged request to be excused and explaining that there was something going on at the church and her mother wanted her to help, or that her mother wanted her excused to drive the auto.

Then she has gone to shows or made dates, and sometimes she has gone to the home of one of the girls. She asked, a little time ago, to stay down overnight with one of the girls because the teacher in English wanted the class to read a certain book in groups of two or three. Mrs. Dougan agreed, on Esther's promising that they would study and not go anywhere or have any boys there. Esther made this request and agreed to the conditions in a delightful sweet mode. She at once went to the Bank and conferred with a boy (one of the young clerks who is sweet on her), and they arranged a date. He took her to Rockford. She never studied a minute that night and kept this from us until last night when Mrs. Dougan demanded of her to tell just how much she had been with this young man unbeknownst to us. She told of this, and other times. We think she has told all in this respect. (This boy is of a good family and is all right so far as we know, but that does not lessen the danger of a young girl like her planning and making her own dates unbeknown to her elders.)

We have talked kindly to Esther, showed her the danger, and held up to her the possibilities of becoming a good, well educated, and accomplished woman. She seems to want to start anew and do better. We will give her another chance. This is our plan for the present:

1st. We have instructed the principal of the school to expect her in school every minute during school hours; to mail her report card (she has signed and returned her own card once at least); and not to accept any oral or written excuses.

2nd. She is not to go to any show of any kind for at least six months, unless we take her to some we deem educational.

3rd. She is not to make any "dates."

4th. She must go and come from school in the regular bus. (She has been letting others bring her from school. Three or four boys and girls pile into a two passenger Ford, or one or two boys bring her home. We have never liked it. Now it must stop.)

Should you deem any of these rules too severe, or unnecessary, or should you want to suggest any others, we will be glad to confer with you.

I have told Esther that if in a single incident she violates these rules, I will at once report the matter to you, and abide by your decision.

We will surely have to make some other arrangement for Esther's

> schooling, before Fall, unless she mends decidedly. The opportunities for deceit are too great in the High School. Some boarding school might be better. We will talk this over when we see you, and after Esther has had a chance to make good.
>
> Sincerely yours,
>
> W. J. Dougan
>
> The incidents and facts as reported in this letter are true and correct.

Only four days after this letter, Esther becomes ill. Eunice writes to Trever:

> I must tell you about Esther. Thursday she felt kind of sick and had a sore throat. Friday she had to go to bed and have the doctor. Saturday she had a fever of 104 ¼ and felt terrible. I sent for the doctor again and he examined her and said it looked suspicious. Sunday he brought Dr. Field out and they both pronounced it scarlet fever. She was not very bad today but the doctor said she must leave home and go to the detention hospital. She will have to stay there four weeks. She doesn't seem to care. She has a young nurse, and if she is not bad she will soon be helping her, cooking and waiting on the other patients. We fumigated her room and sprayed lisol on all her bedding and clothing, and I guess nobody else will get it. . . . It seems so queer to think Esther is over there. Am so sorry.

Esther isn't treated at home on account of the danger of contagion to the milk. Not everyone with scarlet fever goes to the pesthouse. Eloise hadn't, the previous year, because she was too sick to be moved. But her father, who milked the Marston cows, had had to stay out of the house for four weeks. He put his plate on the kitchen step and went away while Lura, or his mother, Mrs. Smith, put his meal on it. Then he returned and fetched it. He slept in the milkhouse and talked to his wife through an open window. Had he gone into the house, the milk couldn't have been sold.

But Esther is not too sick, and the Big House is filled with men who handle the milk. It's sensible for her to be the one to leave. And for Esther, being at the pesthouse is a reprieve. She's freed from school for a while, freed from the heavy load of housework she does at home, and freed from opprobrium. Her parents' rules are more oppressive than a house of detention.

She is released from the pesthouse the end of April. On May 25, Eddie Pfaff, one of the hired men who lives in the Big House, returns late from town. He sees Floyd Peters, another boarder, crawl out of Esther's window, cross the roof, and climb into his own window. The next day, he reports it to Daddy Dougan. Wesson and Eunice can scarcely believe it. They don't want to believe it.

"Wait and watch yourself," Eddie advises.

Esther's bedroom is a small one behind her father's. Its only entrance is through his room. That night, after Esther is in bed, Wesson makes his usual bedtime preparations but lies down in his clothes. Eunice's room is across the staircase, so Esther doesn't know that her mother, instead of going to bed, is outside watching her window from the bushes by the milkhouse.

The house settles down to sleep. After a bit, Eunice sees Floyd emerge from his window, cross the roof, and slide into Esther's window. She stands in the dark several moments, breathing hard and holding her arms tightly around herself; then she enters the house, goes rapidly to Wesson's room, and shakes his shoulder. The two fling open Esther's door and switch on the light. They surprise Esther and Floyd together in bed.

The pair can't deny the situation. But Esther cries, says that they have done nothing wrong, that they care for each other but they have no place to meet, no place to sit, and so Floyd has come to her bedroom. She looks straight in her father's face, with her large, tear-brimmed eyes, and swears their innocence.

Wesson, white faced, fires Floyd on the spot. "If Esther turns out to be pregnant," he roars, "she is a minor and a ward of the state. I will see you go to the penitentiary!"

Floyd leaves but sneaks onto the farm the next day and beats up Eddie Pfaff. Wesson mails him his final paycheck.

Esther is not pregnant. Eunice reports to Lura and Mrs. Smith, "Esther just swore that they hadn't done a thing wrong at all, just cozied up in bed because it was chilly." Eunice believes Esther. Mrs. Smith, Lura, and Eloise do not, but they have learned long since not to say anything.

Esther spends a restricted summer and starts her junior year. She's been studying piano with Vera, but this fall she goes into town and takes lessons from Vinola Seaver. Each week she's given fifty cents to give to her teacher. It's three months before Miss Seaver, a timid woman, screws up her courage and calls Eunice to ask when the Dougans are going to pay for Esther's lessons. That money and other money, Eloise knows, is going toward a Gruen watch that Esther is having held for her at a jeweler's. On the noon hour, Eloise sometimes goes with Esther while Esther pays on it. Its price is thirty-seven dollars and fifty cents, and she plans to give it to Floyd Peters for Christmas. His wages, in the six months he worked on the Dougan farm, were forty-five dollars a month; had he not had room and board he would have received sixty dollars. The watch represents more than two weeks' pay.

Later, when Wesson and Eunice learn about the watch, and W. J. asks the jeweler how he could have let a sixteen-year-old schoolgirl buy an expensive item like that, he responds, "But she's a Dougan, and the Dougan name is as good as gold!"

Eloise has gone out several times with Paul Erickson, one of the young farmworkers. He suggests that they bring Esther along with them one evening. It will look like he's squiring both girls, but they'll pick up Floyd in town for a double date. Eloise is uncomfortable with the idea and makes an excuse not to go, so the plan falls through.

Christmas comes and goes. As the new year progresses, Esther, always lovely, becomes daily more radiant. Wesson puts his arm around her, pulls her to his knee and says, "Little lass, you're blossoming into a bonnie woman!" Eunice fumes. She tells Wess sharply not to say such things. "It'll go to her head, all you men fussing over her looks and praising her all the time!" she cries, and her hand jabs and jabs as she spells the reprimand out to Wesson on her flashing fingers.

In March Esther is driving to town and stops at Eloise's. Out by the mailbox they chat. Eloise says, "At school they're saying again that you're pregnant." Esther doesn't laugh this time. She cries and says, "Why do they always say these terrible things about me?" She raises her large eyes to Eloise and asks point-blank, "You don't think I'm pregnant, do you?"

"No," says Eloise, and believes her.

By spring, Esther's social life has ceased. Her boyfriends, including Russ Baumann, the one she's told Eloise she is crazy about, have nothing to do with her. There are no more dates. A dentist's son, Eldon Freebach, had been trying to go out with her. She had thought him too juvenile. But now she's in need of fun and telephones him several times. Repeatedly, he refuses to come to the phone. His mother tells Eloise's mother, "I don't know what's gone wrong with him—he's had such a crush on Esther Dougan, and now he won't have a thing to do with her, and it's embarrassing. I know the Dougans must wonder what's wrong with him. . . ."

Esther turns seventeen in June. All spring and early summer, with no male diversion, Esther turns to Eloise for recreation. Eunice says to Eloise, "Esther's been more a friend to you this summer than she's been in a long time." She goes on to Lura, "She's been more of a daughter to me. She's been so pleased with everything I've sewed for her—before, she's always wanted everything so tight, and we'd fight about it. Now, she agrees with me and thinks tight looks cheap, and she wants me to make her dresses loose."

In July Eloise goes with her parents to Camp Byron, a Methodist camp for all ages. Eloise waits on tables in exchange for her meals in the big mess hall. There are dormitories, but there are also tiny cottages on the grounds, for rent or privately owned, where families can come and stay and participate in the preaching and programs, the meals, and the recreation. Eloise's grandparents have rented such a cottage, two sleeping rooms separated by a long curtain the width of the little building. Nellie Needham, Wesson's second cousin, owns a cottage. Wesson and Eunice and Esther come up near the end of July for a brief visit. With Nellie and her sister there, too, the tiny cottage is crowded; Esther asks Eloise if she can stay with her. Eloise consents, and Esther runs back and tells her parents. She and Eloise attend the camp meeting in the large tabernacle but leave before the adults. Back at Eloise's cottage Esther says, "It's so lovely and moonlight out, let's not light the lamp." Eloise agrees. The girls undress and go to bed in the dark. In the morning, when Eloise awakens, Esther is already up and dressed. At one point during the day, Eloise puts her arm around her friend's waist and is puzzled to find Esther's body as rigid and hard as a marble statue. She doesn't know that Esther has wrapped herself with five yards of muslin.

Back in Beloit, in mid-August, Floyd Peters's mother comes to Lura. She tells her that Esther is pregnant and that the Dougans don't know. She knows, because Floyd told her before he left town.

"Daddy Dougan will have me in the penitentiary," he'd said. "Mom, you do the best you can." She asks Lura's advice.

"Talk to Esther," says Lura.

Mrs. Peters says she's telephoned several times to ask Esther to meet with her, but Esther pretends her caller is a salesperson. "No . . . no . . . no, we're not interested," Esther will say and hang up.

Lura then advises her to go straight to Eunice.

From a friend who has a job selling Realsilk hosiery door to door, Mrs. Peters borrows a suitcase of samples. She knocks on the Dougan door. Esther answers. "We don't want any," she states. But Eunice comes to the door and asks her in—Realsilk is a fine product. Esther stays in the room, behind her mother and outside her vision. She shakes and shakes her head and glares with her large eyes whenever Mrs. Peters pauses in her sales pitch. Quailed, Mrs. Peters takes Eunice's generous order and leaves without delivering her message.

She next goes to the Dougans' pastor, the Reverend Mr. Misdal, at the Methodist church. She tells him the story. Mr. Misdal comes out to the farm. He tells Wesson and Eunice about Mrs. Peters's visit. Esther is called in and, in the presence of her parents and minister, hears the minister repeat the story. She breaks down and cries. They call Dr. Thayer, and he comes out immediately. He takes Esther up to her room to examine her. When he comes back down, he confirms the allegation. He says Esther is more than seven months pregnant.

The day after her parents learn of Esther's pregnancy, Wesson finds a letter on his desk in his bedroom, a large pencil scrawl on farm stationery:

> My dearest Daddy—
>
> I love you and know you care for me—and now I will tell you everything truthfully—since last night I have felt much better—more at ease—to have you know the truth about Floyd—now in regard to anyone else—no one else has ever had sexual relations with me but Floyd—all my school boyfriends have been just good pals and have always treated me very well—
>
> I will confess though that once when I was going to kindergarten when I was living in Stoughton a larger boy followed me home from school and attacked me—I told my older sister and she used to have my brother wait for me at school or another sister so I wouldn't have to come home alone.
>
> In regard to Walter Lake. He suggested to me, asking me to go for a walk in the garden with him etc.,—but I refused—he paid little more attention to me. And O. J.—he never did suggest it with words—but he came to my room that night—and he was leaning over my bed—I pushed him off—and told him to leave immediately or I would call you—he would say—but listen, I have something to tell you—I told him to leave immediately—he finally went over by the door—and I said

leave the room—he said he was afraid you'd wake up—I told him—if you didn't I would awaken you anyway—and—after standing listening to whether you were asleep or not—after a while—he left my room, closed the door, and crawled out on his hands and knees through your room.

Most all boys "try" a girl to see what she is like—and when I went with Russie Baumann—he told me he respected me more than any other girl because I held myself aloof and respected myself so much. Jim Delaney said I was different from most modern girls—and he liked me on that account—I always could hold myself aloof from any boy except Floyd—somehow I couldn't resist him—I don't know why it was and I have wished thousands of times I had won in resisting him—I am glad though that seeing I didn't that I got into trouble or likely no one would have ever known—and I feel better about it to have my sin told to someone who understands and is considerate.

I really feel as though I am nearer to being a Christian now than I ever have been. I see things so much differently—and feel a much greater responsibility.

I feel nearer to God than ever before—for anyone in my condition never knows her outcome—and she needs God's strength as well as the love of those dear to her—

Now Daddy dear I have made my confession and feel quite assured that you will stand by me in the coming crisis altho' I don't see how you can be *so* forgiving—after the great sin I have been keeping back so long—

For when Floyd used to come to my room, he came several times—we had sexual relations then and when I met him after choir it happened again—But God forgive me—because I truly am repentant and see my great mistake. I know though my future life will not be ruined by it—I am going to strive for higher things and overcome my great mistake in the past—for I know I can depend on you and Mother and with the help of God I will do my best.

Another letter appears a few days later.

Dear Daddy—

I really believe that I had better try to get along without all of yours and mother's combined efforts—I really am not worthy of them all. Mother says it will be harder for you two than for me—socially, etc.—but everyone knows I am only taken into your home and it wouldn't be such a reflection on you two if I were to go away somewhere and never return—I love you and appreciate everything you've done for me, but all I've been is worry, heartache and expense—I want my baby to be with me and if I could only go somewhere where I could have my babe and then work and care for it—I ought to do something like that because I'm to blame and should be able to take the consequences. Another thing it's too much expense for you folks and if I could work and get money to pay for it all. The only thing I'm good for anyway is housework—because it was born in me to be a domestic I guess.

This is the way I feel—that the burden is too much upon yours and mother's shoulders and that you're doing too much for me—

I am of course willing to do as you say—but God grant me find a place where I can take care of my baby—

I hope you do not misunderstand this note and my motive in writing it.

Word of Esther's condition has spread instantly. Lura says to the Marston family, "I don't believe *Eloise* could have gone through seven months of pregnancy without my knowing it," and she reports other churchwomen asserting the same thing. It does seem incredible. Eloise hears Eunice defend herself to Lura by telling about the menstrual cloths.

When Esther and Eloise both began to menstruate, near their thirteenth birthdays, each girl's mother gave her the standard supplies: a kit of bird's-eye pads to wear. It was Eloise's responsibility to set her soiled pads to soak in a mop pail of cold water, swish them around some, and leave them for her mother to finish in the washing machine. Esther's requirements, she knew, were more stringent. From her first period, she was to be responsible for the washing and wringing of her pads herself, getting out every trace of blood and keeping them in a place where none of the men could ever see them. Then she was to present them on washday to go into the machine.

Eunice tells Lura, "I noticed that I hadn't had any of Esther's pads for quite a while, and on washday I said to her, 'Where are your pads?' and she said, 'Oh, I've neglected to take care of them,' and after a bit she brought them down to me all wet and wrung out, and after that they were always on time, as punctual as clockwork." She adds, "And then she bound herself so tightly . . . and never had a sick day. . . ."

Wesson spends sleepless nights and anguished days on the problem of Esther and her baby. Eunice is so beside herself that he can't hold a reasonable conversation with her. He confides to Vera, living beyond the milkhouse in the Little House, who had typed up his letter of the previous year to Mrs. Grube. Now she types for him a letter to himself, as he thinks out loud what the family's options are in the present situation. One option is that Mrs. Peters has offered to take Esther and the baby into her own home or to take just the baby and raise it if the Dougans want to separate Esther from her child.

> *Thoughts on our difficult problem.*
>
> I am writing because all of our nerves and tempers are wrought up and on the hair trigger. It is so easy to have a misunderstanding and say things that hurt.
>
> This to me seems an ideal plan:
>
> To have Esther go to the State School for confinement, give the babe to Mrs. Peters, or better, to some unknown person. Then Esther come home, live a quiet life, taking some private or correspondence course of study, and music, and helping in the home. We to give her the affection, sympathy and loving direction she needs, some of us going with her wherever she goes outside of the home; not to watch her but to show her and others we care for her and stand by her. Then if she deceives us or fails again under the influences for us to follow the teachings of the Master in answer to the question, "How often shall I forgive?" "I say unto thee not seven times but seventy times seven (490)." Then I imagine if the Master were speaking in this age with its temptations and all thought and actions in big figures, He would multiply this to infinity.
>
> If we were able to carry out this plan, I would be glad; but I fear it is too ideal to fit human nature. Only an unusual supply of divine grace could help us to submerge the human feelings and tendencies. I can see a multitude of difficulties in it. Esther has had a good chance. Mother

took her in good faith and has tried to be a real mother to her. She has forgiven almost up to the limit of seventy times seven, and it is not strange that she has lost confidence and hope, and cannot give the mother affection to Esther now in her trouble. It is difficult and dangerous for me and the other men of the family to stand alone in doing this.

I confess I have a tender feeling toward Motherhood. I am almost nutty on this subject. I cannot harm a mother mouse, I save the homes of mother birds, not because I want their young rascals to strip my corn and steal my berries and cherries, but because I respect the mother spirit. And, with the domestic animals, I take great delight in observing the mother pig, getting her confidence and helping her in caring for her litter. Especially does the baby heifer going through her first experience of motherhood appeal to me; and I try to heed Mr. Hoard's injunction, "The cow is a mother, treat her as such."

When it comes to the motherhood of the humans, my thought and respect is only deepened and intensified. The pregnant mother is beautiful to me. This prudishness about seclusion would not be, if men and women could revere motherhood.

I mention this feeling of mine to explain my tender feeling toward our unfortunate little girl at this time, and also the danger of my manifesting this feeling as I would like to. Therefore I am convinced that under all the circumstances it is best for Esther and all concerned that she be cared for hereafter away from us. *But she must be cared for!*

The plan of going to Peters' is only an easy, cheap, and cowardly thing to do. There are three possible outcomes to it:

First, that F. returns and they marry.

Second, that F. returns and refuses to marry her, or she cannot bring herself to accept him.

Third, that F. never returns.

In the first: We all know he is a drinker, liar, gambler, prostitute, ignorant, suspicious, and an infernal coward devoid of every sense of moral obligation. Can we throw our little Esther into the hands of such and expect her to develop to a pure and useful woman?

In the second case: Esther would be there helpless, dependent, and under his evil sway. We can all imagine the result: a ruined life,—then open profligacy or prostitution.

The third alternative is the most pleasing. Then she might become the

> "Hester Prynne" of *The Scarlet Letter,* truly repentant, doing deeds of charity and kindness to all, caring for her refractory child, but a pitiable figure and a blighted life.
>
> The only plan I can see at present is to have Mrs. Grube take Esther to the Hospital, then we find a suitable home for Esther and help with her support, and Mrs. Grube will give the child to Mrs. Peters. This will separate the child from Esther, will give us a chance to keep an interest in her, and will help Esther to regain a normal girl's life. This plan would hold for a year or two, and then the future would be determined by the circumstances as Esther makes good.

Esther is aware of the storm raging about her and the various options being considered. She knows that her father has written to a Roman Catholic home for unwed mothers in Michigan and is glad when they refuse to take her in. She wants to have her baby at Peterses'; she rejects the Beloit Hospital because births there are announced in the paper. She writes a letter to Eunice and leaves it on her bed:

> Mother dear—
>
> You probably do not realize that I have seen through the past years your efforts to keep me dressed and looking so up to the minute as possible, —and all your carings for me since I was about six years old. I can see how much you took upon your hands when you took me in—and I have always wished to be a real daughter and do as you wished—even if it does seem as though I have been a miserable failure—
>
> This past summer and spring, I have really led a more sincere life than I ever have before. I have seen things through a different light. I cannot explain why and I have turned it over in my mind numberless times, why I ever let Floyd convince me, and why I yielded to temptation. It has always been farthest from my thoughts, anything of that kind—and why it happened I have tried to solve many times. Mother, I know you feel terrible for many reasons, but I want your and Daddy's help and I know I will turn out to be the right kind of woman—with your forgiveness.
>
> In regard to my baby—I love it and have always wanted one—to say was mine. I am extremely happy to think I will have one—but the conditions of course should not be as they are—nevertheless I am willing to take what comes and know God will help me—and guide me—

> I think Mrs. Peters will make it enjoyable for both me and the baby—and care for the baby especially—I think that is the best plan—but about marrying Floyd I cannot decide to do it—that will work out for itself later, possibly—
>
> Now, Mother dear, please help me and I will do my best—

But Eunice, along with Wesson, goes up to Sparta to confer with the officials of the orphanage. There they learn about Esther's biological mother, that she ran off with another man, leaving a family of four or five young children. The father, unable to cope, put them all in the state institution.

They come back and drive into the Marston dooryard. Wesson goes into the barn with Albert while Eunice comes into the house and pours out the results of the visit to Lura and Mrs. Smith. She cries and cries. "It's in the blood," Eunice wails. "Like mother, like daughter. There's nothing we could have done, nothing. . . ."

At home she tells Wesson that blood will tell and that she will not allow Esther to have her baby at the farm. She doesn't want Esther and the baby returning to the farm nor for Esther to return alone. She washes her hands of her. She's convinced that bad seed is irredeemable.

Although the Peters scenario is not what Wesson wants for Esther, he has no more alternatives. On September 26, Esther's labor begins, and he drives her over to the Peterses' home in nearby Shopiere. Dr. Thayer is called. He stops by the farm and picks up Vera. At the Peterses' house, Wesson, his face heavy, says to Vera, "I would stay, but with Eunice feeling as she does, I cannot." He returns home.

During her labor Esther writes a letter home, remembering the things she had promised to do for Trever. She's not yet aware that Eunice has refused to have her back.

> My dearest Mother and Daddy—
>
> Since I have arrived here I have had but one pain and it's past six—I don't really know if that was a false alarm or not—

> Oh! I love you two so and know how you care for me and miss you both tremendously already.
>
> I am thankful to Vera and appreciate it so much to think she is here with me. She certainly is darling to do it and give me some of her baby clothes.
>
> Mother and Daddy dear—please don't feel so brokenhearted—because I am out of my home, because I am coming back and let you know I can be a real daughter.—
>
> As far as marrying Floyd goes—I do not want to—I want to be single and finish my education as I planned. I know I can do it—and Mother I know I'll be a real help to you in every way—because I do not intend to have this ruin my life—and Daddy has given me such wonderful things to think about—I love you both immensely.
>
> Trev wanted his tux shirt and tie sent to him and his sweaters put in the cedar chest.
>
> Mother, could you send some handkerchiefs—my nightgown, petticoat, and teddy—If you could get me a brassiere, size 36 or 38, I really need one as soon as I am up and around—
>
> All my love and remember my promise—
>
> Your daughter, Esther

Mrs. Peters cooks a supper of pork chops for Vera; the doctor; her husband; Georgia, her youngest child, who is near Esther's age; and Herbert, an older son who is currently living at home. Herbert has also been a boarder at the Dougan farm, his work time roughly coinciding with his brother's, though he started some months earlier, left before Floyd's nocturnal visits, and came back as a day laborer through the summer after Floyd's firing. Ronald stops by early in the evening, holds his little sister's hand for a while, and returns home.

Esther's labor picks up. Vera administers the chloroform when Dr. Thayer directs. Esther suffers pain, but her labor is not unusually long nor difficult. Before midnight, she's delivered of a healthy boy, one with Esther's same large beautiful eyes.

"His name is Russell," Esther whispers.

In the days following, Mrs. Peters acts as nurse to Esther and the baby.

Georgia and Herbert frequently tiptoe in and peek at the little face. Wesson visits, and Ronald and Vera, and Floyd's other brother, Ross, and his sister, Leora. Eloise comes, too.

Esther says, "It was so funny. I just didn't show it till the last six weeks, and then it just popped."

"Well, you know," says Eloise, "I told you two times that people thought you were pregnant, and I thought maybe you were, and the third time, when you actually were, I didn't think so."

Eunice sends gifts, but she can't bring herself to come. At the Big House, on the Sunday after the birth, she serves everyone a big Sunday dinner. Besides Wesson and the hired men, Ida and Hazel and Lillian are out from town, and Ronald and Vera and little Joan are over from the Little House. In the midst of the meal, the phone rings. It hangs on the wall in the dining room. Eunice gets up and answers it. Everyone falls silent so that Eunice will be able to hear. She suddenly slams the receiver onto its hook and spins around, her face flaming and contorted with shock and rage. Her mouth works; she is incoherent.

"What is it, dearie?" cries Wesson in alarm.

Eunice's hand flies, she splutters and cries, and the story comes out bit by bit. She'd put the receiver to her ear and a woman's voice had said, "Judge not lest ye be judged; forgive, and ye shall be forgiven," and abruptly hung up. It's hours before Eunice is even partially calmed down. Nobody ever knows who made the call.

The next day Esther writes a despondent letter:

> My Dearest Mother and Daddy,
>
> It seems as if you have forgotten me entirely. Yesterday and today have been so lonesome—especially Sunday—for I rather thought you would be over for sure Sunday—
>
> My problems are so many and I sometimes think I just can't stand it another minute.

Baby is really growing and he seems exceedingly smart. He's such a darling.

I started reading *High Fires*—read two chapters and my eyes began to hurt so decided it wasn't best, but the book is very interesting.

Herbert, Ross, and Leora and her husband came yesterday—

Mother, you paid more than $5.00 for baby things, I don't see as I ought to have another $5.00. The baby layette is darling—it was so wonderful of you.

I would like some bedroom slippers if you could get them—maybe you could get them and then I will pay for them out of this money—I would like a pair with low heels and real light soles, if possible, about size seven—not so very wide. I will really need them badly when I begin taking care of baby nights.

My mind seems a jumble—things look so hard—and look harder every day. I just can't decide what is best or what to do—it seems as though at night I can't stand it—during the day it's not nearly as bad.

I do love you so and need your help and mostly your advice, for I want to become the kind of woman you want me to be,—for I certainly have made a terrible mistake.

Ross said that Floyd went to Chicago to find work—couldn't find any, so got discouraged and started bumming west—he said until he could get some money to come back a little respectable he wouldn't come. He said he didn't intend to leave me but expected to get a job and come back after me. Maybe he means it and maybe not, I don't know.

It's getting too dark in here to write more—please come and talk to me—

All my love—

Esther

Esther soon realizes she will not be coming back to the farm. When the baby is about three weeks old, she writes her father her thoughts:

Sunday, Oct. 17, 1926

My Dearest Daddy—

I have been thinking hard ever since our talk last Sunday, and I think I have decided my future—as far as I can—I am positive that this is the best place for me—for I am sure Floyd will come home before long, and I want to be here when he comes. Then if Floyd and I decide not to marry—then I have made up my mind to finish high school. There is a good opening for me—Mrs. Tonolen says that they will probably be living in Rockford next year and she would like to have me live with her and finish High—she always keeps some girl with her that helps her, stays with the children, and goes to school—if I went down to Helen's this could not be worked out—of course everything's going to come out all right, I'm sure—and if Floyd comes back and we marry, I know he'll make a wonderful husband and I'm sure we'll be happy. But when he comes we may decide not to marry—things like that will have to be worked out yet, so I'm sure this is the best place for me—and all the Peters would like to have me stay. I know your viewpoint and you said if Floyd came back and didn't want to marry he could convince his mother that he wasn't the "only one"—Floyd knows he is or he wouldn't have run away—he knows the baby is his and mine only and so does God, so everything's coming out all right if I stay right here—I'm well convinced that my decision is right—and things will work out better this way—hope I hear from you soon—

Love,

Your daughter

Esther G.

Heretofore, when she has signed her notes at all, it's been simply "Esther" or "Your daughter, Esther." She signs this letter "Love, Esther G.," then goes back and squeezes "Your daughter" between the "Love" and her signature. Her father knows that Esther has always been aware that Groose is her legal name. And Aunt Lillian has never let her forget it.

A letter from Sparta carries on the story.

Oct. 16/26

Dear Mr. Dougan,

I have been waiting a long time to hear from you in regard to Esther and her baby, understood you were to send me a copy of her letters she wrote you and Mrs. Dougan, also what her future plans were to be. . . . Trust she has not given up her advanced education.

Best wishes for you and your family.

Mrs. Ada E. Grube

But a fourth scenario, one Wesson did not anticipate in his letter to himself, comes into play. Floyd's brother, Herbert, is a plodder. He has none of Floyd's sexy charm. But he has a fiancée, and they've been putting money down on some furniture at Leath's: chairs, a table, a couch, a bedroom suite. As soon as they have it all paid for, they'll marry.

The fiancée lives on a farm west of town, works in town, and rides back and forth with a widower who lives nearby. On a Thursday, she and Herbert make their final payment. They plan to be married the following week.

That Friday she doesn't return from work. Neither does the widower. They've driven to Dubuque, over the river in Iowa, where there is no waiting period, and gotten married.

Herbert is shattered. It's only a few weeks after this that Esther arrives at Shopiere and has her baby. Herbert, when he was at the Big House, had always found Esther attractive—her vivacity and beauty, her laughter, her flirtatious way of joking with the boarders. He had admired how hard she worked, up at five before school to help with breakfasts for all the men; the many hours he saw her doing the dishes, dusting, vacuuming, ironing, hanging out the wash. Although Eunice always had a hired woman, there was work aplenty for three. And Esther went to school besides. Now he admires still more her courage and spunk, cast out by the Dougans, deserted by his brother, at only seventeen having a baby alone. He and Georgia sit in the bedroom evenings, and the three chat. They laugh and play games. Herbert watches Esther care tenderly for his tiny nephew. Though they never discuss it, he knows that Esther is all sympathy and indignation for the wrong that has been done to him, and she knows he feels reciprocally. It's very soon that he proposes marriage.

Again there is a letter from Ada Grube at Sparta:

> If Floyd's brother is willing to marry Esther and you say he is a good moral fellow and she likes him well enough to marry him, why wouldn't it be a good idea. The other fellow (Floyd) is a dirty skunk. Why wasn't he man enough to come back, for I feel he has been kept informed of everything all along, and give himself up and take Esther and her baby and make a home for them.

Esther accepts Herbert. He rents a small house near his parents. His share of the refund on the Leath furniture purchases a set of more modest furniture from the same establishment. The couple are married in mid-November in a parson's parlor in Shopiere. They have only Herbert's brother Ross and sister Georgia standing up with them. But afterward, there's a merry dinner at the Turtle Grange hall, put on by Eunice and Wesson. The Peters family attends, except for the baby, whom a neighbor is watching. Herbert's friends come, and from Esther's side, besides Eunice and Wesson, Ronald and Vera; Trever, down from school; Aunt Ida, Aunt Lillian, and Hazel, out from town; the help from the farm; and Eloise and the Marstons and Smiths. Wesson gives a little speech about wishing the couple happiness and includes a few earnest lines about the responsibilities of marriage and the importance of being loving helpmeets. Eunice says, "Well, Esther, you have a second chance, and you are lucky. Herbert is the finer man."

The only one missing is Floyd. He's not actually missing. He's sitting outside in the dark, in his car.

After the reception, the couple go to their little home. In the middle of their wedding night, the bedroom door bursts open and Floyd is standing there. He orders Herbert out of the bed. The brothers fight, Esther screams, the baby wakes and cries. Herbert manages to throw Floyd out but has to call for help to keep him out. It's an inauspicious ending to a happy day.

Wesson, whose frequent communications to Trever at the university rarely mention family affairs but concentrate almost wholly on Trever's studies, spending, and character, in a letter dated November 21, 1926, includes a brief and weary account:

> Well, I have had a full week regarding Esther. She is married to Herbert, then the next day F. turned up. I am glad she is settled. Floyd stayed only one day. I wanted to get an appointment to see him but when I proposed this he skud again.

Helen Clarke, Director of the Child Placing Department at the State Public School for Dependent and Neglected Children, is not aware of the latest developments when she writes from Sparta on November 24:

> Dear Mr. Dougan:
>
> You were indeed patient and kind and your attitude showed toward me and Esther was more than a little appreciated. I realize the strain you were under and, therefore, doubly value your cooperation.
>
> I very much hope that Esther and Herbert are going to be happy and that their future will be rosy. . . . I shall always value the contact that I had with you because of your fine Christian attitude toward your problem.

But Sparta learns of the situation, and the superintendent of the orphanage writes Wesson in January, after Wesson writes Mrs. Grube about Floyd's return and subsequent behavior:

> I greatly fear that we have made somewhat of a difficult problem of Esther's case and I don't know what to advise. While the state released the guardianship at the time of the marriage of Esther, we are still interested. I am inclined to believe that we would take steps to prosecute the boy, Floyd, unless he leaves the vicinity and ceases his attentions to Esther, regardless of her feelings in the matter. Should you see this young man it might be well to inform him on the former charge of his intimacy with

Post. When Jackie is six, Eloise marries an engineer, and Jackie is flower girl at their wedding. The couple live now and again in Beloit but mostly all over the globe. Their two children are born in faraway places.

The four Dougan children grow up playing occasionally with Russell, when he and Esther visit the farm. Jackie knows that there is something odd about her cousin besides his large, strange eyes, that he is not-quite-a-cousin, nor Esther quite their aunt, but she's hazy as to what causes the difference. In church, when she and her sisters sit in the pew beside Grama and draw during the sermon, a standard picture they produce is of a hill with a rock part way up it, and a girl tripping on the rock. She and Patsy snicker over "Esther Falling on Fool's Hill" though they don't know what they are snickering at.

Esther divorces Floyd after ten years. Grama, on a trip out west with Grampa visiting Trever and his family, writes back to Ronald and Vera in May 1939:

> Then we got a long letter from Esther. She has her divorce and is happy. She is to have Russell and I am sure she would be better off without him. He will be but a big expense and maybe trouble. They are on their way to Chicago.

Esther marries again. She has a home in Shopiere with white ruffled curtains, polished floors, and snowy throw rugs. Jackie goes along when Grama visits and is given the grand tour. And in summer of 1942, Grama writes Jackie, who's away at camp: "We had a fine dinner at Art and Esther's, and Trever thought she has a lovely home."

Over the years Esther works at various jobs. At one time, she's the beautiful and gracious hostess at the area's finest restaurant, the Wagon Wheel. At another, she works in the Fairbanks Morse factory. For years she manages the general store in Shopiere. When she sells candy in a Fannie May store in Beloit, she assures her friends, as she presses gifts of candy on them, that employees have an allowance. Eloise is reminded of noon hours at Merrill School.

When Russell is grown he fathers two sons in separate marriages, enters the service, and is killed in Korea. Esther's third marriage ends; the reasons are unclear. There's a brief fourth marriage, in which she is perhaps mistreated. Her last husband, Clifford Cox, outlives her. They have a number of happy years.

She has also been happy in her grandsons, whom she helps to raise, and who grow up loving and attentive. Both become pro football players, one with the Green Bay Packers, one with the Washington Redskins. The newspaper, always alert for a good story, runs an article which features a smiling Esther holding large photos of the brothers. Esther and her husband take Trever and his wife to a football game when the Redskins play in Chicago. It's a proud day for Esther.

Esther dies, unexpectedly, at sixty-seven. Her memorial service is at the Shopiere Methodist Church, and it is packed to overflowing. Afterward, there is a community potluck in the church basement. Affectionate words are said about Esther. It is obvious she was loved.

Later, Eloise says to Ronald and Vera, "I never knew anyone like her. She could look you straight in the eye and tell you black was white, and you'd believe her, because you wanted to believe her."

Eloise also says, "All her sins were warmhearted ones. Somehow, when someone steals something to give it to someone else, it doesn't seem to be as bad."

Esther leaves her body to science. Eloise says, "She was generous to the end."

45 A GREAT PIG

Jackie is grown, married, away. She is visiting at Chez Nous. She pokes in a dusty box in the corner of the attic. She discovers it's filled with family papers. Among the papers is a letter from Grampa to Trever, when Trever was a young man. Jackie knows the background of the letter:

Trever is following Ronald's footsteps. He cuts out of college in the middle of his junior year and goes to see the world. He travels across the country with friends, finding short-term employment here and there and having adventures that would fill a book. Finally, his watch pawned and down to his last dollar, he stands in an employment line in San Francisco. A man comes down the line, plunking certain men on the shoulder. "You. You. You. You." Trever is one of the ones plunked. The group follows the man and finds that they are shipping out on a two-masted schooner for Alaska, to work in a salmon-canning factory in the Aleutian Islands.

Grampa writes Trever letters warning him of the dangers of his present life but also urging him to take advantage of its opportunities. He tells him to work hard, live clean, and be an example to the other men. He indicates that Trever can learn from the lowliest job and from any man in whatever walk of life. In the same way, others can learn from him. Let the lessons they learn from Trever be true and valuable ones.

Now Trever is thinking about returning to the States. He may even return to school. Grampa writes him the letter Jackie finds. It's dated June 23, 1925.

> My Dear Boy Trever,
>
> I want to talk to you very much but some way I can't write. You know all about us and we want to know all about you—but questions seem futile with time and distance so great before any answer.
>
> Regarding your school next year. You must plan now and get in and

work hard. Get a real education; a mental training that will fit you for big things in life. That training can be secured almost anywhere if one has the right aim. Don't make any definite arrangements regarding school until you get home. This year is pretty hard on me. I am working harder than ever and have some little worries.

I am very grateful that Ronald finished college this year. It is going to do him a great deal of good. He carried heavy work and did it extremely well.

Do you remember that front page picture in one of the farm papers that I used in a talk at Janesville? It is of a ruddy-faced aristocratic farmer at a county fair with his little white pig under his arm and displaying a large blue ribbon. His expression is remarkable. It is first of surprise and then of confidence. He seems to be saying, "Well, by George! I am surprised." Then he straightens up and with confidence seems to say, "But of course, I always knew he was a *great* pig."

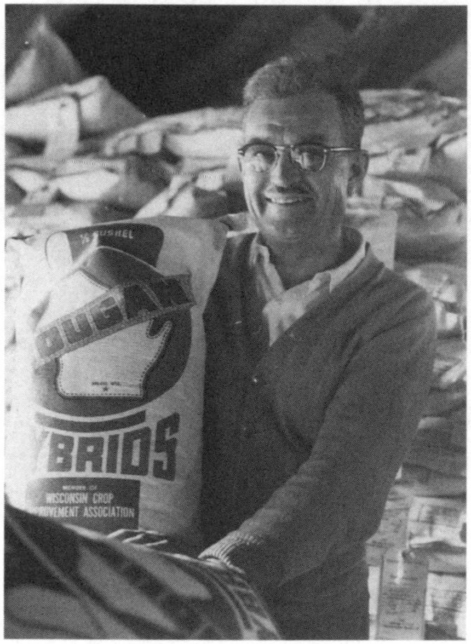

Ron in the seed house, holding a bag of Dougan Hybrid Seed Corn.

Perhaps a great pig!

In the case of Ronald having the best standings in the B.S. division and only one point below the top of the whole senior class I confess *confidentially* I am surprised. Also I am conscious of the other expression, "I always knew I had a great pig." Yes, I have confidence in my boys even when they fall short of my ideal for them. I know they are going to find themselves and be good and great men.

It is rather fortunate that Ronald is ready to get into farmwork and help me with the lift and management. I especially need help in handling men. My hearing is becoming a greater barrier to me every year in every way. It is hard for the help and for the family. On this account I am dropping much of my public work. I do not think I should do much talking hereafter. I wish I could get started at writing for publication.

You must plan to give us a few days before getting into school.

I think of you very often and pray for your protection especially that you may be great enough to live clean and true.

I will not write more tonight. If you have any questions to put up to me I will write so you can get it in San Francisco when you get there. Your splendid descriptive letters are highly enjoyed.

Write to me as freely as you do to Ronald. I feel a little jealous that he should get letters I cannot know.

Your loving dad,

W. J. Dougan

Jackie is filled with tenderness toward Grampa and with delight at his words about Daddy. She goes downstairs and reads the letter out loud to Daddy and Mother.

They're delighted, too. Daddy looks as smug as Wilbur in *Charlotte's Web.* Imagine his father, way back then, calling him "a great pig!"

"Do you think I've lived up to his expectations?" he asks Mother and Jackie. "Do you think I'm a great pig?"

Mother purses her lips. "Well, if not *great,* at least a *pretty good* pig."

"Life's not over yet," says Daddy.

46 THE CEMETERY TOMATO

It's an early evening in August, eleven or twelve years since Grampa has died. Mother and Daddy have eaten out in Beloit. Daddy is going too fast down Clary Street toward Colley Road. The cemetery is on their left. Daddy approaches the entrance and suddenly banks in onto the one-lane brick drive, past the ornamental brick office of the caretaker.

Mother, thrown against the door, grabs the armrest. "Ron, what are you doing?"

"I want to see the family plot," Daddy says, slowing to a sedate pace over the uneven pavement. "I want to see how Grampa's tomato is doing."

"But the cemetery closes at eight," Mother objects. "It's five to eight right now."

"They never close these places right on time," says Daddy. "Anyway, we'll only be five minutes."

He drives to the family plot. It's right along the fence, as close to Colley Road as a plot can be. Grampa and Grama are buried here; and Grampa's mother, Delceyetta, who hid Ronald and Trever's toys; and Grampa's sisters Aunt Lillian and Aunt Ida, whose life together was a constant quarrel. Aunt Lillian originally wanted to be buried here but changed her mind and wrote a note asking to be interred at the Grove Prairie cemetery near Lowell, where her father, Arthur, was buried, and a sister, Agnes Augusta, who died at three. But the note was filed and forgotten, and she was buried here willy-nilly and alongside Aunt Ida. On Aunt Ida's other side lies her husband, James Croft, who dropped dead of a heart attack in Horace White Park when Ronald was a boy and who used to say, when he went into Murray and Frank Johnson's grocery store, "This place smells like a high-holer's nest!"

Mother and Daddy, admiring a prize cow and her calf. Daddy is perhaps quoting Mr. Hoard, of Hoard's Dairyman: *"The cow is a mother, treat her as such!"*

Mother's mother is also buried here. There is space for more family, though Daddy fancies a handsome crypt at the far end of the cemetery whose roof is held up by a row of angels like Greek caryatids. "Now there's a fine place to be laid away, if one has to be laid away," he'd say, driving some grandchild past it on one of his occasional but fruitless searches for the tombstone in the cemetery that reputedly says on it, "James Wilson, Murdered."

In the middle of the family plot is a concrete planter. It stands on a pedestal and is as big as a lard-rendering kettle though more nicely decorated, with concrete loops and garlands chasing its edges. Some years, flowers get planted in it on Memorial Day and even watered occasionally. Some years, it remains empty, filled with the previous year's dry and tangled stalks. This year, Daddy has planted a tomato in it.

During June and July, the tomato flourished and was thick with yellow blossoms. Any casual observer would suppose it to be an acceptable cemetery-type plant. Daddy tended it sporadically and poked in a few sticks to tie up the vines. Now he's well pleased. He walks all around it. The plant is heavy with small to medium-sized to large green globes blending with the foliage. A few are beginning to blush red.

"I'm sure Gramp is enjoying his tomato," he says. "Better than flowers! Maybe I'll try a pumpkin next year." He goes to get some water from a nearby spigot.

Mother gets out of the car, admires the tomato plant, and wanders the family graves. Daddy waters the tomato. Then they both return to the car and drive to the exit. The gate is closed and locked.

"It's only eight five!" Daddy says. "They never lock these places on time!"

"They did tonight," Mother says.

Daddy looks all around, but no one's in sight. He tries the door of the cemetery office. It's locked, too. He rattles the gate, to no avail. The cemetery is surrounded with a high wire fence; there is no climbing it. He stands at the gate and waves his arms. Traffic on Clary Street is sparse; what there is doesn't notice him. Daddy yells. Mother leans on the horn a few times. Finally a man comes out of a house across the street. He says he saw the caretaker just leave, and he'll call him at home. He disappears. Mother stays in the car; Daddy walks around and reads inscriptions. Twenty minutes pass. Dusk is falling.

Daddy goes and leans on the horn. The man returns, seems surprised to see them there. "I called and left word," he says.

"Maybe you should call the police," Daddy says.

The man disappears. In a few minutes, a squad car pulls up. Daddy from his side of the gate tells the two policemen he got locked in watering his father's tomato. The police fill out all the vital statistics on Daddy and the car. They say they haven't a key, but there's one down at the station. While they radio for it, Daddy looks at more tombstones. It's now almost too dark to tell who died and when. The policemen return to the gate and chat. Daddy discovers that one worked on the farm, fifteen years ago. He finds police work less strenuous than farmwork.

A second squad car pulls up. Two policemen jump out, all efficiency. They have the key. It doesn't work; it's the wrong key.

The first officers radio the station again, give more explicit directions on where the right key might be. Daddy and the four policemen stand at the gate and talk. The police tell stories of various absurd situations they've encountered, and Daddy can match each one. The man across the street walks over, and some of the other neighbors, to see what's going on. Kids pull up on their bicycles. Cars stop. It's getting to be a party.

A third squad car arrives. The two men inside say they've searched and searched, and they can't find any key. Everyone has a plan for what to do. Most are for breaking the lock on the gate. But the gate is an ornate one, and the lock is part of the ornamentation. Daddy is reluctant; he's the one who'll have to pay for repairs.

"We may be staying here all night," he tells Mother. "But it's warm."

Mother doesn't think much of this solution.

Just then another car pulls up. It's the custodian with the key. He unlocks the gate, lets Daddy and Mother out, and locks the gate behind them while Daddy tenders his thanks. The police leave, and the crowd disperses.

A week or so later Daddy visits the cemetery again, this time in the middle of the day. He likes communing with his father beside the tomato plant. Also, he figures the first tomatoes are ready for harvesting, and he can take a few home for dinner. He can drop some off at the cemetery office, too, and tell the caretaker to help himself. But the concrete planter is empty; the tomato plant is gone.

Daddy looks around for the remains. A few graves away, he finds one small green tomato. He pockets it. He drives around the cemetery till he finds the out-of-the-way spot where dead flowers and grass cuttings are piled. There's no evidence of the tomato plant among the recent refuse.

At home he cuts the small tomato up and adds it to his salad plate. "Somebody mowing the grass must have finally noticed that plant, and thought it was a mistake," he tells Mother with regret. "Next time I'll put a sign on it: W. J. DOUGAN MEMORIAL TOMATO. Then they won't dare disturb it."

He ponders. "But you know—it wasn't just torn out. It was deliberately dug up and carried away. Maybe I should call the police."

Mother says, "I think the police have had quite enough of us for a while."

ABOUT THE AUTHOR

Jacqueline Dougan Jackson published her first story at age ten and has since written eleven books in addition to *Stories from the Round Barn*. She teaches at the University of Illinois at Springfield.